# Shadows

Megan Wolters

First Edition

Edited by Sharina Wunderink

To Amber and Emy,

In 2012, you were there when I first thought of Souls. And you're still here, 10 years later, at its conclusion.

*To give light to them that sit in darkness and in the shadow of death, to guide our feet into the way of peace.*

*Luke 1:79*

# CONTENTS

# TRIGGER WARNINGS

*Sexual Assault (no scenes)*
*Alcohol Consumption*
*Demons*
*Witchcraft*
*Abuse*
*Blood*
*Guns/Knives*
*Death*
*Torture*
*Brainwashing*
*Intrusive Thoughts*
*Anxiety*
*Depression*
*Suicide*

# SOULS BREAKDOWN

**The First Deal**

Five-year-old Adia makes a deal with Shemu—a shadow demon—in order to save her mother in exchange for her soul. Adia's and Shemu's souls (now bounded together) create a Shadow World.

**Shadow World**

Within the Shadow World there are realms (City of Souls, Consumption, Alternate Earth, and Echo). Adia creates the Edge, which borders Consumption, to escape Shemu. The Edge makes it so Shemu has no access to Consumption (a hell within a hell). Then she creates Alternate Earth unknowingly, believing she had broken the deal with Shemu and returned to her body. Echo is where souls' memories are stored/altered.

**Monster Hunter**

Lamarse—an Eternal Guardian having entered Adia and Shemu's Shadow World to fight the demons from within, trains Adia to defend herself from Shemu's monsters in Alternate Earth. Her first boyfriend, Cameron Mathewson gets possessed by a smoke creature (a monster born from a piece of a human's soul and Shemu's soul) and Adia is forced to kill him. She separates herself from Lamarse and targets smoke creatures. She joins a team of hunters led by Lamarse.

**Austin**

Austin and Adia's story before the Second Deal will be addressed in *Hunters*. Here's a brief summary that was revealed in *Souls*: Austin moves in next door to Adia in Alternate Earth. He becomes possessed by a smoke creature and fights Adia. He manages to survive and gains knowledge to the Shadow World because of a piece of Shemu's soul who had possessed him. He also gained True Sight—seeing people or creatures for what they truly are. Adia trains him to be a hunter and they grow close.

**The Second Deal**

Austin saves Adia from being burned by a draemaki (human dragon). Austin's wounds are fatal. Adia makes a deal with Shemu to spare him in exchange for her soul. She does not know she is already in the Shadow World. Since she has power/pull in the Shadow World, Shemu needs her to go to the City of Souls willingly. Austin and Adia get married and spend six years together before Shemu alters her memories after a car accident.

## Alternate Life

Shemu—going by Sam—manipulates Adia's memories and steals Austin's spot in her life. She believes she is an FBI agent and the love she feels for Austin is now for Sam. Alternate Earth becomes hazy due to Adia losing creative control after Sam changed her memories in Echo. Lamarse speaks to her telepathically but her altered mind blocks his attempts and she suffers hallucinations. Sam fakes his death, and a demon offers Adia a deal to trade her soul to save him. She is sent to the City of Souls.

## City of Souls

Adia returns to where she and Shemu first started after the first deal —the City of Souls. Shemu uses one of his monsters to pose as the King Demon. Austin also made a deal with Shemu that if he could go where Adia went, he would work for him. He must pretend not to know Adia, who believes a lot of her memories were with Sam, not Austin. Still, Austin and Adia become close. Adia learns that she has been in the Shadow World since her first deal (age five). Understanding she has power equal to Shemu's, she's able to break the Shadow World in an act of death.

## The Awakening

Before Adia breaks the Shadow World, Austin is consumed and sent to Consumption. A piece of his soul is locked in Consumption while the rest of his soul is returned to his body on Earth. On Earth, he believes he is still dating Judy—his ex-girlfriend. He has no memories of the Shadow World, and he gets held in a government facility against his will. Also on Earth, having escaped the Shadow World and awakened, Adia learns that Sam is still attached to her soul.

# HUNTERS BREAKDOWN

**Broken Shadow World**

Any soul consumed before Adia escaped is split in two, one piece returning to their body (if still alive) and the other remaining in the now broken Shadow World. Austin having been consumed at the end of *Souls*, has a piece of himself still trapped in the Shadow World. He meets Lamarse and other hunters there, as well as a piece of Adia's soul who had been tortured by monsters in Consumption. Lamarse helps that version of Adia heal.

**Somewhere Else**

Adia's soul is still attached to Sam's. She sees him, but no one else can. When she has an adrenaline rush, he tries to possess her body but instead it brings both of their souls into an alternate reality. Truly, they are in a broken version of Echo Memory (Shadow World). There, he can alter what she sees and pretends to be Austin. He is unable to possess her unless she grants him permission.

**Castle**

Austin, without memories of his time in the Shadow World, is taken to a government facility run by Lamarse's sister, Ebony. She collects those who have no memory of the Shadow World and tries connecting them with the other piece of their soul. You later discover that Ebony is possessed by shadows. They are replacing the souls of their victims with the souls of monsters having been released from Sam's Shadow World (dark souls). They bring Austin's soul into the Shadow World, where he meets the piece of Adia still there. Then he enters Echo and relives memories from the Shadow World. The shadows' main objectives for building Castle are to build an army of dark souls, learn what they can of humans, and manipulate Austin/Adia to eventually make her a Seven Core.

**Dallas Meets Cora**

Cora (Lamarse's other sister) and Dallas rescue hunters being attacked by dark souls. Cora has the gift of foresight. She used to only see visions here and there, but after Ebony killed her, she was Reborn with an enhanced gift. She can now Vision Walk, dream the close future and relive it many times so she can predict the multiple outcomes. They build a team of hunters from those they rescue. Cora had overseen Earth Guardianship, but Ebony turned the Mortal Guards against Orion (their father and Master of the Universe) and Cora. After Ebony killed Cora, the shadows use Earth Guardianship's resources to run/control Earth.

## Adia Comes to Castle

Ebony/the shadows kept Adia in an insane asylum, experimenting on her connection with Sam. Discovering adrenaline is the key to merge the two souls together, sending them to Somewhere Else, they bring Adia to Castle. Ebony sends Austin's soul to the Shadow World at the same time they shoot Adia with adrenaline. When Austin is reliving his memories in Echo, he discovers Adia had been there as well, reliving the same memory. Each time Austin travels to the Shadow World, he merges more and more with his other soul. He gains his muscle memory to fight and True Sight (ability to see auras/true nature). He is also able to see Sam.

## Adia Makes Another Deal

The Shadow World trips are slowly killing Austin. The shadows know this and use it to manipulate Adia into making another deal. She grants Sam permission to possess her body. Sam terrorizes Castle, the dark souls joining his side in fighting. For show, he kills Ebony but really grants permission for them to make Adia a Seven Core. He then kills Austin out of spite and because he is in love with Adia. In Echo, Sam tries to convince Adia to stay in the Shadow World with him. She attacks him and he disappears. When she returns to her body, he is nowhere to be seen. She is unaware the shadows are attached to her soul.

## Austin is Reborn

Austin learns in Passage (place between Heaven and Life where time doesn't move) that he had also died in the Shadow World when he was possessed by a smoke creature. He was given True Sight and is secretly an Eternal Guardian. His father tells him he has a great purpose but won't remember their conversation once he is Reborn. When he comes to, his True Sight is enhanced, and he can see through darkness. Adia, being the daughter of Lamarse, can sense others' emotions. Although she had never died, she was granted this gift at birth but didn't have it in the Shadow World. She doesn't know Lamarse is her father. She believes her gift is a side effect of Sam being attached to her soul. If the emotion is powerful, she can sometimes see into their memories.

## Adia is a Seven Core

The Shadow Universe is run by seven core souls. They govern the shadows. Ebony became a Seven Core when she made a deal, which gives shadows the right to possess her body at will. When dark souls come to attack (not wanting to return to the Shadow World) Austin, Lou, and Adia fight them off. Adia gets possessed and kills the dark souls. Austin can see them controlling her actions. He speaks to Cora and discovers that this was the plan all along, for Adia to become a Seven Core so she can destroy the Shadow Universe from within. He has a choice to run or stay and chooses to stay by her side, even though it could kill him.

## Timeline Clarity

*Shadows* will deal with two timelines, past (Lamarse's story) and present (events following *Hunters*). Adia was five years old during her first deal. *48 Years Before Adia's First Deal* is 75 Years before the conclusion of *Hunters*.

# CHAPTER SONG PLAYLIST
*Available on Spotify*

1. *Ain't No Rest for the Wicked* by Cage the Elephant
2. *House of the Rising Sun* by The Animals
3. *Follow You* by Imagine Dragons
4. *Migraine* by Twenty-One Pilots
5. *Welcome Home* by Radical Face
6. *Darkside by Neoni*
7. *Kingdom* by Charli XCX and Simon Le Bon
8. *Zombie* by Damned Anthem
9. *An Evening I Will Not Forget* by Dermot Kennedy
10. *Save Your Soul* by Damned Anthem
11. *Sleep Alone* by Bat for Lashes
12. *Bartholomew* by the Silent Comedy
13. *The Chain* by Fleetwood Mac
14. *Hell's Comin' with Me by Poor Mans Poison*
15. *Team* by Lorde
16. *The Planets Bend Between Us* by Snow Patrol
17. *Shooting the Moon* by Ok Go
18. *Gods & Monsters* by Lana Del Rey
19. *Dog Days Are Over* by Florence + The Machine
20. *Darker Side* by RHODES
21. *Death and All His Friends* by Coldplay
22. *Till Forever Falls Apart* by Ashe, FINNEAS
23. *Work Song* by Hozier
24. *Lost and Found* by Katie Herzig
25. *Spirits* by Strumbellas
26. *Just Say Yes* by Snow Patrol
27. *Adia* by Sarah McLachlan
28. *Smile* by Mikky Ekko
29. *Safe & Sound* by Taylor Swift, The Civil Wars

30. *Gallows* by Katie Garfield
31. *Where the Shadow Ends* by BANNERS
32. *Seven Devils* by Florence + The Machine
33. *Demons* by Neoni
34. *Fade* by Lewis Capaldi
35. *The Monster* by Eminem, Rihanna
36. *Cosmic Love* by Florence + The Machine
37. *Raise Hell* by Brandi Carlile
38. *Power Hungry Animals* by The Apache Relay
39. *Fire* by Barns Courtney
40. *Never Let Me Go* by Florence + The Machine
41. *Bet My Life by Imagine Dragons*

# CHAPTER ONE

## Ain't No Rest for the Wicked

**Lamarse** *(Point of View)*
**Matadon** *(Location)*
**48 Years Before Adia's First Deal** *(Point in Time)*

The smell of sweat, smoke, and death overwhelmed Lamarse as he walked into the tavern. He squeezed past a passionate couple and bumped into a lady blowing fire against the rocks. She stared in a daze at the scorch marks and a laugh bubbled out of her. She fell onto her hands and knees, coughing up blood. Lamarse helped her to her feet only to be shoved away. She spat a curse at him, saliva and blood landing on his neck. Still, he helped her to the nearest table.

"You look like Master Orion," she slurred. She stumbled into a chair and started laughing again.

It wasn't the first time he had been told he resembled his father. He doubted the woman would be kind if he revealed his identity, so he kept his expression neutral. The children of Orion had a blessing on their names. No one remembered who he really was—an Eternal Guardian and the son of Orion —unless he told them willingly. Any pictures or books labeling them the children of Orion were faceless or their names blurred to all except those they chose to reveal to. It came in handy when walking through worlds like Matadon that detested the Guardianship.

Lamarse held his breath as he brushed past several people until he came to a balcony. He let out a long sigh, his eyes landing on his sister down below.

Cora stood in a circle of men, all holding out their fists. In turns, each revealed the stone in their palm. A worried expression crossed Cora's delicate face. Lamarse was reminded of a time when they were children, and she would have nightmarish visions.

*What have you gotten yourself into?* Lamarse was tempted to send those words to her telepathically. He stepped forward, ready to rescue her from the horrid men, when she uncurled her fingers, revealing a white pebble in the center of her palm. A collective sound of moans and grunts came from the men. His sister's face lit up, feigning surprise.

"Cheater!" a few said.

Cora beamed. "Pay up, monsters."

Lamarse's body tensed when a man grabbed his petite sister by the waist, throwing her over his shoulder.

Cora no longer smiled as she curled her arm back around the man's neck—an impossible feat if Cora was mortal—and choked the man until he dropped her. Another man charged at her with a knife.

Lamarse pulled out his weapon—a black pistol with special armor-piercing rounds capable of penetrating steel with ease. He fired at the ceiling, causing a hole the size of a basketball.

Cora's wide eyes were fixed on her brother. "Idiot," she muttered.

Lamarse paid no attention to the grimy men and women moving to take him down on the balcony.

"If it is a fight you desire," he called down to those holding Cora in place, "then challenge me."

"How noble!" one shouted up to Lamarse.

"I will allow you to live," Lamarse stated. "Fight *her* and she will give you no tomorrow."

Before the men comprehended Lamarse's meaning, Cora

twisted out of their hold. She jumped up on the table, kicking a man's head so strongly, his jaw broke. She disarmed another and used his own knife to puncture his jugular. She was already killing the third man before the second finished bleeding out.

The fourth, fifth, and sixth kill happened in a matter of a minute.

Three men closed in on Lamarse, thinking his attention was distracted. He had them unconscious on the balcony without touching or even looking at them.

"H-how did you do that?" a bystander asked.

Lamarse ignored the question. He lifted himself up on the rail and jumped down the twenty feet, landing with the agility of a cat.

"Was that necessary?" he asked his sister, stepping over a dead body. "I could have stopped them without the bloodshed."

Cora tilted her head, taking in Lamarse's appearance. He wondered how different he looked since they last had seen each other. She had changed plenty. Her brown hair was mostly red and purple with several thin braids. She also had new tattoos. He was jealous. His tattoos disappeared after being Reborn. Only the family crest on his wrist remained because of magic. It was visible to those who knew his identity.

"Did you read their minds?" Cora asked.

Lamarse narrowed one eye. "I was still reeling from your insult to think about entering their minds. I am not an *idiot*."

"You were far above me when I whispered that." Her eyes danced across his features again, speculating. "Sorry I missed your resurrection celebration. Was there good wine at least?"

Lamarse's stony expression broke into a smirk. "I died twice, so you missed two rituals. The wine was decent enough." He tapped his left ear. "I was gifted enhanced hearing and—"

Footsteps thumped toward them. Lamarse entered their minds as easily as opening a door. The men halted before collapsing to the ground.

"Impressive. How long until they awake?" She raised her

brows. "Or are they dead?"

"They will be asleep for an hour."

"Can you kill with that ability?"

"Yes."

"You are becoming a true god."

He didn't like the disappointed look in her eyes. "And *you* are becoming blood thirsty." His eyes fell on the blade strapped to her hip. "It is one thing to contradict Father's teachings," Lamarse said through his teeth, "but to lose sight of the value of life—"

Her nostrils flared. "If you had read their minds, you would know these men are beyond evil. You can drop that self-righteous gleam in your eyes. I am working."

"For Father?"

She scoffed.

"Assassin work?"

"Not that I have to explain my ways," she replied, "but a child was abducted. These men work for King Tyron. They are in the business of selling anything and anyone. I figured I would steal their money before I killed them. I already saved the child— children."

He softened his expression.

"Why are you here?" She crossed her arms. "Did Father send you?"

Although the tavern was mostly emptied now, a few spied from the shadows above them. Lamarse reached their minds to see if any were a credible threat.

"I sent myself."

"I guess I was foolish to think Father sent help. Saving children is beneath the greater good."

"This is your anger talking," Lamarse stated. "The universe is a large place. Too many souls to protect to—"

"Unless the whole planet is in danger of extinction, the innocents are left to fend for themselves." Her eyes lit with anger. "There are worse things than extinction. Ask those children I saved."

"I would have helped you," he muttered. "All you needed to do was ask."

Her throat bobbed.

Lamarse blew out a breath and ran a hand through his long, blond hair. "I found you because I have news..." He was unsure of what her reaction would be. They were no longer the close siblings they had been growing up. Ebony had been born years before Lamarse. He shared a childhood with Cora and felt protective over her.

Concerned flashed in her expression. "Is it Ebony?"

"I am getting married," he announced.

She stared back at him.

"I know you don't want to come home," his heart raced at her silence, "but know that you are welcomed at my wedding." When she still didn't respond, he quietly pleaded, "Please come to my wedding."

# CHAPTER TWO

## *House of the Rising Sun*

**Lamarse**
**The Draken**
**48 Years Before Adia's First Deal**

Cora wrung her hands, staring out the window of Lamarse's spaceship. The Draken had the ability to teleport port-to-port, and they were only two away from home—a home that Cora hadn't been to since their mother's murder.

Lamarse pressed a firm hand on top of his younger sister's fidgeting fingers. "Reya is excited to meet you."

"When did Father have you working with Earth Guardianship?"

He removed his hand. "She is from Lehran." He saw a flicker of surprise in Cora's expression. "Why did you think she was from Earth?"

Cora returned to staring out the window. "I misunderstood."

Though Lamarse did not read minds unless necessary, the temptation was there. He shifted his attention to the streaking lights out the window and fell silent. They only had one more port to go until they were home.

\* \* \*

**Lamarse**
**Carinthia**
**48 Years Before Adia's First Deal**

Cora stayed by the ship, not ready to face their father. Lamarse offered to wait with her, but she assured him she only needed time to collect her thoughts. Part of him expected her to steal his ship and bail, but he ignored that intrusive thought and continued over the bridge to Alexon Manor. He spotted Reya sitting by a tree made of gold. It had been a gift from their father's longtime friend, Aurum—the god of Gold.

Reya's long, white hair was in a single braid, and she was wearing his favorite dress. She also wore their family's ring as a symbol of their impending marriage. She was solely focused on the book lying in her lap and didn't look up until his shadow fell over her. She let out a squeal before scrambling to her feet to hug him.

Lamarse sighed as he breathed in her flowery scent. Reya glanced around at the grounds. "Is she not here?" she asked in Lehranian. It was a beautiful language, especially spoken in her lovely voice.

"She is waiting by the Draken."

Reya's face dropped into worry. "This must be difficult for her."

"What about your brother?" Lamarse hadn't dropped his hands from her waist. They had only been separated for a week, but it felt like ages had passed since seeing her fair, beautiful face.

Reya stepped away and tears sprung to her silver eyes, a slight pink tinting her cheeks. "He chose not to come."

A quiet growl rumbled in the back of Lamarse's throat. "I will speak to him."

"No." Reya placed a gentle hand against his cheek and smiled through her tears. "It is his choice. I have faith that he and I will make amends one day, but it will not be before our nuptials. He will regret not attending but that will be his mistake to bear." She kissed Lamarse and the anger boiling inside of him eased. "Now, we must prepare your father for Cora's arrival. I will not have him making her feel uncomfortable."

Determination tightened Reya's face as she turned from Lamarse to the castle's entrance. He caught her by the arm and spun her back to him. She let out an adorable gasp before being silenced by a long-lasting kiss.

* * *

**Lamarse**
**Consumption**
**52 Days After the Awakening (AA)**

Lamarse shifted from a lion to a man before stepping down the steps that led to the dungeon. He passed several glass prisons holding monsters before stopping in front of Coye's. Lamarse stared into the silver eyes of Reya's brother as the floor of the dungeon rumbled.

"Adia has become a Seven Core," Coye spoke. "They are coming for you."

Lamarse said nothing as they stared at each other. The ground continued to quake. Monsters thrashed against their glass prisons, knowing they would soon be released. Lamarse shifted back into his lion form before running up the stairs. The ground quaked as he stepped outside of the mansion. The purple sky flashed yellow streaks like lightning. He looked at the armed hunters gathered in the grass. He would not let them see the fear and heartbreak in his eyes.

His daughter was now a Seven Core. He knew it would happen—that it needed to happen. Ever since Adia had made a deal with Shemu, it was never a matter of saving her body, but her soul.

Black smoke clouds rolled across the thundering sky, dropping dark figures. Chilled to the bone, Lamarse fought to remain stoic as the Shadow Core surrounded him.

A few hunters made to fight, but Lamarse shook his head. In an act of respect to Lamarse, Elizabeth dropped to her knees with Garrett following. The hunters pounded a fist over their heart.

Monstrous sounds grew louder before creatures he had kept locked in glass cages charged out of the mansion, some breaking through windows. Talena, one of the Seven, fought for internal control over Lamarse. Although he could easily break her mind, he let her win. She hypnotized him, rendering him unable to move as he watched his team be slaughtered or dragged away to the dungeons.

Coye strolled out with his hands tucked in the pockets of his white uniform. His sinister smile grew at the sight of the Shadow Core. He nodded to the mansion. "To the dungeon you go, *Brother*."

# CHAPTER THREE

## *Follow You*

**Adia**
**Malibu, CA**
**200 Days AA**

T he wind swept through Adia's shoulder-length hair. Sitting in the backseat of Cora's car, she smiled at the scenery flying by them. The sun warmed her face, and she remembered how for 180 bells, she lived without sunlight. Austin held her hand, staring over her shoulder at the ocean view.

Cora parked the car, and everyone got out, the beach wind whipping through their hair and clothes.

Austin curled his arm around Adia's waist. "Eat or swim first?" He kissed the corner of her mouth, and a pleasant chill ran down her back.

Austin tightened his grip on her hips as they kissed. Dallas whistled, breaking them apart. She threw him a rude gesture before helping Austin set up their towels on the sand while Dallas and Cora swam. They took turns applying sunscreen, and she laughed when he tickled her neck, which led to more kissing. Her lips tingled as he dug into the cooler and pulled out their sandwiches and drinks.

"They seem happy," Adia stated, nodding to Cora and Dallas.

"I think we all needed a break," Austin replied. "A good day."

"A good day," she repeated, recalling their kiss in the City of Souls on the ice-skating rink. Their kiss that Austin didn't remember.

"The water looks great," he said. "Ready?"

She took his outstretched hand, and they ran to the water. She stopped at the shallow waves, but he kept running. He dove in, submerging his body into the ocean. He surfaced and turned back to her as a wave crashed over him. He popped up several feet away and beckoned for her to join him.

The cold waves breaking at her ankles gave her goosebumps.

"Come on!" Austin shouted.

"It's cold," she said with a laugh.

Austin swam closer to her. He shook the water from his reddish-brown hair and smirked. "You mean to tell me that Adia Dawson will happily charge a monster but is afraid of the ocean?"

She scoffed. "I don't like being cold."

"It's only cold at first. You get used to it."

"I've swam in an ocean before."

"In the Shadow World. Come on, chicken." He grinned.

Her smile grew to match his. "Really? So mature."

"I could help you get used to the water..."

"Don't." She glared in warning, but her lips were still curved, making her expression less menacing and more playful.

He swam to her, but she bolted, running back to their towels. He managed to catch her around the waist. She could have fought him but let herself be carried back to the ocean. His wet, cold arms cradled her body as he stood waist-deep in the water. He moved to kiss her, but a wave crashed over them. She rolled around in the water, not knowing up from down. A hand gripped her wrist and yanked her to the surface. She coughed, rubbing away the salty water that burned her eyes. The hand that still held her wrist tightened to a painful hold. She opened her stinging eyes to see a woman standing before her with soaked hair covering her face. Her skin was gray, and she looked skeletal. She breathed out quick, wheezing breaths that grew louder until it was all Adia could hear.

Adia tried to yank back her hand, but the skeletal fingers cut into her skin, making her bleed black.

"Soon," a voice croaked from behind the curtain of black hair where a blue eye peeked at her, "your happiness will only be a memory. A ghost. A forgotten dream."

Adia spotted Dallas, Cora, and Austin playing in the water a distance away, oblivious to her danger. She screamed for them, but they made no reaction to her cry for help. The skeletal woman sunk into the water, pulling Adia under.

Adia fell through black water until she dropped onto a snowy field. Her breaths came out in rapid puffs. She lunged for the skeletal woman, her hands wrapping around her throat, and she squeezed.

Squeezed.

*Squeezed.*

Adia flinched away. The woman shared her face.

A knife dropped into Adia's palm from nowhere. Before she could drive the blade into her doppelganger, she realized they were not alone. Snow drifted over them as she stared at the tree line with bated breath. Something was there, she could sense the evil watching her. She held the dagger before her, wishing it was a gun.

"You feel them, don't you?" the other Adia croaked.

Adia's quaking jaw clenched as she watched the forest, waiting, but not sure what she was waiting for. Seven shadowy figures stepped out, all sharing Adia's skeletal face. One had her mother in a vice grip. Another had Dallas.

"They will kill them all," the doppelganger said.

Adia took the dagger and slit the other Adia's throat as her features transformed into Austin's. He stared at her in absolute horror as he dropped to his knees, blood spilling from his throat.

"NO!"

Bloodied snow rose to her ankles and then her knees. She screamed as Austin floated in his blood, staring up at the night sky with dead eyes. The red snow reached Adia's chest as arms wrapped around her from behind. She gurgled a scream as she was pulled under to drown in her lover's blood.

\* \* \*

## Austin
## Mount Hood, OR
## 200 Days AA

"Adia! Adia! Adia!"

Adia's eyes were closed as she thrashed in Austin's arms. The blankets and sheets had toppled off the bed in her struggle. Austin's back was positioned against the wall as he held his girlfriend in a vice grip, saying her name repeatedly. He could see the shadows' tendrils touching her mind. They often messed with her dreams, turning them into nightmares. Last week, Austin awoke to find Adia holding a knife to his chest. Another night, she scratched at him, screaming. She never remembered the dreams when she awoke. He told her the scratches were from falling into a rose bush. Adia would question that story, but the shadows controlled her reasoning now.

Austin tightened his hold on her as she continued to wriggle in his arms. Her breaths were quick, and she was drenched in sweat. He wouldn't be surprised if she was running a fever. Her body often treated the shadows' invasion like a virus.

Adia took a ragged breath, blinking at him. He loosened his hold into a softer embrace. He grabbed the blanket from the floor and wrapped it around her shoulders, rubbing her arms.

"Are you real?" she whispered, her teeth chattering.

"I'm real, star," he whispered.

She leaned against him, hugging his arm. He could feel her quick heartbeat. He stroked her sweaty face until her eyes drooped. The shadowy tendrils retreated once she fell back asleep.

Austin carefully moved off the bed. He found Lou sitting at the kitchen table, drinking tea. She pointed at the coffee brewing on the counter.

He filled the biggest mug they had and downed the black liquid, not caring how it scorched his throat. He refilled it before meeting Lou's blue eyes, the same shade as Adia's. Her aura, he couldn't help from noticing, was red with white shining through. Austin wasn't always sure what all the colors meant, but from the weeks he had known Adia's mother, he knew her to be strong, brave, and loving.

"Maybe you should try to get some more sleep," Lou told him after he refilled his mug for a third time.

"She'll have another nightmare," he muttered.

Lou's eyes flicked to the hallway where Adia and Austin's room was. "You could sleep on the couch. I'll take watch."

It wasn't the first time Lou had suggested he sleep in the living room. He traced the design on his mug as he said, "I wouldn't be able to sleep." He recalled the one night he slept away from Adia. He had tossed and turned, his thoughts on the terror the shadows were inflicting in Adia's mind. Lou, though able to comfort Adia, couldn't see what they were doing to her daughter. She wouldn't see if they possessed Adia and wouldn't know when to run. In the short time of knowing Lou, he believed she would stay with Adia through the nightmare, even if it killed her.

At the sound of Adia's muffled cry, Austin abandoned his mug and walked back to his room. He climbed into bed and wrapped his arms around a squirming Adia. He buried his face in the crook of her neck and muttered soothing words.

She stilled before asking, "Are you awake?"

Austin kissed her shoulder. "Yeah."

"Did you have a nightmare?" She brought her body closer to his.

"Yeah, sorry to wake you."

"Don't be."

It wasn't long before her breaths were long and deep. Austin, caffeine fueling his anxiety, spent the rest of the morning watching the shadows move along the walls, preparing for when they would invade Adia's mind again.

# CHAPTER FOUR

## *Migraine*

**Adia**
**Mount Hood, OR**
**203 Days AA**

Adia could sometimes feel dread drop in the pit of her stomach for no reason. She stood in the kitchen, cutting tomatoes for dinner and her hands would not stop shaking. Sweat glistened on her brow as her eyes darted around the kitchen before settling on Austin and then her mother. She sensed calm emotions from them as they worked on their tasks for dinner. Austin was pan frying beef while her mother worked on pasta. Their wounds from the cabin fight over two months ago had healed, but her mother still had a slight limp that she hated discussing. Adia's resilience to show weakness was inherited from her mother.

Something tapped on Adia's shoulder from behind. She spun, holding the knife in defense but nothing was there.

"Adia?" her mother's voice was faint as white noise deafened Adia's ears.

*You are fine. There's no threat here.*

The echoing voice faded as Austin's hands cupped her face. Her brow tightened in confusion as to why he looked concerned. Sound returned and Adia flushed with heat.

"What's wrong?" she asked him.

Austin's throat bobbed as his eyes flicked over her face. "You almost passed out."

"I did?" Adia held her head, sensing another headache coming as her stomach twisted with nausea. She stepped away from him, feeling disoriented. "I think I'm getting sick."

"You should rest," her mother suggested. "I'll finish cutting the vegetables."

*No, you're fine. Stay. Help.*

Austin grabbed Adia's hand, kissing her knuckles. "We got dinner. Go rest."

"I'm fine. I'll stay and help." Adia returned to dicing tomatoes. She could sense Austin and her mother watching her. Her shoulders tensed.

*Why are they worried? Why am I dizzy?* Adia's headache grew as acid crept up her throat. She gagged.

*You're fine.*

*You're fine.*

## *You're fine.*

"Adia?"

"I'm fine!" she snapped at her mother.

"Adia." Austin's eyes sharpened on her knife digging into the cutting board. Her other hand was squeezing half of a tomato, the juice spilling between her fingers, resembling blood.

"I know you're fine," Austin said, but his voice sounded off and his eyes were still focused on the knife she gripped.

Adia stared at the mess in her hand and then at the hole she had stabbed into the cutting board. She crossed the kitchen to the sink. Her head throbbed as she vomited. She rinsed out her mouth then went to the garden without a word.

Adia picked out two small tomatoes, barely registering the hard rain soaking her clothes. Her vision spotted as her headache grew into a migraine. She took several long breaths, trying to ease the nausea. She wanted to dive deeper into what had happened—into why she reacted the way she did.

*Nothing happened.* Those words circled in her head. *You dropped the tomato. That's all.*

Adia entered the kitchen, silencing Austin and her mother's hushed words.

"Sorry, I won't drop these. Promise."

\* \* \*

After taking some medication, Adia went to bed early. Her throat ached and she was sweating. Her temperature was 101°F. Even after digging through the storage closet for her winter clothes and stealing all the extra blankets they had in the cabin, Adia couldn't warm up. She hoped she would feel better by the morning. They hadn't taken any cases since living in Oregon. Cora wanted them to work on strengthening their bodies, and she said she would call when they were needed. They received that call two days ago. A large group of dark souls were hiding in Moorpark, California.

Adia violently shivered as she pulled the three blankets to her neck. She had been trying to fall asleep for only a few minutes when she heard the creaky door open and felt the movements of Austin crawling into bed beside her.

"Can I get you anything?" he asked.

"Can you find me another blanket?"

"Sure."

Adia wasn't sure how long she had slept before heat spread throughout her body. She tossed all but one blanket aside and stripped off her sweater and wool socks.

"Are you okay?" Austin asked, not sounding as though he had been sleeping.

"Can you open the window?" she mumbled, trying not to gag.

He was out of bed and opening the window before she could finish her question. She breathed in the fresh air, grateful for the gentle breeze on her face. It was drizzling outside, and she loved the smell of rain. It helped her drift asleep.

When she awoke, Austin's throat was in her hands.

\* \* \*

## Austin
## Mount Hood, OR
## 204 Days AA

Austin coughed until he could find an easy breathing rhythm. Adia scrambled off their bed. He could see the shadows spinning around her, but they weren't touching her anymore. He had been holding Adia through another nightmare when the shadows forced her hands to his throat.

"I-I-I," Adia stuttered, fighting whatever the shadows were telling her. The shadows curved Adia's lips into an unnatural smile. "I had the strangest dream."

Austin held out his hand, ignoring his burning throat and his instinct to run. The shadows forced her to move forward, and she stumbled into his embrace.

"I'm sorry that I woke you," she spoke against his bare chest. "I had the strangest dream."

Austin could see the shadowy tendrils slipping into her ear. He couldn't help the shakiness in his voice as he said, "It's okay." It hurt to speak.

"Everything is fine," she sighed, shutting her eyes.

Once Austin was sure she was asleep, he stepped out of the room to examine the marks her fingers had caused. Alone in the bathroom, he slid to the floor, wrapping his quaking arms around his knees. He buried his face between his arms and hyperventilated. Anxiety and fear were two familiar companions to him. He had gotten better at pushing them down so Adia wouldn't suspect anything was amiss— not that the shadows would allow her to understand what was happening. Once he caught his breath, he swallowed two painkillers, and splashed cold water on his face. He stared at his reflection until he no longer saw fear in his irritated eyes.

He returned to their room with a glass of water.

Adia had awoken, and she sat on the edge of their bed scowling at her shadow on the wall. No tendrils touched her, but he could sense the internal battle happening inside her mind.

"Maybe you should go to California by yourself," she whispered.

His voice was raspy as he said, "Cora needs both of us." He handed over the glass of water and sat next to her.

She gripped the cup with two shaking hands.

"Are you feeling sick?" he asked, grabbing the thermometer. "Do you need more migraine medicine?"

She continued to stare at her shadow. He knew she was piecing together what was happening. It was the reason for her headaches. Anytime she fought the shadows' control, they hurt her body to weaken her senses.

"Are you ready to go back to sleep?" he asked when he saw that her fever had broken.

"It was easier in the Shadow World," she said quietly. "Lamarse told me not to sleep or Sam would mess with my mind in Echo. I didn't need to sleep because I wasn't in a body. I'm always exhausted here, but I've never slept more." Her lips trembled as she said, "Why am I always tired?" She turned to him and touched the shadows under his eyes. "You look as tired as I feel." She focused on the redness along his throat. "What happened?"

"I fell," he knew the lie wouldn't sell. But as he spoke, he saw the shadows touching her mind.

"How did you—?" She broke her sentence with a yawn. Her eyes drooped as she lethargically placed her cup on the nightstand, water sloshing over her hand.

He helped her back into bed and listened to her breathing. His eyes burned, but he wouldn't let himself fall asleep.

# CHAPTER FIVE

*Welcome Home*

**Cora**
**Carinthia**
**48 Years Before Adia's First Deal**

C ora stood at the edge of Alexon Lake, taking in the view of her family's estate for the first time since her mother's murder.

*The seer will betray her kin, wielding Death to better the eye.*

The haunting words echoed in her mind. If she didn't soon create a distraction, the rest of the prophecy would play on a loop, driving her mad.

*The seer's worth will be judged—*

She turned on her heel, eyes dancing around the trees for anything that would drive her mind away from those words. She spotted a familiar lynx, much larger than any domestic feline. He was curled in a ball at the base of a fruit tree.

"Chancel," Cora greeted.

The cat's eyes met Cora's and then looked away.

Cora hesitated before saying, "I missed you."

The cat huffed a breath and lifted his head before rolling to face the other way.

Cora's stomach dropped. "I did miss you! Look!" She pointed to the small silhouette of Chancel tattooed on her hip. "You are the only one I missed."

When he still didn't acknowledge her presence as she sat down, she sighed. "I did not mean to abandon you." He was half her height in length, and thick with fur and muscle. If the cat desired, he could kill Cora, and she wouldn't blame him.

Chancel continued to ignore her.

"I *am* sorry," Cora insisted. "You know why I left." Although Chancel seemed to understand, he couldn't speak, so her secrets were always safe in his keep. Even Lamarse had tried reading his mind once but only saw flashes of light and indecipherable symbols. "I would have brought you with me, but you are a bit spoiled here. You would not live as a king where I sleep most nights."

Chancel met her eyes for a beat. He offered his head and Cora petted him gently between his perked ears. He curled into a ball next to her and purred.

Cora beamed at the cat. The prophecy's words were far from her mind as she told Chancel about all the places she had visited. It had been dark for a long time. No one had come to get her, although Lamarse would have told everyone she was here.

She was starving, but hunger was a familiar discomfort and a preferred one compared to how she would feel facing her family—her father.

"I have to go inside." Cora bit back a groan and made no move to leave.

Chancel blinked his yellow-green eyes in silent waiting.

"Maybe I can stay out here a bit longer."

Chancel stood and trotted toward the bridge.

"I hate this," she muttered before following. Every step filled her with more anxiety.

Ebony stood in waiting at the front door. Cora's fists were so tight, her nails dug into her palms. She slowed her steps, staring into her sister's blue eyes. Ebony was silent until they were within hugging distance, although they did not embrace.

"Your food is cold."

When Cora made no apology, Ebony scoffed before turning

on her heel and walking into the large entrance.

Alexon Manor was massive, and Cora had spent her childhood exploring every hidden room and tunnel. There were days she missed the smell and the sounds of her footsteps echoing off the stone walls. The nostalgic memories were overshadowed by the last week she'd spent residing in it. Anguish dropped like a stone in her stomach, and she feared she would be sick. She focused on her sister's swishing ponytail as she was led to the banquet hall.

Cora stilled at the archway leading into the vast room, tasting acid. Her hands shook and to avoid meeting her father's eyes, she focused on Lamarse and the woman standing next to him.

She had never seen a more beautiful Lehranian. Bred to be warriors, they weren't known to form relationships of any kind. Lamarse's betrothed had a gentleness about her that was unexpected. Her silver eyes twinkled as Cora approached.

"You must be Reya."

Reya broke from Lamarse's side and pulled her into a strong hug. Cora let out a surprised laugh. She had never known a Lehranian to hug.

"It is wonderful to meet you, Cora," Reya spoke in her native language.

"The pleasure is mine." Cora's Lehranian was flawed, but she knew Reya understood.

"Sit with me," Reya said. "I must see how you enjoy my Cuptka."

Cora raised her brows and her eyes strayed to Lamarse.

"She enjoys cooking," he said. "We have already eaten, but she ensured your meal was warmed."

Reya pulled out a chair and Cora sat, biting back a smile that faded when she saw her father watching in silent contemplation.

"Welcome home, Cora," was all he said when their eyes met.

Cora couldn't stop the trembling in her hands as she reached for her cup of wine and sipped. Feeling braver than she thought she could, Cora's eyes moved to the other end of the table, opposite to where her father sat. Her breathing caught as she imagined her mother there. Her mother's laugh echoed in Cora's memories.

"I hear you were in Matadon," Ebony said.

Cora took a long sip as a servant set down her massive bowl of Cuptka—a noodle dish with orange and yellow spices sprinkled over a white sauce.

"I was," Cora replied at last. She dug into the dish. Ebony was already asking another question, but Cora turned to Reya and said with wide, sincere eyes, "Delicious!"

"You should encourage her to speak in Carinthian," Ebony said, her chin jutting up.

"When did you learn to cook?" Cora asked Reya in Lehranian.

Reya looked between Ebony and Cora before answering in broken Carinthian, "A year ago. We do not cook elaborate meals on Lehran."

"Ah." Cora smiled, hoping to ease the tension in Reya's shoulders as Ebony's eyes bored into Cora. "What is your favorite meal to make?"

"Bos Chi," she answered, clearing her throat. "But anything with pasta is my favorite to eat."

Ebony corrected her pronunciation.

"Let her speak," Cora said.

"It is how she will learn," Ebony argued. "Lehranian culture is unfortunate, but in due time people will forget where she came from."

Cora looked to Lamarse, but his eyes were on their father.

\* \* \*

An ache pressed against Cora's temple as Nexa, a longtime family friend who worked at the castle, finished pinning up her hair. It had been a week since Cora arrived home and a busy one it had been. People had arrived from all over for her brother's wedding. Cora spent most of her time hiding on the grounds with only Chancel for company. Her father had gone away, and Ebony focused all her attention on wedding preparations. Cora welcomed the isolation but didn't mind when Reya accompanied her. Reya had a light to her, and Cora always smiled when they spoke.

"What is this?" Ebony said to Nexa, after barging in the room. "I specifically requested a twisted bun with braids wrapped around her head."

"My hair is too short for that style," Cora cut in, stopping Nexa from undoing the pins. She couldn't take more hair-pulling.

"Extensions." Ebony's eyes blazed as they turned on Nexa. "Dye those ridiculous colors out of her hair."

"It is my hair," Cora said, but her tone wasn't as bold as she had meant it to be. "I prefer it this way."

Ebony breathed through her nose, red splotches on her cheeks. "This is not *your* wedding."

"Correct, it is Reya's. I cannot imagine her opposing to—"

"Fix it, Nexa. Or be banished from the grounds."

Nexa sucked in a breath and undid the pins holding Cora's hair in a half-bun. Cora had never seen Nexa cower. Nexa had always been quick to give her opinion even if it differed from their mother's. Cora eyed Ebony, who stood by the door, looking at Nexa in contempt. She hadn't noticed the change in her sister's demeanor since her mother's funeral—when they discovered Ebony had been adopted. She saw the glint in Ebony's eyes—the hunger to prove she held as much power as Cora and Lamarse. That although she was not the blood daughter of Orion, she was still gifted telekinesis.

"Stress of the wedding does not suit you, Sister," Cora spoke.

Ebony spun on her heel and left.

"I am sorry she treated you that way, Nexa. You do not have to—"

"It is fine, Miss Cora. A lot has changed in the way the

servants are run since your—" Nexa's fearful eyes shifted to the door. "Let me go fetch those extensions. I do hope we have enough time to dye your hair."

"Servants?" Cora questioned after Nexa had left. Her mother had never used that term before.

* * *

Cora clapped as her brother kissed his new wife. Her eyes brimmed with tears as they faced their guests with their hands clasped. Reya beamed and Cora's breath caught. Everyone stood, praising their new marriage as Lamarse and Reya walked through the crowd. Cora, being small and quick, caught up to them and threw her arms around her brother, kissing him on the cheek.

"Congratulations." She turned to Reya and spoke in Lehranian, "Thank you for settling for my brother. Welcome to the family."

"I know I am not the one gifted with foresight," she spoke back in Lehranian, "but I feel as though we will become great sisters."

Cora's headache pulsed. She had hoped it was from lack of sleep, but now she feared it was a vision fighting to be seen.

"I am happy for you, Brother," Cora said.

Ebony cut through the crowd, forcing her way before Lamarse and Reya. "The ceremony was so beautiful! I could not have asked for it to go better!"

"Thank you for your hard work on our wedding day," Reya said in a thick accent, her genuine smile faltering. "I am satisfied."

"*Grateful*," Ebony corrected.

"We must let them be greeted by their guests," Cora said to Ebony.

Ebony glanced at Cora's hardened gaze and scoffed. "Who is more important to have in your presence than *family*?"

"Come, Sister," Cora said.

"Or am I not *family* enough anymore?"

Cora placed a hand on her sister's shoulder, but Ebony shook it off. She stepped closer to Reya and commented on the flower choices.

Reya struggled to keep up with Ebony's quick words. Cora turned her annoyed expression to Lamarse, but he was talking with a guest.

"I am surprised your father did not perform a Union," the guest said to Lamarse.

"I am hoping for one soon," Lamarse said, but his throat bobbed. Cora wondered how many times he asked their father for a Union on their marriage. She returned her attention back to Ebony, seeing that Reya's expression had grown wearier.

"Maybe speak in Lehranian so she can better understand you," Cora said.

"It is how she will *better understand* Carinthian. Immersion. It is how we became experts of hundreds of languages." Ebony gave Cora a pointed look. "You...only thirty."

Cora bit her tongue, refraining from telling Ebony she was fluent in a thousand languages.

"Cora!" It was Chattian, a family friend their mother knew from her childhood. She had long black hair and pale blue skin. "It has been too long. What have you been doing?"

Cora explained, with as little detail as possible, about the most recent dealings she had on Matadon as her siblings moved through the celebrating crowd.

"Matadon, did you say?" Chattian's dark eyes sparked, and Cora braced whatever she was about to say, expecting it to be a lecture. "Were you trying to find Jax?"

Cora shivered as coldness swept through her. "He is in Abyss."

Chattian looked Cora over with considering eyes. "Surely, you know he has escaped?"

Cora's fingers tingled. Her father stood amongst a crowd all trying to converse with him.

"Your father did not tell you?" Chattian spoke the words in a hushed tone, placing a hand on her brow as though faint. "It is not my place then."

Cora didn't excuse herself as she shouldered through the guests and approached her father. She pointed a trembling finger at the Master of the Universe.

"You—"

He gave a polite smile to the Harrodian talking to him and excused himself. He touched Cora's arm before guiding her away from the crowd to a quiet hall.

"When?" Cora asked between shallow breaths. She was too hot in the chilled castle.

"A year ago." His words were soft but not apologetic. The Master of the Universe did not make errors. His actions were always well thought out.

Cora opened her mouth to ask why he hadn't told her when her father answered, "Timing."

It was his go-to response when Cora questioned his methods. *Timing was everything.* He saw many futures and revealed little foresight. As the child who inherited some of his foresight, Cora knew she should understand his actions—or lack thereof—but she didn't.

"We will talk after."

"After what?" Cora's eyes had grown wide, and her head throbbed as sweat glistened at her hairline.

A scream startled Cora, raising the hair on her arms.

"What—" Cora pursed her lips, knowing her father would not divulge the answer. She broke out into a run, pulling up her elaborate dress. She reached the Reception Hall but couldn't see what had happened. Everyone made way as Lamarse carried Reya.

"What has happened?" Cora asked.

Lamarse rushed Reya to where their father still stood. "It is Reya. She..."

Reya's eyes were opened but something was wrong. Reya stared at the ceiling and when Cora waved a hand before her face, she didn't react.

"Her mind…" The blood drained from Lamarse's face. "It has gone quiet."

Their father confirmed something to Lamarse in the privacy of their minds.

Lamarse fell to his knees, Reya still cradled in his arms.

"What is it?" Cora shouted.

"A Lehranian has sold his soul to the shadows," her father answered.

# CHAPTER SIX

## *Darkside*

**Cora**
**Mount Hood, OR**
**205 Days AA**

C ora and Dallas parked at the base of the mountain where Adia and Austin waited by their four-wheeler. Cora noticed the dark circles under both Adia and Austin's eyes. Dallas stiffened next to her.

"They look...exhausted," he said.

Cora kissed his tightened brow. "Remember what we talked about. She may look like death, but she must not sense your worry."

Dallas rolled his shoulders as though the task of not worrying for his two best friends was a heavy burden. They walked to Adia and Austin, hand in hand.

"Hey guys," Austin croaked. "Was the drive down here okay?"

"It was uneventful," Cora answered.

"Gene puking his guts out is uneventful?" Dallas asked before greeting Adia with a hug. "Still don't understand why we couldn't use the ship."

"Too many hunters, not enough ships," Cora said as Adia asked who Gene was.

"New recruit." Dallas gave Adia a pointed look that made her smile. "He asks a lot of questions."

"Questions aren't bad," Adia said.

"You'll have to meet him."

"Where—" Austin cleared his throat, but his voice still came out in a croak as he asked, "Where are the others?"

Cora tried not to focus on the marks around Austin's throat as she said, "Grabbing some supplies at the market."

Dallas looked around. "I thought Lou would be here."

"I told her to stay." Austin gave Cora a meaningful glance before smiling at Adia, who remained oblivious.

Cora was grateful Austin ensured Lou had a break, but she couldn't imagine that conversation going well.

After explaining the route and stops they would make, Cora and Dallas got back in their truck and drove to the market where the other hunters waited. Within the hour, they were all on the road heading toward Moorpark.

"This is a good, easy mission," Dallas said, his eyes focused on Austin and Adia's car ahead of them. "Considering our team, there's no chance at failure. The hunters know to stay away from Adia if she becomes possessed. The amulets will help us not shoot each other in the dark."

Cora didn't speak.

"Yet, I feel like we're headed to our tombs." He eyed her before returning his attention to the road. "Or maybe not our tombs." At her continued silence, he said, "You're lying to me."

"I am not lying."

"Lying by omission then." Dallas' grip on the steering wheel tightened along with the knot in Cora's throat.

"You are going to want to help Austin and Adia in the fight," Cora said, her voice small. "You cannot."

"What?" He choked on the word.

"You must keep your distance. Fight far away from them."

"Cora—"

"The bigger picture, Dallas."

"What if—"

"Dallas, *please.*"

* * *

## Adia
## Moorpark, CA
## 206 Days AA

It was after midnight by the time they reached the neighborhood inhabited by dark souls. Adia had driven most of the way after Austin veered off the road, struggling to keep his eyes open. Although she was far from feeling well rested, adrenaline pumped through her at the knowledge of evil nearby. She touched a hand to her gun attached to her belt as she surveyed the quiet street. None of the houses had their lights on, and aside from a slight glow from nearby lamp posts, it was impossible to see.

Austin touched her shoulder and gestured to a shadowed area. She unhooked her gun and aimed it but still couldn't see what he saw. He stepped forward and shot. He cursed and she knew he had missed. Even in the Shadow World, she had better aim, but with his new capability to see in the dark, he had the advantage.

A scuffling noise sounded in the shadows, but before the dark soul revealed itself, someone charged at Adia from her right. The possessed human was shot from an incredible distance. She had no time to admire the sniper's aim before two other demons attacked. Austin and her fought side-by-side until they were parted, now each fighting two on their own. Cora and Dallas had entered the neighborhood a block away, so they weren't in sight, but she could hear their fighting. A cry that sounded human shook Adia, but she kept focus. Austin had stopped to see who had gotten hurt and his mistake cost him a punch to the jaw. Another three demons pulled Adia into a fight before she could see if he was okay.

Panic made her fighting sloppy, and her breathing was uncontrolled. When she was able to turn her attention away, she saw with spotty vision that Austin was being dragged by two possessed men. A dark soul pulled her into a fight. Then another. She couldn't reach Austin.

*Where was Cora and Dallas?*

**They left you. He will die.**

The intrusive thoughts paused her movements, rendering her unable to block a powerful hit to her head. When she opened her eyes, a knife was coming toward her chest. A gunshot fired but it sounded muted, like she was underwater. The dark soul collapsed. She blinked at her blurry hand holding a smoking gun. She pushed herself up from the road, but her movements were slow and awkward. She froze at the sight of the stars as her world swayed. She couldn't recall where she was or why. All sound was muted except the voice in her head.

*He will die.*

*He will die.*

*He will die.*

Adia jolted when her hearing returned. Chaotic sounds surrounded her. She held up her gun, her eyes wide as someone shot behind her. She swung around in time to see a dark soul drop to the ground and an unfamiliar face smiling at her. He took in whatever startling emotions she was conveying and said,

"Woah! You okay?"

She knew the man wasn't possessed by a dark soul because Cora had given the hunters matching amulets that glowed when near another. Cora explained only those who also wore the necklace could see the light. It was small, no larger than a quarter and could be visible even under clothing.

"I'm Gene." The stranger grinned. "Newish recruit." He offered a hand to shake but Adia ignored it. "Oh! You're bleeding!"

Adia touched her forehead, and her fingers came back black. She blinked and the blood turned back to red. "Where's

Austin?"

Gene pointed to where Austin lay, his neck broken. Gene's mouth moved, but Adia only heard the voice in her head.

*I killed him.*

Adia stared at Austin's distorted body and her vision doubled. She could see him standing, staring back at her, translucent like he was a ghost. The more vivid image was of him lying dead.

*I will kill you too,* Gene seemingly said.

She grabbed Gene by the back of his neck and with strength she didn't know she had, lifted him from the street.

* * *

## Austin
## Moorpark, CA
## 206 Days AA

Austin awoke to being dragged along the road. He twisted out of the dark soul's grip. Hands grabbed for him, but instinct took over. He managed to evade the dark soul's hold and placed it in a headlock. Austin constricted his muscles until he heard the sickening crack of the man's neck breaking. He fought to catch his breath, swaying a bit as he searched around. Through the dark, he saw Cora taking on several dark souls. Dallas fought down the street. Austin's eyes glanced over the dead bodies wearing amulets.

Adia stood next to a hunter, staring back in horror. Austin twisted around, fearing what loomed behind. When he faced forward, Adia held the hunter by the neck.

Austin tripped over his own feet, rushing to them. He saw the shadows lifting her arms as a tendril slipped into her ear.

"Adia! ADIA!" Austin reached her, but her other arm pushed him back with incredible force. He landed on the road, rolling until his back crashed against the sidewalk. He couldn't move or breathe for several terrifying seconds. When he managed to suck in air, he used that breath to shout for Cora's help.

The shadows circled Adia and the hunter. Austin ran to them but held up his hands to show he wasn't going to touch Adia. When her eyes met his, they were white.

"He is a dark soul," her voice echoed as Ebony's had in Castle. "His amulet lies. He must die."

"I'm not p-possessed," the hunter said, choking on the last word. "She—"

Austin sharply shook his head to silence the hunter.

"ADIA!" Dallas shouted from down the street. He shot several dark souls before being tackled. Dallas' gun flew out of reach. Cora managed to break from her fight to help Dallas. Austin gave her a pleading look, but she turned away.

Austin trembled as he met Adia's white eyes. "I think there's a misunderstanding." His eyes moved to the hunter's. "What's your name?"

"Gene." Tears streaked through the blood and dirt on his face.

"Cora told me the amulet wouldn't work for anyone but the hunter and only the hunter could remove it," Austin told the shadows, pretending he was speaking to Adia. "I can also see that he is not possessed."

The shadows forced Adia to smile. "You have True Sight."

His hair rose. The shadows were aware he could see them.

"Let go of Adia," Austin dared to say.

"But it's so fun." Her voice continued to echo. "Every time we make her think you're dead, she breaks. I wonder how she will react to this." Adia's other hand moved to the front of Gene's throat. "Will she care for killing a stranger?"

Austin's hands flew forward. "No!"

The shadows' circle vanished at the sound of Austin's hoarse scream. Gene dropped to the floor at Adia's release. He scrambled to Austin and collapsed at his feet as the shadows returned to swirling around Adia. Her control slipped as tendrils struck her skull. Her back arched as she screamed.

Austin stepped up to the swirling blackness, his hair whipping with the whistling wind. "Adia!" He stepped within the circle. "Adia!"

Her hand flung to his throat. He could no longer talk but instead of struggling, he reached for her wrist and stroked up her arm until he was touching her face. He wanted to tell her so many things but couldn't.

"Stop!" she screamed.

The blue in her irises returned.

Austin dropped to the ground.

Spots clouded his vision as he lifted his head.

Adia's eyes moved to the shadows.

# CHAPTER SEVEN

*Kingdom*

**Adia**
**Moorpark, CA**
**206 Days AA**

Shadowy hands held Adia into place.

In the distance, the fight between hunters and dark souls was still happening. Austin kneeled on the road, staring up at her with widened eyes. She remembered writing on the mirror, telling him to run, but he ignored her warning.

"What is it you want?" she asked the shadows.

A chill crawled up Adia's spine as the shadows formed a face. The eyes were hollowed and black like a skull. It mouthed the word that echoed in her mind,

*You.*

"You already have me," she said. "What is it you want now?"

*To learn.*

**To take.**

## *To play.*

Austin moved to stand, but she shook her head. When her hands choked the life out of him, all she wanted was to stop and they listened. She hadn't won control—they allowed her to speak, so she knew there was something she could offer— something to bargain.

Keeping a stoic expression, she spoke within her mind

saying, *Is there any hope for Earth?*

*We* already *have what we want from Earth. We have taken over similar planets before. You* **have** *something in your blood we desire to...study...to take...to play with.* At Adia's perplexed silence, the demon continued, *During Shemu's trial, he offered some information... Information Ebony was* **cursed** *to conceal. You are* **Orion's granddaughter**.

"Who?" she said the word aloud, and Austin's face tightened with frustration and pain.

*So ignorant.*

*So blind.*

*I don't know—*

# So weak.

Knowing they were only going to continue to insult her, she moved on, hoping she could find the answers some other way. *I want you to leave Earth alone. You want...whatever it is you want. You can get that from me? But you need my willingness?*

*We don't need* **your** *willingness, but it does make it...better. We can take every* **soul** *on this Earth, and when we finish, yours* **will be** *the last to go. Or you can come and live willingly as a Seven Core. Eventually* **a shadow** *will take Carinthia.*

Adia locked eyes with Austin, his eyes were glazed like he was fighting for consciousness.

*Give me a year,* she thought.

The skull growled, vibrating her mind.

*A year to live a human life without your torture. A year to hunt down the dark souls. A year without you attached to me.*

*You are a Seven Core.* The skull laughed. *We will not break* **our bond**. A pause. *Still, we are willing to give you a year. Only if you* **make an Allegiance Bond**.

*What—*

*We cannot make the deal here. We must bring you* **home**.

*Home?*

The skull flew to her, and Adia dropped into cold darkness. When light and warmth returned at last, she stood before a massive castle.

\* \* \*

**Adia**
**Shadow Core**
**206 Days AA**

If Adia didn't recall the skull's evil image, she would have thought she was in Heaven. Every color was vivid, and the sun glistened off the castle's diamond walls. She breathed in citrus and Austin, as though she was wrapped in his embrace.

"Beautiful, isn't it?"

"Yes," Adia couldn't help from saying. She stared at the beautiful woman who spoke. She had golden, flawless skin and vibrant green eyes. The silver crown on top of her red head glistened. "Who are you?"

"Talena," she spoke in a lovely voice. "One of the Seven Shadow Core like you. I'm here to guide you through the Kingdom."

Warmth blossomed inside Adia's chest. A laugh bubbled out.

Talena spoke with a playful smile like they were the oldest of friends. "As a Seven Core, you will live in your own perfect world but come here when called upon. You will reign your paradise as you wish. With whom you wish."

The peace dropped from Adia's senses as she pictured Austin hurt by her hands. She needed to return to him—save him.

"Adia?" Talena's eyes glowed.

"No one else from Earth will be here. Only me."

"As you wish."

"Is Sam here?" Adia's eyes swept the castle's grounds, expecting to see the shadow smirking nearby.

"Shemu was sent to a trial for his unwise actions. You need

not worry."

"He's gone?"

"Does that make your decision easier?" Talena eyed Adia in amusement.

She didn't answer, but the peace had returned as though she had fallen back into a comfortable sleep. They entered a garden blossoming with countless flowers that smelled of spring at her family's cabin. She paused to pick up a rose and her fingers tingled at the silky feel. They took their time strolling until they reached a set of large silver doors that opened upon their arrival.

The walls inside were decorated in extravagant paintings and sculptures of all beings. Adia spent far too long taking it all in before being guided into a vast room. Her eyes fell on the eight thrones and the five demons standing before them. Adia only recognized Ebony.

One demon had purple skin, four eyes, and fangs that reached his unusually shaped jaw. Talena introduced him as Eris.

Another was named Seren—a female with dark skin and hair braided below her silver crown. Her eyes were red and when she smiled, Adia stiffened at the sight of her feline teeth.

Camar was introduced next. His cloak shadowed his face. A sword was strapped to his back. He tilted his head at Adia's perusal, and even though his hood shifted, his face remained in darkness.

Hesta had no face. No eyes, no mouth, nothing. Only wearing the same silver crown as the other Shadow Cores. Their naked body had as little features as their face. They morphed into a beast, letting out a roar so loud, Adia stumbled.

Talena caught her, tsking at the shapeshifter who returned to their featureless state. The peace had gone cold while Adia was taking in the Seven Core who sat before her. The sound of Talena's laugh warmed her, and Adia gave them her best smile.

"Come, my niece." Ebony appeared by Adia's side.

*Niece?* Adia's eyelids fluttered as her mind was swept in a daze. The peace was there but cold reality was creeping along its edges.

"Adia?" Talena held her hand, her face the picture of concern. "Are you ready to sit with your family?"

"I make this…"

"Allegiance Bond," Ebony answered, and Talena shot her a pointed look before smiling.

"I make this bond, and I get a year to rid Earth of dark souls. To be with the ones I love—" Her voice caught, and she had to clear her throat. "And Earth will be left alone from future threats in your control. And you will only possess me with my permission. Those are my conditions."

"Yes, yes," Talena said like they were agreeing on where they would eat dinner, not an entire planet's fate. "Now sit and the bonding will begin."

The peace swept through Adia again and as she walked, she had no anxious thoughts. No doubts. No worry about what she was doing. When her back touched the gold of the center throne, she was electrified. The fear, the doubts, and the realization of what she had done sparked to life in her consciousness as pain tore through her. It was too late to change her mind—to escape.

She damned her soul once again.

# CHAPTER EIGHT

## *Zombie*

**Lamarse**
**Consumption**
**206 Days AA**

L amarse was meditating in his glass prison when footsteps echoed down the dungeon stairs. The steps sounded different than the heavy footfalls of a beast or the quieted ones Coye made. Whoever was coming wore heels that clicked with every step. Lamarse straightened his posture and although he couldn't read the mind of the approaching woman due to the glass that encased him, he knew who it would be.

He had expected her to come sooner.

"Hello, Brother."

Lamarse held back a snarl as he met his sister's eyes.

"I had the pleasure in seeing Adia just now," Ebony said. "She made the Allegiance Bond."

Lamarse stared back at Ebony but refused to speak.

"Surely, you can appear to me in your natural form to chat." When he made no change, she sighed. "I hear Coye has been torturing you, but he does not seem to be doing a good enough job. Shall I call for the Seven to have their fun?

"I do look forward to getting to know Adia," she continued. "Shall I tell her how you settled for her mother when Shemu claimed your first love?"

Lamarse kept his face neutral of any emotions, knowing Ebony was eager for any twitch of a reaction.

"Have you gone dumb, Brother?" Her eyes softened, but he knew it was a tactic to get him to speak. "He should have told me I was adopted. How everything could have been different."

This was hard not to comment on—Lamarse hadn't known of Ebony's adoption until their mother's funeral. In the ceremony of blessing her soul in the afterlife, a light was released to touch on her blood relatives. Ebony was left untouched.

Ebony's eyes darkened, revealing the dark soul she had become. "I told Shemu to make the deal with Coye. To get rid of Lehranian filth like Reya."

Lamarse shifted into his natural form and stepped to the glass. Ebony's lips curled into a triumphant smile, but he could see the uneasiness in her black eyes.

"I know," he said.

\* \* \*

**Lamarse**
**Carinthia**
**48 Years Before Adia's First Deal**

Lamarse carried his unresponsive wife to the medical room.

"Who made the deal?" Lamarse's question was directed to his father.

"You cannot save her."

Lamarse had never fought with his father before. He had seen enough arguments between Cora and him to know it was a futile action. Anger and panic stormed through Lamarse.

He needed to save his wife.

He would not accept this fate.

"Who made the deal?"

"Her brother," was his father's calm reply.

Lamarse placed Reya on the medical bed. She stared at the ceiling with no expression. He tried to read her thoughts, connect to wherever her soul had gone to but couldn't. This was unusual. He had gone to planets before when they were on the brink of destruction due to shadow demons. He had always been able to reach the soul and communicate within the Shadow World.

He would find Coye and make him break his Shadow World.

Make him release Reya's soul.

Lamarse ignored Cora as she followed him. He didn't need her help to find Coye. He passed through guests who tried to congratulate him, not knowing the sinister turn their wedding had taken.

"Where's Reya?"

"Eager to leave, I see!"

"Where's your beautiful bride?"

"Congratulations! Gorgeous ceremony!"

Lamarse ignored them all as he passed. He considered forcing their minds into silence before jerking away from the intrusive thought. He shook as he entered the Draken. If Cora spoke to him, he did not know as he programed the ship's flight mission to Lehran.

\* \* \*

**Lamarse**
**Lehran**
**48 Years Before Adia's First Deal**

Finding Coye was harder than Lamarse expected. After hours of searching, Cora suggested they rest. But he wouldn't stop until his brother in-law was discovered. Most of the people on the street appeared to be asleep, but they walked mindlessly around. He touched a few of their minds and saw them in a dark place, terrified and cold. No one understood what was happening to them. Others believed they had died, and this was their penance. Although most were violent by nature, Lamarse didn't believe they deserved a hell as bleak as Coye's Shadow World.

It was approaching morning when they found Coye wandering along a field, miles from his home.

"Lamarse," Cora breathed. "Maybe we should call Father."

Lamarse connected eyes with his sister, breathed in deeply, and entered Coye's mind.

* * *

**Lamarse**
**Coye's Shadow World**
**48 Years Before Adia's First Deal**

While the other souls had been trapped in cold darkness, Coye lived as a warrior king.

Reya had once told Lamarse that despite their parents pitting them against each other, she had been close to Coye. Until she defeated him in the final battle to rule their world.

*Where is she?* Lamarse sent those words into Coye's mind.

"Show yourself," Coye said, looking around.

Lamarse manifested himself before Coye. "When you made that deal with the shadow, you robbed Reya's soul. Redeem your action and break this world. Before your people—"

"Excuse me," someone said from behind Lamarse, "but who are you? What is this nonsense you speak?"

Lamarse turned on his heel and saw Reya, but she displayed no recognition of Lamarse. He tried to read her mind, but since he was connected to Coye's consciousness, he couldn't extend his ability to hers.

"Are you bothering my brother?" She raised her brows.

"This world," Lamarse turned back to Coye, "is not real. It is a manifestation that will kill your people." His eyes flicked to Reya's, and he found it painful for her not to know him. "Will kill her."

"Are you insane?" Coye asked, his eyes speculating. "Reya, call for Huxley. Have him send this intruder to the medic for his mind to be examined."

"You are not aware of what you have done!" Lamarse stepped forward, prepared to show him what he had seen in the streets of Lehran.

"I wouldn't do that if I were you," Reya said.

When Lamarse met his wife's eyes, they had blackened, and smoke billowed around her.

"What is your name?" the demon asked.

"Where is Reya?"

"In the deepest part of this world. A void." Smoke wafted from the demon's nostrils. "What is your name? How did you get here? I didn't invite you."

"Free these people. Break this bond. I…" Lamarse stopped himself from bargaining. It was one of the earliest lessons his father had taught him. Never make deals with demons.

The shadow blew out a smokey breath before smirking. "I will share my name if you share yours."

"Lamarse Alexon of Carinthia. Son of Orion. Now let these people go." If the demon knew Orion was coming, maybe he would let Reya's people go out of fear.

"I promised you my name and nothing else," the demon said. "Shemu. Now, Son of Orion. Get out of this world and live your life to the fullest. I am coming for *you*." Shemu, still in Reya's image, casted a force so powerful, Lamarse's connection with Coye broke, and he returned to Lehran gasping for breath.

# CHAPTER NINE

*An Evening I Would Not Forget*

**Lamarse**
**Carinthia**
**48 Years Before Adia's First Deal**

L amarse tried to reconnect with Coye. Shemu had done something to ensure he couldn't. Cora convinced him to return home. He walked into the medical room where his wife rested with a heavy weight on his shoulders. He relayed the little he had managed to get from Shemu to his father. He expected to be lectured for giving away his identity.

His father observed Lamarse in silence before placing a hand on his shoulder. "Dark times await, Son." He looked as though he wanted to say more.

Lamarse looked into his wife's soulless eyes and anger poisoned him. He stepped away, causing his father's hand to drop. "You knew this would happen."

"I did."

"When?"

"Since before you were born."

"Leave."

"Son—"

"I SAID LEAVE!" The words had roared out of Lamarse, startling even himself.

Cora's eyes were wide and tearful as she silently guided their father out of the medic room. Lamarse made no apology as they left.

He wanted to break things; wanted to release the rage drowning his other senses. He quivered as he kissed Reya's limp hand. Again he tried to reach her mind, but no number of attempts would connect them.

He spoke to her throughout the night and well into the morning, turning away anyone who came to visit. He refused food and ignored Cora's insistence that he rest. The sky was darkening when Reya's senseless movements stilled. Even though she had not responded to his voice before, Lamarse still called her name.

He listened for her heart, but it had stopped.

\* \* \*

Petals drifted with the wind, touching Lamarse's numb face. Five days had passed since his wife's death—since the ruin of Lehran. *Why*, he asked himself in the privacy of his mind, *hadn't I offered my soul in exchange for Reya's?*

"Lamarse." Cora's hand touched his arm.

Everyone was waiting for him to speak. He stepped to the mantel and took long, slow breaths to ease the building nausea. His eyes landed on his father, and his teeth snapped together. He diverted his attention to stop himself from doing something unwise like ask in front of family, friends, and the Guardianship, how his father lived with himself. How he could know what would happen to Reya's people and not do a thing about it.

Lamarse's breathing picked up and he was close to hyperventilating when he saw the gold tree—Reya's favorite spot on their family's grounds. He conjured an image of her reading under the shade of that tree, smiling as she turned a page.

"Reya," Lamarse said her name, not meaning to start his eulogy. He focused on the ghostly image of his wife as he continued. "Reya was—" An ache grew in his throat at his use of past tense. "I should have better prepared." He coughed and his voice trembled as he managed to say, "She deserves the most beautiful eulogy." He was no longer able to contain the emotion pricking his throat. He muttered an apology and stepped off the mantel.

"Coward," he scorned himself before breaking out into a run.

He found himself in the Draken before making the decision to leave Carinthia. He punched in a flight plan and hesitated. His eyes flickered to Cora crossing the bridge. He flew away before she could reach him.

\* \* \*

**Lamarse**
**Lehran**
**48 Years Before Adia's First Deal**

Lamarse walked up the path to Coye's door and kicked it down. He grabbed a vase of dead flowers and smashed it against the wall. Anything he could pick up he did with violence, making sure nothing stood in his brother in-law's manor without being destroyed. Lamarse roared as he threw a framed painting of Reya's parents over the balcony. He dug out his knife and shredded the curtains, blankets, and rugs. His throat was raw from yelling and only at the sound of the front door opening did Lamarse stop. He expected it to be one of the Mortal Guards assigned to sweep through the desolate planet, but it was Cora.

She stared up at him from the bottom of the stairs. She tucked her hands in her pockets as she said, "A Mortal Guard informed me you were causing quite a disturbance. They feared you would throw them against the wall if they interrupted."

"You find my pain amusing?"

The small smile on Cora's face dropped as she climbed the stairs.

He stared at his bloodied hand, unable to recall what had injured him. Exhaustion overtook him as he slid down against a wall. He stared at the chandelier above him, wishing he had broken that too. Shots blasted the light fixture until it fell with a satisfying crash onto the first floor. Cora pocketed her gun and sat next to him.

"I am sorry about Reya."

"Did you know?" His words sounded hollow and emotionless.

"No." She reached for his hand, but he pulled away. "I promise."

His shoulders eased until he remembered something Cora had said. "You..." He turned and saw tears were overlapping her eyes. "You thought Reya would be of Earth."

Cora's throat bobbed.

"You had a vision."

She stared back at him as several emotions flashed on her face. He itched to know what she was thinking, but he wouldn't cross that line.

"When we were younger," she began, "I saw you living on Earth. You were married, but she was not Reya."

"You knew this, and you did not tell me?"

"What was I supposed to make of that vision? Futures can change—"

"If I had known something would happen to Reya, I would have—"

"Would have what?"

He didn't want to say the words.

"If you knew you were meant for someone else, would that have stopped you from falling in love with Reya?"

"If I knew I was going to feel like this..."

Cora hummed. "You always choose love. Even if it means pain in the end. I know you, Brother."

He scoffed. "What would you have done? Knowing everything you know now. Jax—"

"I did know," she whispered.

Lamarse fisted his shaking hands. "You knew what he would do?"

"No!" She sighed, looking pale and sick. "I had a vision of myself throwing his gold amulet in the lake."

"Why would you still go through with a relationship knowing it would end in pain?"

"Because while I was in it, his love was the best gift. The memories are tainted now, but past-Cora needed him."

Lamarse didn't look at her as he walked down the stairs.

"What are you going to do?" she asked.

If he answered, he knew she would try to convince him it was a foolish mission. She would be correct, because the shadows had been around longer than the Guardianship, and no one had ever come close to destroying them.

# CHAPTER TEN

*Save Your Soul*

**Austin**
**Moorpark, CA**
~~**206 Days AA**~~
**365 Days Left**

A ustin had witnessed the shadows flying into Adia. He watched, unable to speak, as her eyes returned to normal, but her movements slowed. She was a sleepwalker; her soul taken away. He tried to scream, but no noise left him. His vocal cords were damaged from being strangled and the act of trying to scream made him almost faint.

Adia collapsed, and he feared her body had died for a horrifying minute before she jerked to a stand. Her eyes glowed white as she strode toward him. He scrambled to stand, but white-hot pain exploded in his broken wrist. She walked past him and snapped the neck of a dark soul and then another's. She tore through the battle, killing before they could even fight back. Within two minutes, every dark soul had dropped dead. She left the hunters alive. Then she collapsed.

The shadows left her body and disappeared. Austin clenched his teeth as he pushed himself up on his good wrist to a stand. He dropped on the road next to Adia, rasping for breaths, sweat dripping from his brow.

"Adia?" he tried to say but no sound came out. He swallowed but the action ripped through his throat. He stroked her damp forehead.

Adia said something, but Austin's ears were ringing, and he couldn't make it out. He came closer and heard a muffled, "I made a deal."

Dallas helped Adia to a stand while Austin flinched at Cora gently touching his throat. He wanted to know what Adia had meant, but he couldn't voice the question. He tried pleading for her to tell him with his eyes, but she wouldn't look at him.

"Your throat is swelling," Cora told him.

He reached out for Adia, but Dallas carried her away. Austin struggled to break Cora's hold until she shoved a coin-shaped pill between his lips. Drowsiness swept through him as the agonizing pain faded.

* * *

## Adia
## Los Angeles, CA
## 364 Days Left

Adia sat at the edge of Austin's bed and watched him sleep. His throat had severe damage, and if it weren't for the healing medication Cora provided, he would have needed surgery. She held his bandaged hand while Cora stood close by. Although the shadows had agreed to only possess her when permitted, she asked to not be left alone with Austin.

"I'm going to find the rest of the dark souls and use the shadows to fight them," Adia announced.

"I will accompany you," Cora said.

"I don't want anyone near me when I'm possessed."

"Adia." Cora's hand rested on her shoulder. "You are weakened after possession. You will need me. We can leave after Austin awakes and give him a proper timeline on your return."

"I'm not coming back."

"You were granted a year of peace. Why would you not return?"

"I-I don't trust they won't hurt him." She shut her eyes, locking her jaw before containing the emotions strangling her words. "I can't believe he risked being with me, knowing what was attached to my soul. So many nights..." She remembered them all now. Every night she woke up with Austin's throat in her hands. "I could have killed him."

"He knew the risk."

"He should have run when I told him to!"

"He never considered running," Cora said softly. "Not once."

"He should have—"

"Would you have run? Would you want him to fight the dark souls alone?"

Tears sprung to Adia's eyes as she mulled over what she would do if the situation were reversed. "We leave in ten minutes," she said at last.

* * *

## Austin
## Los Angeles, CA
## 363 Days Left

Austin awoke with ice strapped to his throat. He was attached to an IV, and he noticed the bag was filled with blue liquid. He saw Dallas sleeping in the chair by his medic bed. He still couldn't speak, but he could swallow without chronic pain. Austin was covered in bruises and his wrist was wrapped. He used his good hand and knocked on the rail along his bed.

Dallas jerked awake, staring back with unfocused eyes. "I must have fallen asleep." He rubbed his face and yawned.

Austin mouthed, *"Where's Adia?"*

"You should—"

Austin hit the railing and mouthed the words again.

"She made a deal," Dallas replied.

The heart monitor beeped rapidly as Austin sat up.

Adia was in the Shadow Core.

He had lost her.

Dallas pushed him back to a lying position. "She's hunting down the rest of the dark souls with Cora's help. Adia told the shadows she would willingly come to the Shadow Core if they gave her a year."

Austin wanted to ask so many questions, but he couldn't.

"Your vocals are badly bruised, but you have strong meds going through you now. It will quicken the healing process, but you won't be able to speak for a while."

Austin mouthed, *"Take me to Adia."*

"I'm sorry, man. You need to rest and Adia..." Dallas coughed. "She isn't too happy with how we handled her being a Seven Core. She needs time..."

The tightness in Austin's chest deflated with those words. He didn't blame her for being angry with him. Nor did he regret his decision to stay.

*"When?"*

"She'll return in a month." Dallas' face dropped a fraction. "Maybe two."

A soft knock interrupted Austin from replying and Lou entered.

"We can talk later," Dallas said. "Rest as much as you can. Sleep will help you heal faster."

Lou's eyes were intense. "Thank you for being okay."

Austin was touched at how much she cared for him, especially since they hadn't known each other long. She stayed, having a one-sided conversation the best they could until the medicine pulled him into a dreamless sleep.

* * *

## Adia
## Miami, FL
## 360 Days Left

Adia gasped as she came to on a street in Miami. Her vision distorted, she could make out people around her were running and screaming. Adia blinked hard and rubbed at her eyes. She unhinged her jaw, trying to pop her ears, but their screams were still muffled. She tried to stand but ended up falling. Gravel cut into her palms and knees.

Cora helped Adia, guiding her to a dark alleyway.

"What happened?"

"You—the shadows—killed the dark souls hiding here."

Adia recalled the hazy memory of letting the shadows possess her. She held her head with bleeding palms and passed out. When she opened her eyes, they were on a ship.

Adia sat up too fast and stumbled, her vision spotting.

Cora handed Adia a bag seconds before Adia emptied her stomach. She dry-heaved while Cora rubbed her back.

"We can return to California tomorrow morning," Cora said after coming back from the bathroom where she deposited the vomit. "Rest here and—"

"No. We're not done."

"It takes a toll on your body every time you are possessed."

"I want this done." Adia closed her eyes, expecting Cora to argue. Cora was an Eternal Guardian, and Adia didn't have fighting energy. Vibrations of the ship powering on startled her and then they were in flight. Cool air filled the cabinet, and Adia took slow, easy breaths. When the aftermath of vomiting subsided, she felt better but still weak.

"Lamarse is my father," Adia said.

Cora kept her eyes on the sky ahead of them. "Yes."

A thousand images flashed through Adia's mind as the puzzle she didn't realize existed came together.

"He's my father," Adia whispered.

* * *

**Adia**
**Washington D.C.**
**348 Days Left**

Adia threw a dagger straight into a dark soul's heart. It was a small herd of dark souls, so she didn't need the shadows' help. Not with an Eternal Guardian by her side. An Eternal Guardian like her father. For the past couple of days, she focused on regaining her strength, having taken Cora up on resting a bit before their next hunt. In silence, Adia mulled over the realization that the lion who trained her to fight—who protected her until she learned to defend herself—was the man who reprimanded her often as a child.

Arms pulled Adia from stabbing another dark soul, and she struggled against the strong hold. She head-butted her attacker and twisted free before shooting the demon down. She charged at the dark soul fleeing to the public street. Shooting him, although more efficient, wouldn't be as satisfying. She jumped on the demon's back and they fought until her fists were slamming into his face. She drove her knife into his chest.

Adia wiped the blood from her blade along her already stained jeans, catching her breath. She had always been fast and strong compared to other hunters. Although she worked hard for her endurance, she had gifted genetics. The realization squeezed her throat.

Adia's legs wobbled. She dropped to the ground and rested her forearms on her knees as Cora finished the fight.

Cora approached, not saying a word. Without meaning to, Adia sensed Cora's worry. Her empathetic ability came not from Shemu's attachment to her soul but because of her heritage.

"I've always had this resentment toward my father," Adia

said once her breath was caught. "I created this person in my mind of someone who was quick to anger and not loving and —" Emotion struck her throat making her eyes water. "I think I wanted to hate him. It was easier than facing the guilt of choosing to save my mom over him."

"Shemu had no say in who lived or died."

"Still…"

"Lamarse understood your choice."

Adia's jaw quivered. "I had so much guilt in thinking I sacrificed my mom to escape Sam that there was no remorse for him. I turned the guilt into hate. Lamarse did so much for me…" Tears mixed with sweat and slid down her cheeks. "I failed him again after Cameron's death. I said horrible things. I —"

"Lamarse was so proud of how independent you became, even when he was worrying about you. He spoke often of how brave you were. He wanted to be the loving father, but you needed to become a warrior."

"You talked to him a lot when he was in the Shadow World?"

"I did."

"But you can't anymore?"

"Not since you escaped."

"Why couldn't I sense others' emotions in the Shadow World?"

"Our gifts are blessings. They can be taken away and given when needed." Cora's eyes moved away, and Adia sensed her anxiety. "My visions are powerful, but I only see what I am meant to. I suppose you did not have your gift in the Shadow World because Shemu would have been granted it as well."

"What does it matter if he could sense others' emotions?"

"When I was a child, my visions were more like a feeling. I would be walking down a hall and get overwhelmed until I turned back. Then I would discover why it was important to change course. As I grew, so did my gift."

"My gift could grow into something dangerous?"

"Emotions can be powerful."

"You said the gifts can be taken away. Why wasn't Ebony's?"

"I wish I knew," Cora responded.

Adia sensed Cora's frustration. Adia drew back her gift as best she could, trying to respect Cora's privacy, but the feeling of frustration lingered until she wasn't sure if it was her own or Cora's.

"I don't know how to grow my gift or control it," Adia said.

"Your gift is unique to you. Practice when you can. We should wash up in the ship. It will be safe to sleep here tonight."

Adia's body grew heavier with every step toward the ship, which had the camouflage feature on. Cora guided her inside, and Adia fought fatigue as she washed her body in the small shower, desperately wishing it was a bath. Then she collapsed on the bed with her towel still wrapped around her, and Cora tucked a blanket over her. Adia mumbled her thanks. She stared with bleary eyes at the silver crown tattooed on her wrist with seven black jewels on each prong. The symbol of her Allegiance Bond.

# CHAPTER ELEVEN

*Sleep Alone*

**Cora**
**Washington D.C.**
**348 Days Left**

Once Adia was asleep, Cora called Dallas.

"Hey," he answered on the first ring, sounding eager.

"Hi." Cora smiled.

"How did it go?"

"Well."

"How is she doing?" She could hear the worry in his tone.

"She knows Lamarse is her father."

His breath made the speaker crackle. "How did she take it?"

Cora glanced at Adia to ensure she was still sleeping. "She is processing. How is Austin?"

"He's on the mend but still has no voice."

They talked for another hour, mostly catching each other up on their days. Cora was still smiling after Dallas ended the call.

A chime alerted her to a message from her father. Cora's senses sharpened as her stomach dropped.

*Jax is headed to Earth.*

\* \* \*

## Cora
## Carinthia
## 48 Years Before Adia's First Deal

Cora had been summoned by her father, and she assumed it was regarding Lamarse. He hadn't left his quarters in weeks.

Her father sat behind his large, mahogany desk. There were portraits from previous Master Guardians decorating the grand room. He had painted them from visions.

Cora glanced around as she shut the door, noticing no Mortal Guards were present. Her footsteps echoed until she reached the velvet chair.

Her father slid over a chronicle—a small box that stored information for missions. "This is everything I have on Jax."

She went rigid, her heart racing. "You want me to find him?" Her tone was cold. "After not telling me he had escaped?"

"What you were doing was more important."

"You would have sent me assistance if you truly believed that."

"I sent Joran."

Cora's breath hitched. Joran was a reliable ally, feeding her information, and even getting her out of tough situations occasionally. She owed a lot to Joran and her stomach twisted knowing he worked for her father.

"Why not tell me?" Her eyes stung.

"You have always bonded with Helena but never me," he spoke evenly. "She was the nurturing parent, and although I have earned respect, I do not deserve your love. I am losing Lamarse's faith. I am asking for your loyalty. Work for me again."

"Lamarse's faith?" She wasn't expecting him to elaborate. Her father was known to give enough information to grip your attention and then starve you for answers.

"I have dreaded Reya's death since before he was born. Worse times will come, and I need him to be prepared for them."

She winced at the pressure building in her head, a vision fighting to be seen.

"I will give you a moment." Her father exited, his footsteps clanging in Cora's mind as the room tilted. She gasped and gripped the edge of her father's desk.

*A man wearing a tuxedo and a bright smile stood by Cora in a wedding dress. A woman with dark hair and blue eyes hugged her.*

*"Congratulations, Cora," she said. "You chose a great man."*

*"Thank you, Adia." Cora said.*

*Adia turned to the man but as she moved to hug him, their surroundings changed. Adia's eyes glowed white in the darkness. She had the man—Cora's husband—by the neck. Her lips twisted into a smile.*

*She broke his neck.*

*"DALLAS!" Cora's scream was deafening as she dropped to her knees.*

Cora's vision faded, leaving behind overwhelming emotions. "Dallas," she choked.

Her father reentered the room as soon as Cora had caught her breath. "What did I see? Who—"

"I have seen that future too." He reclaimed his seat. "There are alternate paths dependent on choices."

Cora blinked, releasing a couple of tears. "What choices?"

"Start working for me," was all he said.

Cora's jaw trembled as she took the chronicle and opened it. The image of her ex-boyfriend projected above the box.

*Jax Aurumson*
*Convicted Murderer*
*Status: **ESCAPED***

Cora's whole body shook as she swiped for the next image—her mother's bloodied body, killed by Jax's sword.

\* \* \*

## Cora
## Baldah
## 48 Years Before Adia's First Deal

Cora trudged through the high grass, sweat beading at the base of her neck. She used a sword to cut down jungle weeds that became dangerous once touched. She wore a guardian suit—thick material that cooled her skin some, but mostly protected her from bullets and knives. She wasn't sure what Jax's reaction would be in seeing her, but she knew she needed the best of her father's suits to face him. Abyss was a world for the most dangerous of prisoners, and she knew Jax. He was a free spirit who never stayed in one area for long. Cora had no doubt Jax would kill her to avoid returning to Abyss.

Cora crouched behind a tree as she smelled smoke. She pulled out a small eyeglass with x-ray capabilities. She couldn't see Jax but recognized some of his men from the chronicle. She sent a quick message to her father and climbed a tree to better spy.

Something slithered across Cora's boot. Although her reflexes were fast, the jungle weed caught her by the ankle and yanked her off the tree. She hung upside down, six feet from the ground where her sword had dropped. She moved to find her knife when a sharp blade touched her throat.

"Hello, goddess."

"Jax."

"Lovely sword you have here." Jax examined her sword as Cora retrieved the knife clipped to her boot. "You cut your hair. I did prefer the gold, but purple is nice," Jax spoke in Gradian. His deep voice used to make Cora's stomach flutter, but now cold ice doused her senses as she stared into the golden eyes of her mother's killer.

As he reached to stroke her hair, she dug her knife into his hand. The sword he held made a thin slice across her throat as he reacted. She cut the weed that was squeezing her ankles and hit the ground hard.

"That wasn't—"

Cora tripped Jax as she stole the sword back.

He laughed and then rolled, pushing her legs, so she fell in jungle weed. Her movements were frantic as she chopped the wild plants, but she wasn't fast enough. One curled around her throat as two others bound her arms.

Jax stalked to Cora, and she was more worried about his intentions than being strangled by jungle weed. She kicked at the ground, trying to gain enough momentum to escape both Jax and the weed. Jax cut the weed around her throat.

"I worry, goddess..." His sword paused at the weed around her arms. "...that you will capture me once I cut you free. Do I have your promise to have a sensible conversation before dragging me back to Abyss?"

Cora spat in his face. His sword flashed before her eyes. It took two breaths before realizing he had cut the weed. She studied him, trying to find the trick in his actions. His curly, brown hair was wild and damp from the sweat that glistened off his brown skin. He seemed taller somehow but was a lot skinnier than the last time she had seen him.

"The look you gave me at the trial," he said, speaking in Carinthian, his deep accent making her heart ache. She had been teaching him her language before everything changed. He switched back to Gradian and said, "It haunts me, goddess."

Cora was silent as she stood and observed their surroundings. His men weren't far.

"I wished we could have had a proper future together," he said and the pain in his eyes looked genuine.

"You never wanted a future with me," she told him.

He shook a finger and smiled, but it didn't remove the sadness in his eyes. "I never wanted to be married."

Cora kicked him in the stomach. He fell into the jungle weed. She pulled out her chronicle at the same time she heard an aircraft flying overhead.

Jax didn't struggle in the weed. "I really am sorry." He sucked in a large breath as the weed tightened around his throat. "Happy Snakes!"

Jax's men sprang from their hiding spots. Cora jumped behind a tree, but she still suffered a shot to the leg. The suit was impenetrable, but the bullet sent an electric current through her. She collapsed to the ground, unable to breathe. Her eyes filled with angry tears as Jax squatted before her.

"I think this look will haunt me too," he said, and she found his voice to be more serious than she had ever heard it be, even during his trial. "Until we meet again, goddess."

# CHAPTER TWELVE

*Bartholomew*

**Dallas**
**Los Angeles, CA**
**347 Days Left**

"Straighten the arm a bit," Dallas instructed a hunter named Marla. She shot and missed the center of the target by three inches. The names of the hunters who had died at Moorpark resonated in Dallas' mind, making him wonder who else he would train to die.

"Dallas!" another hunter called as Dallas' phone rang. "Some guy named Jax is here to see you!"

Dallas' hands tingled as he glanced at Cora's name flashing on his phone. He ignored her call and stalked toward the hunter. "Where is he?"

"Entrance."

They found Jax lounging in the front desk's chair, flipping through a magazine. He held up a finger and continued reading. He blew a breath, his messy, brown curls moving temporarily from his young face. Like Cora, he looked to be in his early twenties, gifted with eternal youth. If Dallas hadn't known who Jax was, he wouldn't have thought him to be a threat even with the sword strapped to his back. Jax's golden eyes lit with amusement at something he read.

Dallas cocked his gun.

Sighing dramatically, Jax tossed the magazine on the desk. Dallas resisted the urge to step back as Jax swiftly approached. Jax's smile was gone as he looked at Dallas closely. Then Jax laughed as though they were playing a game and he failed to keep a stoic expression.

"Amos Makoa Dallas!" Jax clapped Dallas' shoulder. "Such a pleasure to meet my goddess' husband!"

\* \* \*

## Adia
## Albany, NY
## 347 Days Left

Cora had left Adia in New York when Adia refused to return to California. She couldn't bare seeing Austin yet, or the wounds she had inflicted. Fear held her back, but she blamed it on wanting to fight the dark souls scattered across the world. When Cora had showed her the map of demon hordes, she realized it would be more than a month's work, even with the shadows' help. The World Union had teams in every country targeting dark souls discreetly. Cora was unclear whether they allowed Adia's connection with the shadows to help, or if they were even aware. The world was divided between knowing about the possessed humans and believing the attacks to be a political agenda or conspiracy. Even some cities that were invaded believed people were rioting and feeding into chaos. Many religions preached these were signs of the End of Times. They would never know how close to the truth they were if Adia hadn't made an Allegiance Bond.

Cora arranged for her to stay in a hotel. While Cora was away, Adia promised she would only spy on and not fight the dark souls unless they intended to hurt anyone. The world wasn't back to normal since the Awakening, but there were more businesses now. Buildings were being restored, and some restaurants reopened in privileged areas.

Adia walked along the street; her head tilted up at the cloudy sky. Someone was following her. Her fingers twitched to her weapon, but she made no other show that she was aware of her stalker. She turned into an alleyway and spun, ready to attack but nobody passed. A blade touched her throat, and Adia made a swift evasion, resulting in her neck getting nicked. The gun was kicked out of Adia's hand as she pulled the trigger, the bullet missing the Hispanic woman by inches. Adia blocked three of the woman's hits before managing to kick her leg. The woman recovered before Adia could throw a punch and after breathlessly fighting, the shadows spoke to her mind.

*Let us fight her.*

Adia was taken down. She calmed her breathing, even though her lungs pinched at the pressure of the woman's knee on her chest. She used her legs to rise before swiftly twisting. Adia rolled away from the woman and found her gun, shooting her in the shoulder.

"You fight like your father," the woman said in an unfamiliar accent. She barely reacted to the pain of being shot. "I am an ally to Orion."

Adia narrowed her eyes in distrust. "Then why fight me?"

"I wanted to see his granddaughter fight."

"You're not from Earth?"

"No."

*Don't trust her*, the shadows spoke in Adia's head. Fingers tapped on her mind, asking to relinquish control.

"I could have killed you," Adia said, sweat sliding down her face.

"Your aim needs work if that was your goal."

Adia's jaw locked. Her aim was perfect, so why hadn't she shot to kill? "How did you get here? To Earth?"

"My ship. I have been searching for Cora, but she moves faster than I can track. My ship also doesn't have advanced features like hers. I have been fighting the possessed earthlings, hoping to run across one from your team. I wasn't expecting to find you alone. Adia."

"Why didn't—"

"You have a lot of questions. I'm fine answering, but I am losing a lot of blood."

**Let her bleed.**

The woman smiled. "Are the shadows telling you to kill me?"

Adia tightened her hold on the gun. "How do you—"

"Ally. Of. Orion." She huffed a laugh. "I would think you would want to do anything opposite the shadows demanded. Unless they have darkened your mind?"

*Kill her.*

*Kill her.*

*Kill her.*

Adia lowered her gun.

\* \* \*

### Cora
### Los Angeles, CA
### 347 Days Left

It had been an hour since Cora first called Dallas, and he still wasn't picking up his phone. She tried to Vision Walk, but nothing happened. She stormed into the hunters' warehouse with her gun. "Dallas!"

A chuckle had Cora spinning, and she balked at the sight of Jax behind the front desk. Her heart raced as she removed her eyes from her murderous ex and scanned the warehouse for Dallas. Her shoulders relaxed a fraction at the sight of him exiting the kitchen with two steaming mugs.

"I adore your dramatic entrance." Jax reclined all the way back in his chair and then sprung forward. He bounced a few more times, his brows rising in amusement. "This is so joyful! I love how it squeaks!"

"You learned English?" Cora watched Jax's every move.

Dallas set down the two mugs on the desk. At the sight of fire in Cora's eyes, he held up his hands in defense.

"What's English?" Jax asked, setting the coffee on the desk.

"It is what you are speaking." Cora couldn't contain the viciousness from her voice.

"Oh!" Jax laughed again and Cora imagined throwing him against the room, driving her knife into his throat. "I had a universal translator implanted." He tapped his head three times.

Her watering eyes bore into Jax's golden ones. "Where did you steal one of those from? They're—"

"Your father's technology? I have quite the story for you."

Cora's phone rang. She glanced at the screen and seeing it was Adia, picked up at once.

"A bit rude," Jax muttered.

"Adia. What is wrong?"

"I ran into...someone."

"What? Who?"

"She said she is an ally to Orion. Did he tell you anyone else was coming?"

"No. Do you need my help?" Cora kept her eyes on Jax, not wanting to leave him alone with Dallas but also not wanting him to overhear any vital information.

"I can handle her until you get back." There was a pause. "I'll let you go."

"Call if you need me. I will be there when I can."

Cora pinched the bridge of her nose and turned to Jax.

"How's Adia?" he asked, his smile back now that Cora's attention was solely on him.

"Start talking."

"Or what? You'll shoot me? What good will that do?"

"It will be satisfying."

Jax slapped his thighs before standing. His footsteps were light as he paced back and forth. He picked up his steaming coffee and downed it, not wincing at the hot temperature. His eyes met Cora's and the light in them dimmed. "I didn't kill Helena."

Cora shut her eyes and breathed through her nose. She half-expected Jax to use this moment to attack. When her eyes opened again, his expression was grave as he said,

"Ebony did."

\* \* \*

## Jax
## Abyss
## 49 Years Before Adia's First Deal

Smoke swirled at Jax's feet as he followed the line of prisoners. He couldn't count the years he had spent in this hell. There was no day or night. No tracker of time. It was purgatory for those who had committed the worst of crimes. He didn't blame Orion for casting his wife's murderer in Abyss. Only, he damned the wrong man.

Jax's hands weren't clean. He still recalled every life he had taken over the years. They were necessary kills—a means of survival in a war Orion ignored.

"Move," someone snarled from behind. In Abyss, everyone seemingly spoke the same language, regardless of being from different planets.

Jax lifted his eyes from his feet, realizing he had fallen a few steps behind. "Where are we even going?" he asked, his voice void of all emotion. "What is the point of this?"

"Shut up and move." The man shoved Jax.

Jax raised his hands as if in defeat before turning to grip the prisoner by the hair and kneeing him in the nose. He spat blood and attacked back. Jax fought well, considering the man was twice his size.

A whistle blew overhead, and Jax was pulled from the man. "Okay. Okay. We're done."

Although the other prisoner was left in the line, Jax was being dragged away. He struggled, but the Mortal Guards were equipped with special suits, giving them unnatural strength to handle the most dangerous of prisoners. Jax kicked up the ashy dirt into the Mortal Guard's eyes, who jerked his head back, but it did nothing to free Jax.

Jax saw the cliff ahead.

"Okay. We can talk this through. It was a stupid fight. I'm stupid. But I'm the son of a Ruin witch! You really can't blame me for fighting. Blame my mother!"

When the Mortal Guard made no show of stopping, Jax pleaded, "Oh please. Kind sir of Orion!"

The cliff's drop drew closer.

"Wait. Wait! Please! Plea—ARRRRRGHHH!" Jax spiraled down the cliff and into a black pit. He had seen other men drop, never to be seen again. He expected to pass out from the long fall but didn't. When he landed, he caught his breath long enough to scream again. His eyes were shut, and he thrashed on the floor, not sure what other hell he had been dropped into.

"Be calm," someone spoke.

Jax peeked through the slits of his eyelids and another shock buzzed through him. He was in Orion's office.

\* \* \*

## Jax
## Carinthia
## 49 Years Before Adia's First Deal

"Drink. It will calm your nerves," Orion spoke in Jax's native language having no hint of an accent.

Jax stared at the goblet on Orion's desk, at the floor he was sprawled on, and then up at the ceiling. He expected to see the opening to Abyss there. "How?" His eyes widened. "Did you catch the real killer? Am I freed?"

"Stand."

"Right." Jax laughed and sprang to his feet. He took the goblet and drank it in one swallow. He made a face. "This isn't mead."

"It is tea to help calm your nerves."

"It tastes—great! Well done making this tea. Highest compliments." Jax plopped on the cushioned chair across from Orion. Dust coating his prison attire clouded the air around him. He groaned as he gave into a satisfying stretch. "Where's Cora?"

"She left Carinthia after your trial—four years ago."

"Good. I didn't want to see her anyways. So." Jax clapped his hands. "Who did it then? Whom shall I kill?" At Orion's twitching lips, he amended his words. "I mean escort to Abyss. With kind force." It was a lie. Helena's murderer would suffer.

"I owe you an apology."

"Yes. Yes, you do. But you did lose your wife, so I forgive your blindness. It's always hard to see clearly when we're in grief. When my Felisa died, I couldn't sleep for weeks. She was the best dragon, really. Irreplaceable, although I did try finding a new one. I befriended this draemaki—"

Orion held up his hand to interject. "I knew you were not Helena's murderer from the beginning."

It took Jax a moment to comprehend. "I take back my forgiveness." He made a gesture of stealing the air between them as though his forgiveness was tangible.

"I knew Helena would be killed before I met her."

Jax's mouth slowly worked, digesting those words. "That's... wrong." He looked around, seeing how they were alone. "Did you," his eyes grew large as he mouthed, "*kill her?*"

Orion's features became drawn. It was the same tired look Jax often received.

"I did not kill my wife."

Jax was pleased to hear a sense of mourning in Orion's tone.

"There has been a series of events set into place since before Helena's life," Orion said. "Events that will continue long after her death."

"Events such as...?"

"Time will tell."

"Cora hates it when you say that, and I must agree. You're annoyingly cryptic."

Orion stared back at Jax with unreadable eyes. "Cora must continue to believe you killed her mother."

"No," he drew out. "How about a different plan?"

"I will work with you to ensure you are not caught. I will give you all the necessities to stay in hiding and never return to Abyss."

"I didn't commit the crime, so I am free anyways." Jax stood, brushing more dust from his clothes as he turned for the door.

"You have committed many crimes. You are a thief. You have killed—"

"No one innocent." Jax worked to open the door.

"You are not a judge of a life's value."

"I don't have a choice, do I?"

"You always have a choice," Orion said. "It is the consequences you have no control over."

"Right. No choice." Jax returned to his seat. "Why can't Cora know? She loves me, I mean absolutely adores me. Terrifying how much she wants to marry me."

"You will never marry her."

"I know. She keeps begging but—" Jax's thoughts caught up to his words. "I can't imagine she would stay with me if we *never* married."

"You have no romantic futures together."

Jax's mouth went dry. He downed the rest of the tea as he thought back to his last kiss with Cora. To the way she laughed against his lips. It was a game he used to play with her: What could he get her to do first? Laugh, kiss, or draw her weapon on him?

"I…" Jax rubbed at his aching chest. "*No* futures together?" The air became thin and no matter how many breaths Jax sucked in, it wasn't enough. "I don't think your tea is working."

"Deep breaths."

"I'm trying…" His head spun as the pain in his chest grew. "You can't let her go on thinking I killed her mother!"

"She must or the future we need will not occur."

Jax slammed his fist on Orion's desk. "What future could I possibly want if Cora hates me?"

"It is all to ensure the shadow demons are destroyed."

"Shadow demons? Like in folktales?"

"They are real and need to be stopped."

"How?"

"Through a long, painful journey."

Jax rubbed his aching throat. "I think I'm allergic to your tea."

Orion filled another cup from the kettle. "You are about to cry."

Jax scoffed. "I don't cry." The tightness in his throat shifted to burning as tears flooded his eyes.

\* \* \*

## Cora
## Los Angeles, CA
## 347 Days Left

*Jax speaks the truth. Trust him.*

Cora blinked at the incoming message from her father and then looked at her ex-boyfriend.

"Ebony killed my mother?" Dallas' hand moved to the base of Cora's back. She leaned into his touch as her vision swam with tears. "She framed you?"

Jax nodded.

"You been hiding with my father's help?" She spoke slowly, fighting to believe his story. "Until now? Why?"

"Orion ordered me to come to Earth," Jax said. "He's had me blending in with various enemy groups, gaining intel. No one, and I mean not a single person ever suspected I was a spy. Perfection. I was…"

Jax's words faded as a dull ache pulsed in her head. A vision lit up her mind.

*An unconscious Adia was being carried by someone Cora didn't recognize. She was thrown in a trunk. The woman with demonic eyes threw a hotel blanket on top of Adia and slammed the trunk closed. She got in the car and drove off, smiling in the rearview mirror.*

"Cora? What is it? What did you see?" Dallas held her face as the vision cleared.

"It's Adia," she whispered.

\* \* \*

## Austin
## Portland, OR
## 346 Days Left

The kettle whistled, startling Austin who had dozed off on the couch. His phone fell as he sat up. He scurried to pick it up, the whistle growing louder. He checked his notifications, but still nothing. It had been nineteen days since he last spoke to Adia. He rolled his neck as he walked to the kitchen, pulling the kettle from the stovetop. He had recovered from all his injuries, and although he had his voice back, he rarely used it. He had made tea to wake himself up enough to run but now his motivation dulled. He returned to the couch, his vision clouding. Lou made him eat breakfast, but he had skipped lunch. With a sigh, he ignored his hunger and rolled onto his side.

Adia made a deal with the shadows. Even though he knew the day would come, he was never sure of when. They had 346 days left, and he wanted to spend every one of them with Adia, only she was away.

Not calling him.

It was well into night when a humming awoke him. He opened his heavy eyes, the realization slowly settling. He almost fainted for how fast he stood. He blinked his dizziness away as he ran to the backdoor. Lou was by his side soon, her eyes alert.

Cora stepped out from her ship, looking pale and weary. He hurried past her, but she caught him by the elbow.

"Adia is not in there."

"Where is she?" Austin asked.

"I do not know."

Austin leaned against the ship's door, his eyes scanning inside as though Cora was playing a cruel joke on him. He stared at Adia's jacket on one of the beds.

"Is she possessed?" Lou asked from behind him.

"She has been taken by someone we do not know. I need you both in California to help find her."

"You're psychic," Austin said the words, but he felt disconnected from them, as though part of him believed he would awake from a nightmare. "How can you not know where she is?"

"I will tell you all I know," Cora said.

Austin scoffed.

"Could she be in the Shadow World?" Lou asked.

"They cannot take her until the year is up," Austin said.

"They're shadows," Lou argued. "They lie."

Cora's silence made Austin tear his eyes from the jacket and look at her. Through his teeth, he asked, "What is it?"

"I didn't tell you... I thought *she* should." Cora's shoulders slumped. "She made an Allegiance Bond."

Austin looked between Lou and Cora, hating the beat of silence, knowing it meant something worse than a deal. Something that scared them both.

"What does that mean?"

"She's no longer loyal to us," Lou said, meeting Austin's stare. "She has no will."

"Adia killing them from within the Shadow Core—"

"Is nearly impossible now," Cora finished for him.

"Nearly," Lou emphasized, and she placed a hand on Cora's

shoulder.

Austin cursed as he stepped off the ship. He ran a hand through his already messy hair, not remembering when he last showered.

"She cannot be possessed unless she permits it," Cora said.

"That's good at least." Austin felt faint.

"If her capturer keeps her asleep, she doesn't have the shadows' power," Cora explained.

"Can she be killed?" Lou asked.

"Cora?"

Cora's expression tightened. "I don't know."

# CHAPTER THIRTEEN

## *The Chain*

**Lamarse**
**Hylea**
**47 Years Before Adia's First Deal**

Planet Hylea was almost gone. Lamarse had little time. He traveled from mind to mind, in hopes one of the Hyleans would lead him to the one who damned their planet. Hyleans were peaceful beings, against war and resolved conflict through non-violent solutions.

Lamarse had entered his two hundredth mind, walking the alternate reality where the Hyleans lived in a chaotic society. The soul he connected to was at a table, gambling with a female propped on his lap. Lamarse searched around, hoping to find any clue as to where the shadow could be. He was exhausting his ability.

"Who are you?" the female on the Hylean's lap asked Lamarse.

He hadn't made himself known yet to the mind he had entered. No one should be able to see him. "Shemu."

She laughed. "No. Shemu is…" The shadow considered before her eyes blackened. "Who are you? How do you know of Shemu?"

"We have unfinished business."

"*Unfinished business.* How vague," the shadow said. "I need more than that."

He hesitated, too tired to consider any tactics. He hadn't thought about what he would do when he found the shadow who robbed the Hyleans' souls. He focused on one task at a time. His grief powered his endurance, but now he foolishly had no plan.

The shadow raised her hand, most likely to push him out of her world, so he admitted the truth. "Shemu claimed the soul of my wife. I need to know her soul safely passed on."

"Interesting." She leaned against the male Hylean, who made no notice to Lamarse's presence or their conversation. "I will tell you where Shemu is at the cost of knowledge. What planet are you from?"

"Carinthia."

The female's face shadowed as her smile grew, her black eyes eyeing him with hunger. He had a blessing on his identity, so she couldn't know he was Orion's son, but people knew where Orion resided. No one could enter without permission. It was a heavily blessed planet.

"You can find Shemu on Valithi," the shadow said, her teeth flashing.

* * *

**Lamarse**
**Valithi**
**47 Years Before Adia's First Deal**

Finding the core was impossible, but Lamarse knew if he caused enough trouble in the Shadow World, Shemu would find him. Every mind he invaded, he revealed how their soul was in Hell. He didn't ask questions, only told startling truths. By the tenth soul, Lamarse was discovered.

Reya stood before him, wearing a silver dress and long, white hair. "Shemu sent me to…" She lowered her silver eyes. "I didn't know it would be you."

"Reya." Lamarse pulled her in a tight, breathless hug.

She pulled away and stared at him openly with watery eyes. "It has been so long." Her voice was void of any accent. "I forgot your face."

Lamarse shook his head, squeezing her hands. "You have only been gone a year."

Her face crumpled. "It has been a lifetime of torture, my love."

Lamarse rested his forehead against hers, their lips only a few inches apart. "I have found you. You are safe now."

"You have come to save me?"

"We only need to—" Lamarse was yanked back. He reached out for Reya, but everything was a blur around him as he traveled at high speed until he saw the dark sky of Valithi.

"Reya!" he shouted once he found his breath. "REYA!"

"Son," his father spoke from above him.

"You pulled me out?" Lamarse's surroundings tilted back and forth as he sat up from the grass. "I found her! I—"

"You cannot save her."

Lamarse got to his feet before stumbling. He ignored his father's outstretched hand and walked to a man who stood motionless, staring mindlessly at the streetlight. Gripping his shoulder, he forced a connection.

It didn't work. Lamarse shook his head. He tried a different mind. He stalked back to his father, pointing an accusing finger at him.

"What did you do to me?"

"Gifts can be taken away," his father said. "Stop your crusade. Correct your path." His father gave his son a heavy look before leaving.

Lamarse stayed behind, panicking to reach anyone's mind. Hours he tried to return to Reya, but every thought was silent to him.

* * *

## Lamarse
## Tiaxo
## 47 Years Before Adia's First Deal

Lamarse couldn't find Reya without finding Shemu. He couldn't find Shemu unless he entered someone's mind. His connection to her was lost. It was like losing a limb, not able to touch minds in battle. He was drenched in blood, stabbing foes left and right, breaking necks when the kill was unsatisfying with his weapon.

He had survived far harder battles, fought stronger men. He only accepted this mission because he needed a way to release the tormenting anger. If Reya's soul had passed on, he believed it would be easier to move on. Knowing she was trapped, unable to reach the paradise she deserved, he would never rest until he found a way to save her.

Reya was where Lamarse's thoughts had been when someone attacked him from behind. He tried using his telepathy in defense, remembering too late it was gone.

Lamarse coughed blood, wondering if he had a better chance at rescuing Reya in death. He prayed for his soul to reach Reya and rescue her from within the Shadow Core.

* * *

Sunlight blinded Lamarse. He wasn't sure how many days or weeks had passed since dying. The battle was over, and he was sure they had won. He sat up, stretching his neck and arms. His movements were heavier, slower.

Hoping his telepathy had returned, he listened for anyone's minds.

"We were wondering when you would be Reborn!" A Mortal Guard named Gordan startled Lamarse. "What new ability do you have this time?"

Gordan was yards away, yet Lamarse hadn't heard his mind

or his footfalls approaching. Lamarse stretched his hearing out, but the sound around him wasn't amplified. Swallowing, he approached Gordan, touched his shoulder and focused on reading his mind, ignoring how it was an invasion of privacy.

Silence.

*Gifts can be taken away*, his father had said.

\* \* \*

**Lamarse**
**Matadon**
**20 Years Before Adia's First Deal**

Twenty-seven years had passed since Lamarse had failed Reya.

If he wasn't worthy of a new ability, how was he worthy of being Reborn? What purpose could he possibly have unless it was to save Reya? Every effort toward rescuing her got him killed. Each countless death lost him a gift.

Telepathy.

Enhanced hearing.

His injuries took longer to heal.

He lacked endurance.

He struggled to recall things or retain information.

He lost fifty pounds of muscle.

He needed glasses.

Pollen made him sneeze.

His hands shook when holding a gun.

He had a low pain tolerance.

His beard grew gray hair even though he did not age.

Someone took the chair next to him at the tavern he had been spending most of his days drinking. If they wanted him dead, he would be Reborn. He would be less of the man he was now, if possible. Still, he would return. He wondered how many deaths until it all ended. That's what he wanted now. For it to end. He finished the rest of his drink and summoned the barkeep by lifting his hand. It dropped painfully on the sticky table.

"You look horrible," Cora said.

Lamarse wasn't sure if she was a hallucination. He ignored her either way.

"Someone told me they saw you here," she continued as the barkeep replaced Lamarse's empty glass with a full one. "That you are living here."

He grunted as he knocked over his drink. Alcohol used to not affect his blood. Now he died if he drank too much. Cora held his elbow in place, preventing him from calling for another drink. She still had the gifts blessed upon her at birth. She had never died, so they weren't as advanced as his had been. Now, she could easily defeat him.

He jerked his arm away, but the movement made him vomit.

"Come on." Cora lifted him from the chair as though he weighed nothing. The night breeze touched his face. He rolled from her arms, hitting the ground hard. He had spent the last several nights sleeping on tables and in alleyways that the prickly grass outside the tavern was as good a place as any to fall asleep.

When he awoke, he was on Carinthia.

* * *

**Lamarse**
**Carinthia**
**20 Years Before Adia's First Deal**

Lamarse's head pounded as he stared into the contents of his mushy breakfast. Cora assured him the remedy would help his hangover. He believed her, but he didn't have faith he could keep the mush down long enough for it to work. He straightened his cracked glasses, wondering, absentmindedly, if his father would be kind enough to correct his vision. Caring for glasses was harder than he had expected.

"Why did you bring me here?"

"Father told me to. Eat. You will feel better."

"Why are you obeying orders from him? Why does he want to see me after all this time?" Lamarse rested his screaming head on the marble table, embracing the coldness.

"He said it has been long enough. Now eat, or I will spoon feed you."

"Go ahead." Lamarse opened his mouth wide enough for a spoonful.

Cora pushed the bowl to his nose. "You can suffer, or you can choose to help yourself. Choose to be happy."

"Wise, Sister. Sounding a little too much like Father." He grunted as he lifted his head. He ran a hand over his messy beard. "How, I might ask, do you expect me to find joy when I have lost everything?"

"Not everything." She touched his shoulder and stood to leave. "He wants to see you when you are ready."

Lamarse stared at the bowl of mush before pushing it away.

* * *

Lamarse's headache hadn't dulled by noon. His father ensured he had no access to alcohol. Sweat dampened his dirty, ripped clothes by the time he stepped outside. He planned to wash up and sleep in the Draken, only it wasn't with the other ships. He needed his ship to search for shadow infested planets. He burned with rage before it sizzled. If he was being honest with himself, he had stopped searching years ago.

He had stopped trying to save Reya.

He had simply stopped.

Lamarse walked to the gold tree. His fingers twitched for a drink as he kneeled. The pain of Reya's absence numbed over time, but his loss of faith, his downgraded abilities, and his drinking amplified his suffering.

The emotion stuck in his throat broke. He had been sobbing

when he peeked through his swollen eyelids to see his father looking down at him.

Lamarse unsteadily stood. "I am not ready," he mumbled.

"You are destroying yourself, Son."

Lamarse strode away, not wanting to discuss his failings.

"You have not been excused."

Lamarse turned to him. "Why would I speak to someone who knows every pain I will suffer and not do a *damn* thing to prevent it! This is why you had us children: To fulfill the perfectly orchestrated destiny of your Master Plan!" He jabbed a finger at himself. "*I* have been robbed of my freedom to die! Tell me, why does Reya not get a second chance, but I keep getting Reborn again, and again, and again?

"I will exchange my soul for hers if given the chance! Why would Heaven refuse to let me die if I am such a risk to your kingdom?"

"There is a destiny at work. Correct your path and perhaps you can fulfill it."

Lamarse scoffed.

"*Then* you can save Reya's soul."

\* \* \*

**Lamarse**
**Carinthia**
**11 Years Before Adia's First Deal**

It had been nine years since Cora brought Lamarse home. Nine years since his last drink of alcohol. Since his last death. Since he had been anywhere outside of Carinthia. He had spent that time reconditioning his spirit and mind.

Lamarse flipped the page of the book he was reading, his back against the gold tree. He chuckled, unaware of his surroundings or who was approaching.

"I hear you are returning to the Guardianship," Ebony said.

Lamarse's smile dropped as he shut the book. "Yes."

"How could you…" She gestured to his slim body.

"I am going to train as a Mortal Guard."

"Train?" She laughed. "Even Mortal Guards have more to offer than…"

Lamarse's lips twitched. They had always gotten along fine, until he returned home with no telepathy and little capability.

"Based on my testing, I will be training with Earth Guardianship."

"Humans?" Ebony jerked

"Even Father cannot be so cruel! You will surely be antagonized for being so lowly ranked. You are Orion's son!"

He opened his book, eager for the conversation to end. "My identity will be kept secret under the blessing on our names. I will research Earth to appear as though I am from there."

"Surely some of the Guardianship will still know. How embarrassing!" She looked at the cover of his book. *"Pride and Prejudice?"*

"It was listed as one of Earth's '100 Books to Read Before You Die'. I will be reading the complete collection to better converse with the other humans."

"I wish you blessings, Brother." She sounded amused.

"Thank you, Sister. I do not believe I will need it, as I am sure to advance quickly enough." He returned to reading, relieved when Ebony had left.

# CHAPTER FOURTEEN

*Hell's Comin' with Me*

**Austin**
**Los Angeles, CA**
**320 Days Left**

Twenty-one days. That's how long since Austin had last seen Adia. All he did was eat, sleep, train, and search infested areas they suspected she could be kept. Anywhere a dark soul might hide. That's what Cora suspected—one of the monsters from Shemu's world had taken her.

They had captured a dozen dark souls, holding them for questioning. Each time Jax would come out with blood splattered all over him and shake his head.

They had no information, no leads.

Cora begged her father for help. Austin had never met Orion, but he burned with hatred for him when his answer was to wait.

Sweat coated Austin as he sprinted around the indoor track. He had music thumping in his ears, disconnecting his thoughts from his body. He stopped short, nearly tripping over his footing at the sight of Cora. He yanked out his earbuds.

She gently shook her head and continued toward the back, where he knew Dallas was training recruits. Austin swiped roughly at his brow.

"Chin up, man," Jax said, sprawled out on the mat at the

center of the track. "At least you're sleeping again."

"Excuse me?"

Jax rose using his elbows. "Sleeping. Getting rest."

"Who told you I wasn't sleeping before?"

Jax hummed while he considered. "Cora. Dallas. Shadow-girl's mom. They were all conversing quietly. It was difficult to properly eavesdrop."

Austin stormed toward where Cora had gone. He threw open the door to one of the training rooms, where five recruits were stretching while Dallas and Cora talked quietly in a corner. Dallas looked startled by Austin's entrance while Cora kept her expression neutral.

"Take a water break and stretch," Cora told the hunters.

Austin folded his arms. "Your gift will warn you of me being pissed but won't tell us where Adia is?"

Dallas took a protective step forward. "It doesn't work like that!"

Cora touched Dallas' arm, stopping him. "I understand your frustration," she told Austin, her face the picture of sincerity.

"Are you even trying to find her?"

Dallas balked at Austin's question.

"At least I'm sleeping better while she's gone," Austin said. "You think I'm better off without her. Jax overheard you."

Dallas flushed, his eyes cutting to Jax who shrugged by the door

"We are trying to find her," Cora said calmly. "We should not have said that."

The fire inside of Austin demanded to be released. Angry words came out fast and harsh as he said, "What's the point in having a psychic on the team if we can't even find the most important person?" He breathed through his teeth and added, "Is this part of your *plan*?"

"Not Cora's," Jax said, biting into an apple. He took his time chewing before adding, "She's just following Orion's orders. Same as me. She didn't anticipate the Allegiance Bond. Orion told her to give Adia an *opportunity* to make a deal with the shadows at Moorpark." He continued eating his apple.

"If you could enlighten us instead of playing games with our emotions," Cora said, her calm diminished by Jax's presence.

"I don't know the whole plan, goddess, only my part in it."

"Don't call her that."

"Old habit," Jax said to Dallas, brushing past to stand before Austin. "Your girl being taken is supposed to happen because if it wasn't, Orion would have interfered." He turned to Cora. "He has been working on this *grand destiny plan* for longer than you have been born, god—" Jax coughed a laugh. "It really is an old habit."

"I really am trying to find Adia. My visions are blocked." Cora blew out a breath. "Jax has a point. If this is supposed to happen, then the heavens will not grant me the eye to change the course. Even Vision Walking has been taking an extra toll on me."

"So we just wait? Do nothing?" Austin's anger twisted into anxiety.

"Not nothing," Dallas said. "We work on finding and killing dark souls. We—"

Austin's phone rang. He gaped at the screen and then answered. "Adia?"

"She's asleep," a female's voice said.

Austin fumbled to turn on the speaker phone.

"Who are you?" Austin tried to make his voice steady but failed.

Silence.

"Who are you?" Cora repeated.

"Cora." The woman's breath crackled through the phone's speaker. "Lamarse's plan is flawed. I want Shemu dead. I want them all dead."

Cora's eyes grew wide.

"Come find me, Cora. Before I blow Billings away."

* * *

**Austin**
**Billings, MT**
**319 Days Left**

The freezing air whooshed past Austin, but he was warmed by the adrenaline of at last finding Adia. The street was quiet, having once been dominated by dark souls. Cora explained the hunters had cleared the area of dark souls, but no residents had returned, which was the case for many of the overtaken areas. People believed the dark souls left behind their evil—like the whole city was haunted.

Their team was large, considering it was only one dark soul inhabiting the city. Lou walked beside Austin, wearing a hardened expression. It was her battle face. She wore it the day the dark souls invaded her land.

The snow crunched under their feet and even though the dark soul was aware they were coming, Austin feared every step would doom their plan.

"This is exciting," Jax said on the other side of Austin.

Someone shushed him from up front.

Jax rolled his golden eyes. "She knows we're here. She invited us. HELLO! We're here!"

Cora turned cold eyes on Jax. "What are you doing?"

Jax clicked his tongue. To Austin, he said, "She's only grumpy because she couldn't...what was it called, goddess—I mean Cora? Fate Walking?"

Cora rolled back her shoulders, clutching the weapon attached to her hip. Dallas placed a hand on her back and whispered something to her.

"When Cora and I were together," Jax said, "she would have taken me down if I stopped her from attacking someone who had peeved her." He showed Austin his hand that had a scar at the center of it. "This was the last wound she gave me. Stabbed through my hand. I did have a sword to her throat. I wasn't going to kill her. It's just...sometimes with Cora, you need to fight violence with violence. She went there to bring me to Abyss. Anyways, the wound healed, but I had a witch tattoo the scar as a token of what we once had. Orion said—"

"I don't think this is the time to tell stories," Austin said in a quiet voice.

"Oh, right. We're here to save your shadow lady." A beat of silence passed before Jax said, "You can read auras! Read mine. I have this…" He cleared his throat. "It's a long story. But I am curious how it affects my aura. I think in the grand scheme of things—"

Austin had been too preoccupied following Jax's tangent that he hadn't seen the woman sneaking up on them. She held a dagger to Jax's throat. "Do you ever shut up?"

"Hello, Reya." Jax's frozen surprise thawed to a smirk. "Glad you found us. I was not looking forward to walking in the cold for much longer."

At once, all weapons turned on the dark soul. Austin threw his hands up, stepping before her. "Stop!"

"Move!" Dallas shouted back.

Austin turned to Reya, who glared back. She was indeed a dark soul, but unlike the monsters he usually saw within a possessed body, he saw a woman. White hair, silver eyes, delicate features. Her aura shone bright, but blackness surrounded it like a star—like Adia's aura.

"You aren't going to kill any of us," Austin said to her.

"I'm still deciding on him." Reya's eyes moved to Jax, who grinned. Then she stared at Lou, who didn't have a weapon drawn.

"Of course she's not going to hurt us." Jax's eyes were lit with amusement even though Reya kept her blade to his throat. "She called for our assistance."

"What do you mean?" Cora stepped closer, her gun still on Reya.

"She thought she could keep Adia asleep," Jax began, "and they wouldn't possess her without permission because of the deal. What she wasn't expecting was the growing energy shield the shadows put around Adia. She's not going to blow up this city. The shield will, so she called for us to stop it."

Reya's hold on the dagger tightened. "Didn't you kill Helena? Why are you here?"

"I was framed!" Jax laughed. "Ebony killed Helena. I was in Abyss when—"

"Take us to Adia." Cora ignored Jax's appalled expression at being interrupted.

Reya lowered her weapon. "Follow me."

* * *

## Cora
## Billings, MT
## 319 Days Left

Cora tried one last time to Vision Walk, but an intense zap of pain countered. Her vision blurred. She gave Dallas the best *everything is fine* smile, but he remained concerned. Overwhelming thoughts looped in her mind:

*Reya is a dark soul.*

*Jax didn't kill my mother.*

*Adia made the Allegiance Bond.*

*I have no visions.*

They stopped at a grand building that used to be a grocery store. They climbed over a pile of debris to enter. A buzzing grew louder as the temperature rose. They didn't have to walk far before seeing the orb. It was much smaller than Cora had been expecting, taking up the length of the mattress Adia was unconscious on.

"Can you wake her up?" Lou asked Reya, her voice a whisper.

There was something unsettling in the way Reya's eyes bore into Lou's. "If we wake her, they'll attack me."

"Start running, Reya," Jax said, drawing his sword.

Reya's eyes blackened. "Different. Plan."

Jax tsked at her. "You caused this mess, Reya."

"*Stop* saying my name like you know me."

"Reya. Reya. *Reya*," he sang.

Cora's mind lit up with a vision so suddenly, she fell to her knees. She gasped, not feeling Dallas holding her until the vision faded.

"Prepare to fight," she croaked, aimlessly reaching for her gun.

Everyone drew their weapons at the crash on the backside of the store.

"Your friends are here," Jax crooned to Reya.

"They are not my friends," she said through her teeth.

"Time to get a gun then," was Jax's amused response.

Reya sprinted, disappearing in the darkness the orb's light didn't touch. A body flew to them, landing before Jax, their head twisted. He let out a surprised laugh before running to join the fight.

Hours later, the fight carried on. Even with Reya and Jax, who easily made the most kills, Cora feared they would soon be overcome by the invading dark souls. Cora pressed against the bleeding wound in her stomach as she ran to Adia. She tried to place a bloodied hand against the energy shield but was pushed back, landing on a dead body. She didn't check to see if it was a dark soul or a hunter. She rushed back to the orb.

"I will wake Adia up," Cora said, each breath causing sharp pain in her stomach. "We need her help. We need you!"

With a shaking hand, Cora touched the shield again. Her hand fell through. She stepped into the orb, hearing a distant call from Reya. When she turned, Reya stared back with fury.

"I am sorry." Cora wasn't sure if Reya could hear her. "Please, run!" Cora faced forward, not seeing whether Reya listened or not. She walked to Adia, who had a black metal mask attached to her mouth, administering the sleeping draught in vapor form. Reya must have stolen it from the Guardianship when Ebony was in charge. Cora pressed the three buttons on the side and the device unlocked.

Cora nudged Adia for several minutes, the fighting muffled

around them.

"Adia," Cora pleaded. "Wake up!"

Adia stirred.

"You need to give the shadows permission to take over," Cora said in a rush.

Adia blinked slowly before lurching forward. The shadows dispelled the orb, causing the temperature to drop. Sunlight streamed through broken parts of the building. "What's happening? Where am I?"

"We are being attacked by dark souls. Give the shadows permission!"

Adia blinked and her eyes shined white. A monstrous roar exploded from her as she tore through the dark souls, killing every one of them within minutes.

Except Reya.

"Adia!" Cora shouted. "Adia! The fight is finished! Return! Return!"

Adia sprung forward and Reya stood firm, not attempting to run. She held her head high, twirling her dagger.

Dallas stepped before Reya.

"No!" Cora screamed. She had seen this moment long ago. It was her first vision of Dallas. The memory of seeing his neck break always floated in the back of her mind, reminding her their happiness wasn't promised.

Adia gripped Dallas by the throat, lifting him. Cora sprinted, but she was too far away.

A flash of metal.

A scream.

Dallas fell.

It was difficult to make out what had happened in the dim lighting. Cora's watering eyes took in Jax standing over Adia, his sword aimed down.

And Adia's hand rolled to a stop on the floor.

Cora's heart raced as her mind caught up to what had happened.

Jax cut off Adia's hand.

*He* had been the key to saving Dallas—to changing fate. Not only for the value of Dallas' life, but to change what killing him would have done to Adia.

Austin and Lou rushed to Adia's side. He was quick to grab the hand to reattach it, but skin was already growing at the nub of her wrist.

"No," Adia said softly then again in a demanding voice.

"She's talking to the shadows," Austin said. "If they possess her, her hand would be saved." He swiped at his sweaty forehead, gawking at Adia's severed hand he was holding as though he couldn't quite believe what he was seeing. "She won't risk it."

Jax looked at the floor, a hint of guilt in his golden eyes. Cora stepped to him, and his mouth quirked once she caught his attention. He was about to say something dumb. Cora threw her arms around him, holding him tight for the first time since her mother's murder. His body froze, silently stunned by the embrace.

\* \* \*

## Adia
## Mount Hood, OR
## 317 Days Left

Adia awoke to a blurred person hovering over her. She jolted, pushing them away. That motion felt wrong.

"Adia! It's me!"

Her vision focused on Austin's face. She whimpered and he pulled her into him. Her whole body shook as she lifted her hand from his shoulder and saw that it was missing. There was no pain, and the cut was healed. The Allegiance tattoo of a crown was still present, and Adia was sure it had moved.

"Hey." He cupped her face, forcing her attention away from her missing hand. "You're safe. You're home."

"That woman attacked me."

"Reya." He took a breath, and she could feel his emotions as though they were her own. His fear, relief, and concern twisted inside of her. She caught glimpses of his memories that were triggering those emotions. She saw herself possessed by the shadows and her hand being cut off. "She kept you asleep for weeks. I didn't know where you were."

She stared at her missing hand again.

"Cora—she stopped having visions. We couldn't find you." His voice caught. She shivered, sensing Austin's emotional pain. "Reya called me on your phone. The shadows couldn't possess you because you were asleep. They created a force shield around you, and it was growing. You were in Montana, and we weren't sure how much damage the shadows would make in trying to protect you. Cora managed to get through and woke you up."

The distorted memory of Cora telling her to let the shadows possess her played in her mind. "Who is Reya?"

"She's a dark soul."

Her eyes snapped to his.

"She helped us fight the other dark souls. Cora knows her, but I don't know how or much else."

"Is she here?"

"No. Cora took her to Seattle."

Adia's heart raced. She tried hard not to look at her nub, but it kept calling for her to notice her hand's absence. "I lost my hand fighting dark souls?"

"You—they targeted Reya after the other dark souls had been killed. Dallas blocked them from hurting her."

Her arm hair rose. "Don't say—"

"He's okay, but the shadows were about to kill him. Jax cut your hand off and stopped them."

"I'll have to remember to thank Jax. That was very brave for a new hunter."

"He's not a hunter." Austin let out a breathy laugh. "He's Cora's ex."

"Really?"

"He's... You'll find him annoying." Austin stood from the bed and reached in the top dresser drawer. "Orion sent this for you. It was already here when we got home."

A gentle knock occurred on their door, stopping Adia from forming a question. "Come in."

Her mother stepped into their room.

"I'm okay," Adia said in response to her mother's eyes filling with tears, and she could sense the raw emotions radiating from her. She noticed a swollen cut along her mother's jaw. "Are you?"

Her mother gestured as though her injury was nothing. "I'm making soup if you're hungry." She noticed the prosthetic hand from Orion.

"How many days do I have left?" Adia asked.

"317," Austin answered without hesitation.

"I'll be back," her mother added. When she returned, she had a tray of water, crackers, and soup.

Adia reached for the prosthetic. It was a near replica of her missing hand, only missing freckles and a childhood scar. With Austin's help, they slid the new hand on. It gripped her wrist at the perfect pressure before blending into her wrist, covering the Allegiance tattoo. She held her breath as she moved her new fingers. She picked up her bowl of soup, but the force shattered the glass.

* * *

**Jax**
**Seattle, WA**
**316 Days Left**

Jax rolled his neck and did a few hops before knocking on the door. When no one answered, he knocked again, scoffed, and began pounding.

The door swung open. "What do you want?"

He held up an apple to Reya. "You weren't here for breakfast, and you missed dinner last night. Monsters are easier to tame when fed."

Reya snagged the apple in his hand and slammed the door.

"You're welcome, *Reya*."

Silence pursued.

Jax sent out a message on his wrist's device. *Are you sure about Reya?*

It was well into the night when the Master of the Universe replied, *Yes.*

# CHAPTER FIFTEEN

*Team*

**Lamarse**
**Earth Guardianship**
**10 Years Before Adia's First Deal**

L amarse struggled to gain weight. He was still thirty pounds under his ideal, but he was confident in his fighting ability and endurance. Until he stepped into the training facility of Earth Guardianship.

His eyes ticked over each station.

People were throwing knives as they cartwheeled, hitting each target's center.

Climbing ropes with no safety gear.

Shooting arrows of fire.

Flipping off tall mats and landing with the agility of a cat.

Sword fighting.

Sniper-shooting.

Power lifting.

Everywhere Lamarse looked, people outdid his capabilities.

His nerves tightened as he entered the gun range. He geared up and adjusted his glasses, wishing his father had fixed his vision before training started. A man smaller than Lamarse stepped next to him. He wore a hoodie and baggy pants, standing out from the tighter clothing of the other trainees. The smaller man shot the same hole ten times.

"Nicely done." Lamarse had to shout to be heard above the

shooting and earplugs.

The hooded man unclipped his gun and turned away. He stretched, jumped a few times, and then sprinted around the track, passing the other runners.

Lamarse's chest tightened as he took in everyone training around him. He stayed longer than necessary at the shooting range before moving on to lifting weights. There were Mortal Guards at every station, but Lamarse never saw anyone ask to be instructed. It was up to each individual how to structure their own training until dinner. They were required to attend evening classes.

Lamarse was drenched in sweat only two hours into the day, having done more reps than normal, and went to hydrate. The hooded man still ran laps at a fast pace. Lamarse sat against a wall, his legs unable to stand after the punishment he put them through.

"Just so you know," a female's voice said. "They're watching."

A beautiful woman dressed in a tight tank top and spandex shorts stood by him.

"Who is watching?"

"The ones who recruited us. Your accent is unique. What country are you from?"

"England, but my mother is Russian." It was what his father had told him to say. "What country are you from?"

She laughed. It must have been the wrong question to ask. "Texas." Her smile lingered, and he pictured kissing her before shame washed through him.

"Ah," was all he could think to say.

The woman's ponytail swished as she moved to sit next to him. He observed her toned body and tried his hardest not to linger on her curves.

"My name's Hannah."

"Alex Dawson."

She held her hand out, and he hesitated before shaking it.

"We better get up, Alex. If you want to survive next week.

They cut ten percent before the first competition."

He winced standing up and Hannah fixed him with a stare before she confidently moved to the knife throwing station close by. She whispered something in another man's ear before he stepped away, blushing. She glanced at Lamarse with a sly smile and threw the knife at the target's center.

\* \* \*

The hooded man, who Lamarse learned in the first course was named Miller, did the same routine every day, never taking as much as a water break until mealtimes. Miller shot perfect shots. Ran twenty miles. Practiced throwing knives. Then it was strength-building. Meditation. Archery. The active gun range, which required you to run and shoot your target for five miles. More strength-building.

The only times Lamarse saw Miller sitting idly was during courses and meditation. It was also rare to see him without his hood. He had buzzed hair and never made eye contact. Everyone else took rigorous notes about the Guardianship's history and politics, but the only two with blank pages before them was Lamarse and Miller.

Next week was the start of trials—fighting each other then being ranked. Lamarse had never felt sorer in his life. He often wondered what the point was when his value to the Guardianship was nothing without his gifts.

Lamarse messaged his father asking if he could quit to better prepare for training. The answer came as a simple, *No*. Lamarse decided to quit anyways. He packed his bags one morning, but the Mortal Guards had special instructions to not allow him to leave.

An hour later, Lamarse vomited on the track as Miller sprinted past.

"You were a what?" Lamarse asked Hannah at dinner the same day. His abs hurt with every breath, and he anticipated falling asleep during their evening course.

Hannah giggled and she rested her chin on her palm. "Sometimes, Alex, I swear you were raised under a rock. I know we're from different Earths, but seriously? Your Earth doesn't have CIA? Bill told me his Earth doesn't allow women in the field, so I guess anything is possible. I was part of a special training team operations who recruited young children. Top of my class."

"Exciting."

Hannah's eyes sharpened, displeased by his lack of enthusiasm. He was too exhausted to care. "What were you doing when you were recruited?"

"Fighting," was all Lamarse said.

"Really? That's it?"

"What about you?" Hannah turned to Miller, who had been eating efficiently, not once looking up. Hannah rolled her eyes at the silence before reaching to touch Miller's shoulder. Miller snatched Hannah's wrist, twisting it, eyes still on his plate of food.

Hannah spewed out a string of curses before gasping when Miller released her wrist.

* * *

Day one of the second week arrived, and Lamarse woke up with knots in his stomach. When he arrived at the training facility, all the equipment had been removed and replaced with a matted arena. A Mortal Guard named Cal, who oversaw their trials, explained the fighting rules and how they would be scored. They were allowed any type of fighting, which meant there weren't many rules. Lamarse witnessed ten fights before his nerves began to calm. He was listening to Hannah tell a story about one of her ex-boyfriends, so he hadn't heard his name being called. Someone pushed him toward the mat, indicating it was his turn.

Lamarse's knees wobbled as he undressed from his sweatshirt. His eyes were large and unblinking as Miller stepped into the ring in a fitted tank top and shorts.

"The fight between Alex Dawson," Cal announced, "and Louise Miller is about to begin. Alex and Miller, shake."

Lamarse didn't move as Miller stretched forth *her* hand. Her eyes were a vivid blue as they stared at him—as though she could see into his soul. He would have dreams of those eyes.

Louise gripped his hand for a mere second before dropping it. They took their positions. Lamarse rocked on his heels, running blocking techniques in his mind. At the sound of the whistle, he made the mistake of blinking. He was thrown down. The wind was knocked from his lungs, and Louise's foot was pressed firmly on his chest. He grabbed her ankle, but she twisted out of his grip, kicking him in the head.

He saw sparks in his dark vision.

He swallowed bile.

Lamarse swung his arms, but he moved too slow for Louise, who dodged them with ease. A rapid punch broke his nose. He tasted blood flowing over his lips and swayed at the white-hot pain. She fixed him with an emotionless stare before her fist flew to him, knocking him out.

\* \* \*

Pain pulsed through Lamarse as he blinked up at the ceiling of the medic room. Someone was holding his hand, but his neck was too stiff for him to see who it was. He wished Louise had killed him. At least then he would have been Reborn, his wounds would be healed, and his father would have been forced to pull him from the team.

"Alex?"

Hannah's face hovered over his. She had a cut on her lip and her cheek was bruised. She hugged him, his head pounding as she squealed.

"Oh Alex! I have the best news! They aren't making cuts!"

He groaned as he tried to sit up. "What?"

"It was only a rumor. They're still ranking us, but no one is going home!"

Lamarse sunk into his pillow and stared blankly at the ceiling, wishing it would collapse on him.

* * *

"Spot me?" Hannah asked Lamarse a week later.

When she started her third rep, Lamarse's attention drifted to Louise. She sat crisscrossed on the mat where people stretched. She didn't flinch or seem to notice anyone around her, but when someone's arrow went rogue, she moved her head. The arrow broke the mirror behind her, but Louise kept her eyes closed.

"Alex!"

Lamarse snapped his mouth closed as he lifted the bar crushing Hannah.

* * *

During his fourth week in training, Lamarse found the courage to approach Louise.

She didn't acknowledge his presence as he sat down on the mat, keeping a good distance between them. He mimicked her stretches, finding some of her poses impossible to accomplish. When she was done, he copied her by jumping and shaking out his limbs before running on the track. He couldn't keep her pace, but he planned to increase his mileage every day, only stopping when she did.

His lungs pinched and his legs were like jelly by the time they walked off the track. He hoped Louise would pause to stretch or take a drink, but she went to the knives and started throwing them with incredible accuracy and speed. Hannah leaned against a wall close by, observing Louise with an unkind smirk.

During strengthening, he mimicked her routine. They did sit-ups, push-ups, and lifting weights. Then finished with yoga, which led to meditation.

Lamarse's sweat stung his eyes as he downed his water while she meditated. He filled it up sloppily, his hands shaking. He wondered how Louise could work so hard and not hydrate until meals.

"Alex!" Hannah called at lunch, waving him over to her table.

His lips twitched in an apologetic smile before he sat next to Louise instead of with Hannah. He wanted Louise to talk to him, tell him how she became so strong and motivated. He wondered if she didn't speak English and wanted to ensure her that he spoke many languages. He was too exhausted to force conversation.

\* \* \*

Five months had past, and Lamarse still couldn't keep up with Louise's routine. He was stronger, even winning five of his twenty trials. He wasn't the lowest ranked, but he had far to go before he reached the top where Louise's name firmly remained. Her dark hair had grown, but he rarely saw it because of her hood. He sometimes considered if she was a droid his father implanted to get the trainees to work harder. She always finished first when Cal orchestrated unexpected obstacle courses and never once lost a fight. She was incredibly fast and unpredictable. Even when someone managed to hit her, she bounced back and hit harder.

"Good morning, Louise," Lamarse greeted, knowing she wouldn't respond.

She dropped into a split, arching back and then forward.

Lamarse's mouth went dry. Droid or not, he found her

attractive. He mimicked her stretches, having become more flexible. It also helped his muscle soreness. Stretching was something he never had to consider in his advanced body.

At dinnertime, Hannah dropped her tray next to Lamarse's, making him flinch. He had been caught in a daydream, staring at Louise.

"I know your secret, Miller."

Louise didn't pause her efficient eating.

Hannah rolled her eyes and gave Lamarse a pointed expression. "She's not from Earth."

Lamarse's heart skipped a beat. He cursed in his mind. *She is a droid.*

"She's from Matadon."

The fork in Louise's hand paused an inch from her mouth.

"Don't associate with her, Alex," Hannah said, standing to leave. "She's one of Tyron's assassins."

Lamarse stared at Louise as Hannah walked away. When the silence became tangible between them, he continued eating.

"I saw you."

Lamarse stilled at hearing Louise's voice for the first time. It was quiet and husky, triggering a pleasant chill down his spine. Her words registered in his mind. "You saw me where?" Too late did he realize they were not speaking English, but Mata.

"I was taken as a child from Earth," she continued slowly. "I escaped my capturers, ran into a tavern, and screamed for help. You looked at me. I counted. One. Two. Three. Four. Five. You took another drink. I was dragged back to the pit.

"I am human," she said in English. "You are not."

# CHAPTER SIXTEEN

*Planets Bend Between Us*

**Adia**
**Mount Hood, OR**
**307 Days Left**

Adia stood in the field outside the cabin, staring up at the stars. The glow of Christmas lights reflected off the snow. Her human days were numbered. The harmony she was forced to feel in the Shadow Core scared her—she would lose herself. She would become someone who didn't care about the stars, about her mother, about Austin.

She heard the crunch of drawing footsteps until Austin stood by her side, tilting his head up at the clear night sky. "Cookies are ready."

It was Christmas Eve. One of Adia's vivid memories before her first deal was Christmas at their cabin. Adia stared at Austin and the grief of their numbered days strangled her throat. Before she was aware of the shadows, she believed they had a shot at growing old together. Tears sprung to her eyes as she pictured him moving forward in his life without her. He wouldn't be lucky enough to forget her, but time could numb his pain enough for him to fall in love again. He didn't remember their time in the Shadow World—in the City of Souls. The selfish part of Adia hated knowing that his love for her could fade.

"Do you want to stargaze with me?" she asked.

"I'll get some blankets." His voice was tight like she wasn't the only one with sad thoughts.

"And cookies." She smiled through her tears.

"Hot chocolate?"

"Of course."

Later, when they were sickly full, they lay back in silence, holding each other.

"Tell me a story of us," he said. "Before we fall asleep and freeze to death."

"I'm sure my mom would eventually save us."

He waited, his breaths warming her neck.

"I'm trying to think of one I haven't already told you," she said with a laugh.

He pulled back and reached for his phone. He opened his notes application. "These are the ones you've told me already."

She slowly scrolled down the tabs. "You wrote them down?"

"I don't want to forget them."

She couldn't speak as she continued down the various stories of them. "I don't see paintball on here."

"Paintball?"

"It's a City of Souls memory." She went into as much detail as she could recall, Austin hated not knowing everything. Still, he managed to ask questions along the way, leading to tangent stories and soon they were laughing and wiping their tears away. They held hands as she returned to talking about nearly drowning in the pond after paintball.

"You saw yourself here?"

"My body was here so when I nearly drowned, I saw a glimpse of my surroundings. It's why I always felt cold." She sighed, her breath clouding before her. "We should go inside. I think my mom wanted to watch a movie tonight."

"Next Christmas is going to suck without you." He pressed his palms to his eyes and sniffed.

"I know."

"I would trade if I could."

"I know." She moved so their foreheads touched. "We have 307 good days left. They will go fast, and it will suck when it's over. Let's remember this Christmas when we're in the depths of our sorrow." She pulled his face to hers and they kissed until they could no longer bear the cold.

Her mother was reading *Pride and Prejudice* on the couch. She looked up at them entering. "You look freezing! Go stand by the fire. I'll heat up the kettle."

They removed their heavy jackets and boots by the door and then put away their dishes and blankets. They were warming by the fire when the kettle whistled.

"What movie did you want to watch, Mom?" Adia poured hot water into three mugs.

"*It's a Wonderful Life*," she answered without hesitation. "It was your father's favorite."

Adia traced a mechanical finger along her mug, having mastered the use of her new hand without breaking dishes. She had yet to speak to her mother about Lamarse. She sensed her mother's emotional pain any time his name was brought into conversation.

"Did he love Christmas?"

"It was his favorite thing about Earth."

"I had this aunt who Sam created to make me suffer." Adia continued tracing her mug, keeping her eyes away from her mother's. "She didn't take good care of me, and we didn't do holidays. I believed in Santa Claus longer than most children because there were always presents on my bed. I thought I was special since Santa also gave me gifts for my birthday. Monsters were real so why couldn't Santa Clause be as well? After I left on my own to hunt, I woke up that Christmas morning without a present. I wished I had gotten to know him outside of the Shadow World." At last, she met her mother's tearful eyes. "Will you tell me about him?"

Adia sat sipping hot chocolate while Christmas music played, and they exchanged stories about her father.

* * *

## Austin
## Mount Hood, OR
## 306 Days Left

Adia hadn't had a night terror since the Allegiance Bond. Austin stared at the crown with black jewels tattooed on Adia's wrist. Dark tendrils danced along her arm, taunting Austin's anxiety. He kissed her head before getting out of bed to brush his teeth. He was preparing breakfast when Lou entered from the back door, wearing a hoodie covered in snow.

"You ran on Christmas?"

"Running keeps the nightmares away." She had told them briefly of her abduction as a child—being kept in a pit, trained to survive on little. She eyed the sizzling bacon with a grin. "That smells delicious. Is Adia awake?"

"Still sleeping."

She gave him a knowing smile. "Are you nervous?"

"Of course." He rubbed the back of his neck. His hands tingled with anticipation.

Lou kicked off the last of the snow from her boots before placing another log into the fire. They made breakfast together and she told him more of her time as a Mortal Guard. They set the table before entering where Adia still slept. They shared a devious smile before Lou jumped on Adia, who startled awake, groaned, and then laughed.

"Merry Christmas!" Lou sang.

"Merry Christmas." Adia rubbed her eyes and then winced.

"Austin made crepes and bacon!"

Snow drifted outside the kitchen window as they ate. Adia's cheeks were a beautiful red as she went into detail about a time when Dallas and Austin tried decorating a Christmas tree. Austin smiled through the story but ached wishing he could remember.

"Presents!" Lou announced, shooting Austin a secretive smile.

Adia busied herself clearing the table, and Austin shook the nervous energy from his hands. Adia sat close to him on the couch as Lou opened her presents from the recliner. They gifted her a new gun and a special snow jacket from the Guardianship.

Adia gave Austin books he favored in the Shadow World.

Austin's throat tightened as Adia reached for her present. He stared, unblinking, as she pulled the small box from the larger one. Her eyes caught on his for a beat before she lifted the black velvet lid.

"How?" The ring box shook in her palm.

"Cora and Dallas helped me duplicate the design."

"You want to marry me?" Her voice wavered.

Austin was quick to nod. He could hear his heart pulsing in his ears.

"We won't have much time," she told him.

He kneeled before her and took her hand. "This ring is my promise: Our life on Earth won't be long, but my soul will find you again." He reached for the ring, his vision blurring with tears. "Will you marry me, Adia?"

At her nod, he slipped the ring on her finger. They kissed as Lou cheered.

There was a knock at the door. When Lou left to answer, Adia said to him,

"I hope you're right about our souls finding each other again, but I don't want you to wait—"

"Even if there is the lowest possible chance of seeing you again, I will wait." He ran a finger over her diamond ring. "I vow it."

Her throat bobbed. He could see she wanted to argue. "I would wait for you too."

They meant to kiss again, but Cora and Dallas walked in with presents in their arms, singing their congratulations.

# CHAPTER SEVENTEEN

*Shooting the Moon*

**Lamarse**
**Earth Guardianship**
**10 Years Before Adia's First Deal**

Louise *hated* him.

Lamarse had been so consumed with shame for failing Reya, he was blind to others' needs. He tried to think back to a time when he heard someone cry for help but there wasn't one. Those memories were lost in his drunken haze.

Guilt gnawed at him until he could no longer breathe. He stopped on the track, hands on his knees, and heaved. He sat to the side as Louise finished her twenty miles. She never once looked at him.

At lunch, he approached her table, not daring to sit down. "Louise. Can I talk to you?"

When he caught her attention, he saw not hate, not pity, but indifference. He wanted to vomit.

"I am sorry," he said in English. "I want to explain everything to you. I can tell you who I—"

Louise spoke in Mata, "I don't want to know anything about you."

He flinched. "I am sorry for what you—"

"Don't feel sorry for me." Her eyes blazed. "Feel sorry for the children who weren't strong enough to survive the pit. The children who were too beautiful to be fighters, so they used them until their beauty was spent."

Lamarse rubbed at his face as frustration electrified his senses. He punched the wall on his way out of the cafeteria, breaking the skin on his knuckles. Blood dripped off his fingers as he walked with a broken hand, horrified by what Louise had said. He saw it rather clearly now—the path his father had warned him not to take. He had let Reya's fate consume him. He knew now why he was sent here to train with the Mortal Guards.

Louise was his punishment.

\* \* \*

**Lou**
**Earth Guardianship**
**10 Years Before Adia's First Deal**

Lou thrashed around, fighting off the lingering demons from her nightmare. She stared wide-eyed at the dark ceiling as she counted her breaths:

*One.*
*Two.*
*I am safe.*
*Three.*
*Four.*
*I am strong.*
*Five.*
*Six.*
*I am no longer trapped in the pit.*
*Seven.*
*Eight.*
*My friends are dead.*
*Nine.*
*Ten.*

*They can no longer be harmed.*

Lou used her blanket to mop the sweat from her face and neck. She had survived. Only five did out of the hundred from her group. Lou chewed on her nails before she stopped herself. Having chewed nail beds was proof of her anxiety—of her fears. She fisted her hands. The clock showed she still had three hours before her run. Sleep was vital to her strength and routines kept her sane. It was only the idea of running without Alex trailing behind her that got her leaving her room to start the day early.

She stretched in the empty training facility, wondering why she had never thought to awake this early before. She stepped into a run and her body hummed as she increased her speed. Flashes from her nightmares fed her adrenaline. She breathed through her nose, making sure to exhale longer than she breathed in. She slowed on the last mile; her mind eased of the past. She was stretching when more people arrived for their routine. She sensed Alex's approach. She bit back the desire to throttle him and masked her anger with a blank expression.

"My wife's soul was taken," Alex spoke the words in Mata. "Day of our wedding."

Lou could see it: The damage beneath his friendly persona. The pain behind his blue eyes that were always watching her. Lou hid her pain by not showing any emotion. Alex overcompensated his by smiling.

"You are right." He leaned closer, whispering his words. "I am not human. I used to be something more. I lost myself and was punished—am being punished."

"If it's my forgiveness you're after, it's granted." She looked him over. "If it's friendship you seek—I am no one's friend." Her only purpose was to save as many lives as she had taken.

Alex's words were muffled by an alarm. He stepped before her as armed Mortal Guards cascaded in. Cal's voice replaced the alarms.

"Guards in training—this is a simulation. Your mission is to Reach and Return. Your placement will alter your rank significantly."

An arrow marked a door toward the back of the gym. Lou sprinted for it, turning down the hall at the direction of another marker. The holographic arrow had a number within it signifying how far until the Reach.

Twenty miles.

\* \* \*

**Lamarse**
**Earth Guardianship**
**10 Years Before Adia's First Deal**

Lamarse followed Lou, amazed he could keep her pace as they broke through the ship's doors. The icy air stole his breath away. He was still dressed in his hoodie and sweatpants, but some ran in only shorts.

"Did you wake up early so you could run without me?" He caught the slight movement of her throat as she swallowed. "You—"

"Stop. Talking." She shot him a hard look. "And run."

By the next arrow, the silence was driving him insane. "I can let someone know you already ran today. You should not be ranked with the others. If this were any other day, you would be leading the run."

She made no change in her expression.

"Reya was my wife's name." He wanted to tell her everything. "She was…" Bitter emotions twisted his stomach. "She was a warrior—best one I knew." He went on about minor details he had been afraid to forget. Her favorite color being gold. How difficult her childhood had been with her brother as a competitor. How brave she was to leave the kingdom she knew. How much she enjoyed cooking. Talking about her made time move faster, but as the miles ticked down to ten left, Louise's posture had slumped, and her breaths came out as rasps.

"We can walk," he suggested.

She shook her head. She was too out of breath to speak. They were going at a strong pace for him, but he could talk. There were some trainees behind him, but less than he had expected with Louise by his side. Her jaw ticked with every person who passed them.

Five miles later, Louise's feet were dragging, barely lifting off the ground. The cold numbed Lamarse's body, making each movement heavy. He could barely open his eyes as snow fell hard on them.

"Three more miles," he rasped. Runners were passing them on their way back, shooting them pitiful glances. Forty miles in total they would have to run. Louise fell to her knees. With quaking arms, Lamarse lifted her to a stand. He wrapped an arm around her waist, pulling her into his side as they stepped toward the glowing arrow, directing them to return. Letting out a grunt, Lamarse reached out a swollen, numbed hand, brushing snow from Louise's closed eyes.

"We have to go back." He licked his cracked lips, tasting blood.

Louise slipped from his hold. He searched around, spotting some trainees approaching. They turned on the path without meeting Lamarse's pleading eyes and ran back.

"This is ridiculous," Lamarse muttered, trying to get Louise to a stand.

She jolted before vomiting.

"We have to get up," he told her, each word painful to say.

He tried to nudge her to a stand, but she went limp. He shouted her name to wake her.

"Help! Help!" His voice was losing volume as the wind whirled snow around them. They were going to die. He may come back but would Louise? He shed off his sweatshirt and sweatpants and gave her an extra layer. He doubted his soaked clothes would do much for her, so he also brought his body over hers and prayed he could keep her alive long enough for someone to come.

\* \* \*

**Lou**
**Earth Guardianship**
**10 Years Before Adia's First Deal**

Lou stared at the board projected on the wall by the track. It was the next day after awaking in her room, dry and warm. It was an endurance test. Lou stared at her name next to Alex's at the bottom. They were the first to fail. They were the weakest.

*I am weak.*

The words swirled in Lou's mind, alternating between English and Mata. She turned her sharp eyes to Alex as he stepped to her side.

"You would think your run before the test would have granted you more points."

"You were the idiot who took his clothes off," Hannah said from behind them. "You could have ranked higher if you had walked back as far as you could. Alone." Hannah's eyes cut to Lou's before smiling at Alex. She placed a hand on his bicep, and Lou dropped her eyes, willing herself not to roll them. She needed to show no emotion. "Remember that next time."

Alex stepped closer to Lou, and Hannah's hand dropped. She walked off, her ponytail swishing with every step. Alex turned to Lou, examining her as though he expected her to be hurt.

She made the mistake of locking eyes with him. Her stomach tightened as her anger eased into something unknown.

"Do you want coffee? Or tea?" His voice was gentle. "Even after that medicated bath, I cannot stop shivering."

Lou stared back at her name below Alex's. Sucking in a sharp breath, she ran toward the track. No one else was training today. Cal announced they were owed a day of rest after yesterday's trial. She was done with her first lap when she heard Alex's footfalls behind her.

She pictured him lying on top of her in the snowy road. He thought they were dying, and he sacrificed his clothes—his life —to give her a longer chance at survival. She had stirred on the road as the Mortal Guards arrived to transport them back. The memory of a pale Alex with blue cracked lips caused her to slow her pace until he was running by her side, staring at her in disbelief.

# CHAPTER EIGHTEEN

*Gods & Monsters*

**Adia**
**Mount Hood, OR**
**290 Days Left**

Adia stood, arms folded, feeling the breeze on her face as she stared out at the snowy field where her wedding to Austin would take place tomorrow. She wanted to grasp onto the smell of trees and the slight pain of icy air filling her lungs. The door creaked and arms enclosed around her.

"Did you hear back from your mother?" she asked Austin.

"She's not coming."

Adia masked her relief with a frown.

"She went on and on about how I ditched the job Grant got me. How I haven't called in months." Adia felt the rise and fall of his chest as he sighed. "Anyways, it's fine."

"It's not."

"She went to our first wedding, so maybe—"

"She didn't." Adia turned to him.

"She didn't?"

"No."

His throat bobbed.

"We did elope," she reasoned.

"Did I invite her?"

Adia's mouth tightened before nodding.

"I can't believe—her only child!"

Adia's mother stepped out. "They'll be here soon. I'm going to drive down to the market. Anything you want added to the list?"

"Cookies. Austin ate the rest yesterday," Adia teased.

He shot Adia a look. "You said—"

"He wouldn't even let me have any." Adia raised her brows dramatically. "Very rude and inconsiderate."

Her mother played along, tsking. "You should really consider if that's the man you want as your husband."

"Cookies, Lou. Lots and lots of cookies." Austin lifted Adia over his shoulder. "And maybe some beets—her favorite."

"I'll make sure to check whether they have beet-cookies. In case we don't have enough money to get both." Her mother let out an evil laugh as she left. Adia pretended to gag.

Austin, still holding Adia over his shoulder, sped down the steps. She attacked his sides. He squirmed and then slipped, taking her down with him. She gathered a handful of snow and threw it at his face.

"Oh." He brushed the snow from his eyes. "It's on."

She tried to evade his snowball, but it landed at the back of her head, ice falling down her shirt. She gasped but was quick to retaliate. Austin dodged the flying snow, so she hurried toward him, making sure her next throw was aimed at his neck, so he too could feel snow down his shirt. Austin caught Adia by the waist, and they fell again. She desperately wished she could take a picture of his beaming, flushed face and keep it with her through Hell like the tokens they had in the City of Souls.

Austin wiped snow from her eyelashes before his lips were on hers, soft at first and then hard as though he too wanted to hold onto this memory forever.

"This is cute."

They broke apart, seeing Jax leaning against the back porch's railing. Reya stood not far from him, twirling a blade against her gloved palm.

Cora and Dallas appeared from the path that wrapped around the cabin, carrying chairs.

"We could only fit fifty in the ship!" Cora called, grinning at them.

"Let me help." Austin swept the snow from his chest as he walked with Dallas and Cora to the front of the cabin. Adia meant to follow but Reya's brown eyes caught hers. Reya—Adia had learned from her mother—was not only her father's first wife but Coye's sister.

"How's the hand?" Jax asked Adia.

Adia's steps were forceful as she closed the distance between her and Jax and from the corner of her eye, saw Reya's dagger shift.

Adia held out her prosthetic hand for Jax to shake.

"Thank you for saving Dallas."

Jax nodded his welcome and examined her new hand. "A gift from Orion?"

"Yes." To Reya, who hadn't relaxed her guarded posture, Adia said, "Nobody wants the shadows gone more than me. I couldn't say I wouldn't do the same if our positions were reversed." Her mother had explained some of Reya's story, and although Adia wouldn't trust the dark soul, she was trying to be understanding. There was a reason Cora wanted Reya part of the team. Adia stuck out her hand for Reya to shake.

Reya rejected the gesture. "Don't be so sure it wasn't personal."

Jax huffed a laugh, stepping between the two glaring women. "Reya. That wasn't nice."

"You are a repulsive being," she snarled at Jax.

He slowly turned to Reya, brows raised, and golden eyes lit with dark amusement. "And you were brainwashed by a demon. No one's perfect."

Reya's eyes blackened. She let out a throaty growl as her blade flashed toward Jax, who dodged it as though he anticipated the attack.

Austin hurried down the path, no chairs in hand. He skidded in the snow, joining Adia's side. He eyed Reya, who bared her teeth at him. "Everything okay?"

"Yes, yes. Reya needs food is all," Jax said.

Reya swung her dagger at Jax again.

"Woah!" Jax raised his weaponless hands to Reya, having stepped out of her reach.

"Cora!" Adia called.

"Sure, get the psychic," Reya spat, maneuvering around Jax, and slicing his arm. "I have some fight for her too."

Something changed in Jax at her words. He caught Reya's wrist and twirled her into his arms, his sword at her throat. Adia wasn't sure how he had retrieved the weapon. Austin held Adia, silently asking her not to join the fight. They stepped away, easing toward the path around the cabin.

Jax slid around Reya, evading the swipe of her dagger by half an inch. "Please be careful. I really don't feel like washing blood off today."

She growled in response.

Witnessing them fight felt more like watching a dance. Adia tried to follow each technique, filing it away to practice later. Jax jerked away, cursing at his bleeding stomach. Adia hadn't seen Reya stab him, but they were moving too fast to catch every move.

Jax sighed and somehow his golden eyes glowed in the dimming sunlight. A growl rumbled as he drew his smaller sword so there was a weapon in each hand. Reya also retrieved a second dagger that had been hidden somewhere in her clothes. They charged at one another, and the chaotic dance of weapons continued.

"We need to get Cora," Adia said to Austin.

They continued down the path, meeting Cora and Dallas at the front of the cabin. They were sitting in two of the wedding chairs, smiles on their faces.

"Is there a reason we are letting them kill each other?" Adia asked, eyes intent on Cora to study her reaction. "I know he's your ex, but he seems useful enough. When he's not talking."

Cora laughed, no touch of anxiety on her face. "She can't kill him."

A deep scream from Reya echoed around them.

"You sure about that?" Austin asked, and Adia could tell he was fighting to be peacekeeper.

Reya sprinted past them, coated in blood and seething.

Adia stepped forward, fingers tingling to grip her gun, but Cora raised a hand, silently asking her to wait.

Jax stumbled toward them, his breaths rattled before easing into a silent rhythm. He rolled his dislocated shoulder back into place. He touched the deep gash that ran along his throat. A golden light shined from his injuries, and Adia's mind went to souls being consumed in the Shadow World. The light diminished.

Jax straightened, still coated with blood but no longer injured.

Adia's eyes locked on Cora.

"He's the son of Aurum, the god of gold."

"He's a god?" Austin's eyes were large and Jax looked pleased by his reaction.

"Yep," Jax answered as Cora said, "More like a demigod."

"Forgotten son of Aurum," Jax said, wiping blood from his mouth. "Mistake. Bastard. I'm also cursed. Although, not as badly as my sister is cursed. She got murdered by her lover and then reincarnated as a mortal. Then she got murdered by the same lover. Reincarnated. Murdered. Vicious cycle, really. There's also this—"

"Story for another time," Cora said.

Jax laughed. "*You* don't even know the whole story, goddess."

Dallas shot him a look.

"Cora," Jax amended. He turned to Adia and Austin. "I'm starved. When's dinner?"

"Lou is getting groceries," Austin said.

"I don't know if I can wait until she gets back." A low rumble sounded, and Jax gritted his teeth. "Healing burns a lot of calories. It's why I never gain weight."

"Because someone is always stabbing you," Cora teased.

Jax's eyes shined with amusement before he held his growling stomach. "Hunger pains are so much worse than being stabbed. Part of my curse."

Austin gestured to the forest. "What are we going to do about Reya? She tried to kill one of us."

Jax gaped at Austin as though he was in awe at being considered part of the team. Clearing his throat, Jax said, "She'll return. I'm eager to see her face when she discovers I'm still alive."

Adia crossed her arms. "She can't possibly be welcomed back after trying to kill you."

"It was only an episode." Jax ran a finger over the tear in his shirt. "You don't by chance have some clothes I could borrow, Austin?"

"I already called Lou," Cora said. "She's getting you some things at the market."

"If she wasn't loyally Lamarse's," Jax said, "I would kiss her."

Adia fixed Jax with a hard stare. Pain pulsed in her head where a small voice said,

*Let's test how immortal he truly is.*

"Speaking of episodes." Jax narrowed his golden eyes at Adia. "If you're going to let them harm me, please wait until after I eat. I really don't think I can burn more calories without losing my amusing temperament. I'm not really going to kiss your mother. They were only words."

Adia eased her expression, but the small voice returned.

*Only need a command.*

Austin held Adia's hand, and the pulsing headache dulled.

"I'm going inside," Adia said, tasting acid.

"Go in and rest," Dallas told her. "We'll set up the chairs and the tent outside."

* * *

**Reya**
**Carinthia**
**48 Years Before Adia's First Deal**

Reya blinked, a headache forming that she hid with a bright smile. She squeezed Lamarse's hand as an older man gripped her chin, shouting unfamiliar words in a praising tone. She normally could understand Carinthian well enough but not when everyone tried to speak above their neighbor. She also hadn't slept last night, her dreams riddled with anxiety for their wedding. She had never been allowed to romanticize life growing up. She was taught to fight but never how to love.

Until Lamarse.

Reya's eyes shifted around the group of friends and family celebrating their romance. A small broken piece of her heart still expected to see Coye amongst the crowd. He would mock everything, giving her that critical eye she hated but was also familiar to her.

*Where was Cora?* In her attempt to find her sister in-law, Reya spotted the gold tree and longed to be under its shade, escaping in a good book. Her smile grew more forced by each person who touched her, and she had to shove down the version of her who wanted to twist their clingy hands until bones cracked.

Lamarse kissed her cheek, and she was pulled back into the person she worked so hard to become. A guest asked her a question, but she was slow to translate their meaning.

"Soon, but hopefully not too soon," Lamarse answered for her. "We want some time together before we bring children into the mix."

*Children.* The idea strangled her throat, but she masked her emotions with delicate longing. How could she strive to be a loving mother when she was barely grasping what love was?

She pictured raising children with Lamarse. She had never met Lamarse's mother, but Orion seemed to want not much less than what her parents expected from Coye and Reya—to become warriors.

Reya's head spun as she breathed deeply through her nose. It all became too much as fingers pinched her cheek. Mouths touched her hands. She turned to Lamarse, interrupting his conversation with an elderly woman. "I need to sit."

Lamarse guided her through the crowd. The guests followed like they were tethered to them. Whispered laughing surrounded her, and she tried to see who it belonged to, but when she went to sit, she fell through the chair. Through the ground. Greasy cords snaked around her, wrapping around her mouth and throat.

She dropped on a cold, wet floor. In the dim light she could see clumps of slime slipping down the walls. The cords fell loose, slithering away.

An echoing laugh jerked her to attention. Her hands slid in slime as she crawled to the nearest wall. The laughing silenced and she could see a silhouette of someone standing before her, appearing out of nothing.

"Welcome new soul," the chilling voice of a woman spoke. She stepped forward, revealing her face that was identical to Reya's. "To your brother's Shadow World."

# CHAPTER NINETEEN

*Dog Days are Over*

**Reya**
**Mount Hood, OR**
**290 Days Left**

Snow-filled branches caught on Reya's clothes which were drenched with Jax's blood. A string of profanity circled her mind, alternating between languages. Shemu had bestowed on her a gift to learn languages quickly. Gift was the wrong word—she purchased the talent with her loyalty. After her planet's souls were collected and Shemu bound his soul with another core, Reya was kept locked as prisoner while the other souls passed on. She was tortured and manipulated until Shemu tricked her into believing his altered image was someone new and rescued her from her prison. She believed she owed him a debt. She chose to remain by his side, realizing too late she had fallen in love with the shadow.

She now saw the manipulations—the brainwashing as Jax had deemed it. She could separate herself from Shemu long enough to understand that it wasn't her fault. She was a victim—a toy to Shemu. Not everything was a trigger but when she felt the slimy walls closing in on her, her mind shut off and darkness moved through her.

Jax was annoying, but he didn't deserve to die. Another scream escaped from Reya as she fell on her knees, pulling and ripping at vines. Cora would never let her come back.

She wouldn't be allowed the resources of the Guardianship. Her plan to destroy the shadows nearly blew up in her face, costing more innocent lives in the process. She was a lost soul with nowhere to go. Maybe the Hell that awaited her when her soul was finally judged would be better than Shemu's Shadow World. Better than the guilt strangling her breaths as the image of slicing Jax's throat played on repeat in her mind.

A twig broke and Reya shot up, bloodied daggers at the ready. In the distance, a large dog watched her, head bowed. The dog took a small step forward, then another, letting out a short, high-pitched whine with the third step.

The darkness that clouded Reya's vision cleared, and her heart rate calmed as she held out a trembling hand. The dog limped forward before collapsing. Reya crawled cautiously until she was close enough for the dog to sniff her hand. She inspected him, seeing a nasty tear along his paw and an infected wound on his belly.

Reya scooped up the malnourished dog and ran. When the cabin came into view, she quickened her pace, slipping a few times in the snow.

"Cora! Cora!"

The front door swung open, and Reya nearly dropped the dog at seeing Jax alive. She blinked several times, wondering if she had fainted in the forest and was having a vivid dream.

"Who do you have there?" Jax's enjoyment in seeing her shocked by his survival was enough evidence for Reya to know this wasn't a dream.

"Earth dog. He's hurt."

Jax hummed as his fingers brushed through the black and brown fur that was caked with mud and blood, examining wounds Reya hadn't initially seen. "Cora has some medicine on the ship."

"That medicine must be Ruin magic to bring you back." Her voice was tight, and she held back the emotion threatening to rise. She would not let Jax see her cry.

"Although Ruin magic is *partly* how I'm still standing, the medicine came from the Guardianship. Let's not let this poor creature suffer any longer. *Reya.*" He gestured for her to lead the way.

She breathed through her teeth, hating the way he said her name with familiarity. She adjusted the dog in her arms and stepped to the ship's door, but it wouldn't open until Jax's approach.

"They were a bit concerned you might steal the ship," he explained.

Reya bit back a response and lay the dog down on the nearest bed. "Where's Cora?" She refused to look at Jax's smug expression as he washed his hands.

"Inside eating dinner. Don't worry, *Reya.*" He leaned forward so to catch her eyes and grinned when he succeeded. "I know what I'm doing."

Reya stepped back and crossed her arms.

Jax shaved and cleaned the dog's wounds. They discovered several more infected cuts under the matted fur. The dog held mostly still, but Jax gave him a sedative when it was time to clean and stitch the wound.

"He's going to be fine," Jax said, plucking out maggots and dropping them in a pan of hot water. "The medicine will quicken his healing process. What are you going to call him?"

Reya had thought of a name, but she wasn't ready to admit it to Jax. "How did you heal so fast? Was it really dark magic?"

"I'm immortal," Jax paused to take in her reaction.

Reya kept her expression stoic to not give him anything to be amused by. Still, his ever-smiling lips curved.

"Immortal how?"

"I'll tell you my story, every detail of it, but I want yours as payment."

Blackness edged her vision until she could no longer see. Jax took her hand, but she flinched away as though he had burned her. His long fingers gently wrapped around her wrist, and he moved her hand to touch between the dog's floppy ears. She swallowed, her brows dipping in confusion as Jax set his hand over hers. Together they stroked the dog's head.

He removed his hand, but she continued petting.

"You saved him," Jax said, his voice soft and serious.

The dark in her vision cleared.

Jax returned to plucking out maggots. He started spraying the wounds with a blue substance.

"I'm sorry I triggered you," Jax said. "You don't have to owe me anything. I can tell you my story free of cost."

The door opened, and Lou popped her head in the ship, her eyes catching on Reya's before moving to the sleeping dog. She held up a woven bag with the Portland Market's logo embroidered on it. "I brought some items Cora requested. The dog food makes sense now. I also have some clean clothes for the both of you. You can give back Austin's shirt, Jax."

"Amazing!" Jax said, grinning. "Although I do favor this shirt."

Reya felt Lou's attention but refused to look.

"I also got a grooming kit," Lou said. "We can give the dog a bath when she is ready."

"He," Reya corrected and then regretted speaking.

"You're welcome to wash up inside too," Lou said to Reya. "I hope the clothes I picked are to your liking."

"I'm sure they're fine." Reya meant to sound grateful, but her tone was dry of emotion.

"There's also a plate ready for when you're hungry."

Reya looked up in time to see Lou leaving. Adia stood close to the ship's entrance with hands on her hips.

Reya's stomach grumbled at the thought of food.

"There's a shower in the ship," Jax said. "It's too small for the dog, but it will work for you."

"Why are you being nice to me? I would have killed you if you were mortal."

"You needed a release. Better me than my friend Austin."

"You provoked me on purpose?"

"I'll do it again in time. Just need to make sure I have food. I turn into a short-tempered monster when I can't eat after healing. Not too differently from yourself, so we're both cursed."

"You'd really do it again? Allow me to fight you?"

"I work for Orion. My assignment is to..." He puckered his lips, seemingly searching for the correct words. "...help you. These episodes aren't your fault. It's the price you're paying for —"

"Allying myself with a demon?"

"For surviving the Shadow World."

"I could have passed on. I could have not followed him. I could be at peace. I don't deserve—"

A laugh broke from Jax. "Oh *Reya*. If you really believe that you had a choice in any of this, then why would Orion—*the Master of the Universe*—send me to be your stabbing bag?"

Reya jerked back, bile creeping up her throat. "Stabbing bag?" Emotion was tight in her throat, and she would need to either cry or scream soon.

"Whatever you want to call it. I'm here to help you manage your inner demon. It's hard being a monster with a conscience."

Reya took shallow breaths through her teeth. "Why does he care?"

"You are his family in a way."

"Why does he care?" she asked again, not accepting his answer.

"I don't know. He doesn't speak in whys." Jax's eyes moved over her, considering. "I have a theory: We are all pawns in this puzzle that leads to one future he is ensuring will happen. Doesn't matter who or what gets destroyed in the process. He needs that one outcome—the Shadow Core to be destroyed."

Something shifted in Reya's chest, but she wouldn't allow herself to hope. If the Shadow Core ever did get destroyed, she doubted she would be alive to see it. "What's your story?"

"My father was a god," Jax began. "Cheated on his goddess with a Ruin witch—my mother. She found out he was married. He chose his goddess. She chose to sacrifice her soul to curse his family. I used to believe she didn't know it meant cursing me as well, but I've grown pessimistic."

"How are you cursed?"

"I'm a monster with a conscience. I'll wash the dog while you shower."

"Hal Rees," she said.

He looked at her strangely. "What do you mean by gold tree?"

"You know Hal Rees means gold tree in Lehranian?"

His eyes lit with understanding. "I have a universal translator in my head. Why are we talking about gold trees?"

"The dog's name. Hal."

"Gold?"

"Hal."

"Gold," he said in the same slow manner she had spoken.

She blew out a breath. "Is there a way to turn off that translator?"

"Beats me." He flashed her a toothy smile and picked up the sleeping dog. "Come on, Gold. Let's get your stinky butt washed."

"You are so strange."

"But I'm a fun strange," Jax said over his shoulder as he exited the ship.

# CHAPTER TWENTY

*Darker Side*

**Jax**
**Mount Hood, OR**
**290 Days Left**

"How's the animal doing?" Cora asked, kneeling to pet between Gold's floppy ears.

"Should be awake soon to eat," Jax answered.

"I meant you."

They shared an amused smile. "I am…" He had lied so often to Cora that he had vowed never to do it again. Anything she asked, he would give her absolute truth—unless Orion made it so he couldn't. "…tired and sore." He rubbed at his healed stab wound. "Usually normal for a couple of days. Like a phantom wound."

"My father told me what you're doing for Reya."

"I'm always getting stabbed, or my bones broken. It will be a pleasant change to receive them from someone so—" He was going to say beautiful, but realization hit him hard in the gut, stealing his ability to breathe. He had lived so long without Cora it was surreal speaking to her now. So much had changed in their time apart. The way she spoke, and her mannerisms differed from the rebellious spirit he loved to tease. What had remained was the light in her eyes as she smiled. He had been staring too long and cleared his throat, diverting his attention back to Gold.

"She named the dog Gold," Jax informed her, hoping she wouldn't fixate on what he had meant to say. "Strange coincidence."

The smile remained on Cora's face. It was the same smile she often wore when she had seen a vision and was keeping a pleasant surprise from him.

"Her favorite spot on Carinthia was your father's gold tree. I also know you weren't ordered to help Reya. You volunteered."

Jax placed a finger on his lips. "Our little secret."

Gold stirred. "Better return him to the ship so he can eat. Was there anything you needed help with for the wedding?"

"I will send you my list." Cora stood to leave. "I made sure Reya has been assigned the same tasks."

"Very funny."

Cora's smile faltered. She fixed him with a sorrowful look. "I am sorry for hating you for so long."

"If you didn't hate me then you wouldn't have moved on."

"Why did my father order me to find you on Baldah? If you were allied with him."

"To give you a purpose to return to the Guardianship. And some of my men were suspicious how easily we were evading being caught. I also wanted to see you. Orion knew that."

Cora gave a curt nod and left. Jax turned to Gold and scratched between his ears. "Come on, let's get you some food."

Jax held Gold as he approached the ship's entrance. His phone beeped, and he assumed it was Cora's list. He never cared for weddings but would help Cora. It was part of his vow to serve her—to honor whatever love they once shared. He stepped up the ramp and halted. Reya sat on one of the beds, brushing through her wet hair with her fingers. His heart thumped faster as he buried the nerves twisting inside his stomach with a smile.

"Gold is awake but a bit groggy." Jax made sure his tone sounded casual. "He's hungry too."

"I already have a bowl ready for him." She stood, pulling her wet hair in a ponytail, triggering his mouth to water. She wore a simple t-shirt and loose pants. There was something about how comfortable she looked that he found amazing. He was seeing someone who rarely let her guard down in pajamas.

"Why are you staring?" Her nostrils flared and her chin was jutted.

"I enjoy pissing you off." It wasn't the answer she demanded, but it was a truth.

Gold let out a deep sound as he rose his head, trying to wiggle out of Jax's arms. He let him down on a bed. Reya had changed the sheets and cleaned out the maggot pan. She sat down next to Gold, her features transitioning to concern. Jax was amazed by how quickly she formed an attachment to an animal.

Jax handed Reya a treat to feed Gold. Her lips curved into a half-smile as Gold ate from her palm. Gold ate three more biscuits before he was strong enough to walk to his bowl where he drank water.

"This is a good sign," Jax said.

Reya's eyes cut to him as though she wished he wasn't there.

"The medicine must be working if he already has an appetite," Jax continued.

"I'll stay with him tonight in the ship."

"I'm staying in here as well."

Panic flashed in her eyes.

"It's a small cabin," he reasoned. "Dallas and Cora are sleeping on the couches. The ship has two beds. We are also sharing a list of things to do for the wedding." He pulled out his phone before quickly pocketing it.

The first item listed was, *Kiss Reya before cutting the cake.*

"We can go over the list tomorrow morning," he said.

"Why would I help people I don't know?"

"Why would you abduct a woman you don't know?"

She returned her attention on Gold scarfing down the dog food, her jaw ticking.

"Were you feeling vengeful? She is Lamarse's daughter." He

eyed her, ready to catch any slight change in her demeanor.

Silence followed and he regretted his words. He hated the quiet.

Reya brushed through the patches of fur Gold had left.

"Austin said he thinks he's a Bernese Mountain Dog," Jax said, still watching her. "Or a mix of one."

"He's beautiful."

"True. But Austin is taken."

Reya's annoyed look returned.

"I'll go get you some dinner before you slice my throat again."

"Why would you get me food?"

"So you don't eat Gold's," he said, not missing a beat. "You can come with me."

"I think I'll turn in soon. I'm not that hungry."

"Nonsense. I'll get you food."

Her throat bobbed as she stared at the ship's door, shoulders tightening. He brushed past her, exiting the ship. She had followed, taking confident strides toward the cabin, no trace of the fear she had showed earlier. Austin was the first they saw, leaning on the front porch railing, sipping from a mug.

"Just getting the dark soul some food," Jax announced, ignoring Reya's murderous stare.

Austin's smile dropped. "Of course. We made plenty."

Jax reached for Reya's hand. She could have maneuvered away, but she allowed him to guide her inside. The living room was warmer than the ship, the smell of the fireplace and garlic was divine. Reya's eyes glazed with hunger.

Adia stepped into the living room from the kitchen, holding a mug. Unlike Austin, she didn't hide her wariness with a greeting smile. She continued to the door, joining Austin outside.

"Ay-oh!" Jax sang, before opening the kitchen door.

Lou lowered her book at their entrance. "I'll reheat your spaghetti and garlic bread. Do you want any steamed veggies?"

Reya made no response, so Jax said, "Sure."

He guided Reya into a chair, her posture curved as if she would bolt soon. He helped Lou gather the food, making her laugh as he pretended to drop the garlic bread but catching it with his quick reflexes. When he placed the plate in front of Reya, she stared at a picture of Lamarse, Lou, and little Adia on the fridge. Reya scratched at her palm, irritating her skin.

She took polite bites at first before shoveling the food into her mouth. Lou was setting down a second plate as Reya chewed the last of her bread.

"I'm sorry," Reya said to Lou, slowing down her eating.

Lou sat down, reached for Reya's hand that wasn't holding the fork, and clasped it between her palms. "*You* have nothing to be sorry about."

"I'm not talking about Adia in Montana."

"You told Shemu to go after our child when his plan was Lamarse," Lou stated.

The fork in Reya's hand rattled against the plate. "How do you know that?"

Lou leaned back against her chair, letting go of Reya's hand. "For a long time, Lamarse kept communication with me through Cora. I would write him novels worth of letters for him to read during those first miserable years. He didn't tell me much in return. Not even that Adia was a core. He was trying to protect me. He knew I wouldn't hesitate to make a deal if I knew how in danger Adia was, and he needed Shemu not to be aware of his presence. Cora filled in what I didn't know eventually. Including your involvement in Shemu's plan. What he made you become.

"Lamarse blamed himself. He thought he was too late." Lou leaned in close, and Jax held his breath, worried that Reya would stab Lou. "I told Cora not to give up on you. I had drowned in similar darkness, so I know how evil sticks with you, tries to drag you back under." Lou nodded to Jax. "He's here to help with that. You have my help too, if you'd like. But try to murder my daughter again, and I will unleash the darkness I've buried deep within me."

Reya jumped to her feet, nearly knocking over her water glass. Lou didn't flinch but Jax moved to grab Reya.

"Thank you." Reya hugged Lou. "The food is delicious."

"Adia and Austin made most of it." Lou patted Reya's back before pulling out of the hug. "Leave the dishes for Jax. He'll take care of it."

"I will?" Jax's smile was genuine. "I mean, of course." He eyed the sink.

Once Lou left, Jax felt Reya's stare as he fiddled with the faucet knobs. He cursed when cold water splashed onto his shirt. He pumped a few of the containers, smelling some before turning to Reya and saying, "I have no idea what I'm doing."

"I'm sure Gold could teach you."

"He does have better patience than you."

She laughed and the sound lit up Jax's mind.

Side by side, they washed the dishes the best they could before returning to the ship. Gold had chewed through a blanket and properly slobbered all over the pillows.

"Floor it is," Jax said, watching Gold circle around the bed Jax had planned to sleep on before digging his claws further into the mattress. He managed to snag the damp pillow from the bed before the dog could rip through it and dropped it onto the floor, next to Reya's bed. He removed the pillowcase and flipped it to the least wet side. "I don't take kindly to being ambushed while I sleep. When I awake, you may stab me as you wish."

Reya used a towel to cover her slobbery pillow.

"I was only joking." At her continued silence, he tapped his fingers along his chest and stomach. "The wedding should be fun."

She rolled over, her back now to him. The ship, as if knowing she preferred sleep over conversation, dimmed.

"I don't normally sleep so early," he said.

"Try." Reya's voice sounded muffled and when he squinted at her through the darkness, he could see she had brought the blanket over her head.

"Tell me a bedtime story," he joked. He would give anything

to hear her laugh again.

Silence.

"Reya?"

More silence.

Reya's breaths became slow and longer. "You're faking sleep to avoid talking to me."

She let out a muffled groan.

"What type of cake do you think there will be tomorrow?" he asked.

"Jax."

He resisted sighing at her saying his name. "Do you think Austin will make me his best man? I've never had a close friend who got married before. But I watched this one movie to prepare. Just in case he asked me."

Reya rose and light brightened the ship. Gold was already sleeping on his chewed-up mattress. She fumbled around for something in the medicine cabinet while Jax rattled on.

"Do you think Adia has an ex-boyfriend who will object? I really want to protect Austin from any unnecessary drama. But it would make for an exciting—"

Reya sprayed him, and he realized it was the same medicine he had used to sedate Gold. She nestled back under her blanket.

"No," she spoke, and his vision pulsed as the room grew dark again. "I don't think Austin will make you his best man. We are not their friends. We are not their family. We shouldn't even be at this damned wedding."

Jax moved his lips, not sure if any sound came as he was pulled into sleep.

\* \* \*

Someone hollered, making Jax shoot up in panic. He fumbled around, his eyes stinging as he peeked around, expecting to find a foe. They were alone. Gold was barking as Reya thrashed in her sleep. Jax's consciousness blinked in and out as he moved to her. By the time he awoke next, he couldn't remember why he was in her bed. She was curved into him, hugging the arm that was wrapped around her. He shut his eyes, memorizing the feel of her before moving back to the floor.

# CHAPTER TWENTY-ONE

*Death and All His Friends*

**Austin**
**Mount Hood, OR**
**289 Days Left**

Austin reached, tucking hair behind Adia's ear as she stirred. Today was their wedding day. A nervous but wonderful energy vibrated through him at the idea of marrying her. It was quickly shadowed by the thought of losing her in less than ten months.

Their love always formed around a ticking time bomb. First it was Adia waiting for Shemu to claim her soul after saving Austin. Then it was their numbered days in the City of Souls. Followed by their time in Castle. Now it was the ultimate time bomb. Austin craved to remember their previous life in the Shadow World. Hearing Adia recount their life—their misfortunes—would never be enough. It wasn't tangible to him. Adia held years of memories that would be drowned in eternity of darkness, and still, he envied her having those memories at all.

Cora had everything planned for today. She made it so they didn't have to stress, but Austin still did. He didn't want to think about his mother not attending, but the sting of her absence buried deep within him.

Adia touched his forehead, smoothing out the wrinkle. "Second thoughts?" she asked, her lips quirking into a small smile.

He shook his head, and she slid her finger down to his lips. He kissed the tip of her finger and then her palm.

"You're worried about your mom," she said, no hint of a question in her tone. Her ability to detect strong emotions was jarring.

"I think I want to clear the air with her before you're—" He bit his words off, emotion pricking his eyes. "I worry that, uh," he cleared his throat, "she may only be apologetic once you're —"

"Gone." Adia ran her fingers through his hair, and he shivered. "She will most definitely have an Oscar-worthy apology prepared."

"I believe we will defeat the shadows," he said after a long pause. "There're too many variables that have been in the works long before we existed for this not to end in our favor. But..."

"Time."

The lump in his throat thickened. "I have to believe we will find each other again, but I suspect I'll have the rest of my life here without you."

"Since we are discussing depressing things," she began, her voice quiet, "I have this thought—this idea ever since learning about Reya. If we do find each other again in another world, we won't be the same people. I don't want you to wait for me."

That took the breath from his lungs.

"If you have the chance at happiness with someone else, take it."

"Adia—"

"I doubt Reya even cares about the woman whose body she's in. There's too much darkness in her to consider a stranger's life. She stabbed Jax when triggered. I will be worse at the end of all of this. When I went to the Shadow Core, I was calm— I felt peace there. I won't be who I am now when or even if I ever see you again. The time we have spent together will be fragmented as you get older. Don't hold yourself back. Don't—"

He kissed her, rolling her onto her back, his cheeks wetting with either her tears or his own. "This is our wedding day," he muttered against her lips. "You will be my wife today, here, and in all other worlds. You are my purpose. You are my star. No matter who you become."

They kissed deeply, losing time until a knock sounded.

"Breakfast for the bride and groom!" Lou called. "Hurry before Jax eats it all."

\* \* \*

## Adia
## Mount Hood, OR
## 289 Days Left

The heaviness of her conversation with Austin weighed Adia down as she stepped into the kitchen. Reya's eyes moved to hers, paused, then returned to her plate of food. They shared too much in common and yet, Adia struggled accepting Reya. She was unpredictable, and Adia felt on edge whenever around her. Adia saw her as one of Shemu's monsters, and she knew Reya viewed Adia the same.

"Happy wedding day!" Cora sang.

A blast of happiness rolled through Adia, sensing Cora's emotions. "After you eat, we will start getting you ready. Austin, you will need to practice your vows. Reya and Jax will set up chairs, and Lou and I will work on the flower arrangements. Dallas, please don't forget about defrosting the chicken." She continued listing off other things as Adia scooped eggs onto her plate. She doubted she could eat much.

Reya's dog curled at Adia's feet, and she started dropping pieces of bacon for him. Austin forced Lou to sit, and he took over scrambling eggs. Adia wasn't sure there was enough food in the world to feed Jax, who was already loading his third plate. Adia leaned back, scratching the dog's ears as she observed. She had been doing this more lately—reflecting on moments as they happened. She doubted she would be able to keep these memories in the Shadow Core. Still, she studied every detail, soaking it all in.

Her mother smiled at her, and Adia caught a fleeting sensation of concern. Her mother was good at not showing her emotions. Adia had been trying to control her ability, but there was little time to concern herself with something she may not have in the Shadow Core. Adia squeezed her mother's hand and said, "Thanks for breakfast."

"You're not eating much."

"Butterflies."

Her mother's eyes narrowed in disbelief.

Adia turned to Dallas and said, "Your wife is a saint for planning everything."

"She makes it seem easy. I think benefiting from foreseeing wedding disasters helps."

"Has her visions been getting better?"

"She said she was able to foresee some of today." Something shadowed in his expression.

"What is it?" Adia lowered her voice, but her mother's eyes fixated on Dallas, having heard her.

"Cora hasn't been dreaming."

"That's bad?"

"It's not bad nor good. It's nothing." He looked over at Cora who was rolling her eyes at something Jax had said as she placed another stack of pancakes on his plate. "Her abilities are gifts, and they only go so far. If we aren't supposed to intervene, we can't."

The dog nudged Adia's hand, and she dropped another bacon his way. She watched Austin's back as he scooped more eggs into the glass pan. She reached for his emotions but sensed little. He must be content, which made her smile despite what Dallas had said.

A knock occurred on the door and Adia stood to answer. She heard Cora call her name in warning.

On the doorstep stood Sam.

Adia pulled out her gun, but before she could pull the trigger, Austin had her by the waist, spinning her away. "It's not him. It's not him," he said against her ear, lowering her gun. "It's okay."

Adia's heart stuttered; her knees weakened.

"Shemu replicated my image out of mockery. I am Orion." He had his arms folded behind his back, a serene smile resting on his face.

Adia gaped at her grandfather.

Her mother stepped to her side. "Orion," she greeted before giving him a hug.

Adia's mind fought to understand. The facts were there, but she struggled looking at Orion without seeing Sam. He was dressed in a blue tunic and gray dress pants. She stared at the sword strapped to his back, sheathed in black leather. He wore a gold wrist band that had strange markings. When her eyes scanned up to his face. Not only did Sam and Orion's smiles not match, but she could see her father in the way his eyes moved to meet hers.

"I would like to speak to you when you have collected your emotions," Orion said and held out his hand for her mother to take. She guided him inside.

Adia sucked in a jagged breath.

"I am so sorry," Cora said, rushing to her side. "I did not see him coming until he was already here."

Austin rubbed Adia's arms. She couldn't stop shivering.

"I'm fine," Adia muttered.

From the concern she sensed from Austin, she knew he didn't believe her.

"Come on." He guided her to their room. The little eggs and bacon she had eaten threatened to come up.

"He copied Orion's image," Adia said slowly as Austin threw a blanket over her.

"Yes."

"Sam's gone."

"Yes."

Adia buried her face in the blanket so Austin wouldn't see the tears falling as her emotions broke. He rubbed her back as she cried, embarrassed by how weak she had become in the face of meeting Orion. When the coldness had left Adia, and her cheeks were rubbed raw from crying, she sat up.

"He shouldn't have surprised you like that," Austin said, having stayed quiet during her meltdown. "He knows your history with—he knows how you would have reacted. A little warning would have been more appropriate."

She agreed but was too tired to fixate on that. Nerves were sparking at the idea she would need to speak to Orion. Adia stepped out to see Cora waiting in the hall for her. She apologized again.

"You have nothing to be sorry about." Adia smiled, even though she was sure the aftermath of her breakdown was evident on her face. She strode in the kitchen and the conversation between her mother, Jax, and Orion halted. Reya and the dog were nowhere to be seen.

"Adia," Orion greeted, his smile and tone kind.

She straightened her shoulders and stared back. Austin was right; Orion should have given her a warning.

*Let us talk to him.*

Adia locked her jaw and forced the shadows' small voice to the back of her mind. Orion watched her and she could see the intelligence in his stare. What he must know—what she craved to know was in his mind.

"Shall we talk?" he said, his words laced with authority as though he could see into her faltering mind. Her mother guided Jax out, and Adia was surprised he left the kitchen without a remark.

Austin touched her arm. She shot him an assuring smile, and he gave her a pointed look, silently asking if she wanted him to stay. The temptation rolled in her mind before mouthing that she was fine, and Austin left her alone with her grandfather.

"Take a seat," Orion said, his voice soft.

Adia remained standing, her hands on her hips. Orion didn't ask again, accepting her stance. He placed a small black box on the kitchen table and an electric current buzzed through Adia. Her eyes snapped to his, but before she could demand an answer, he said,

"To ensure our conversation remains private. I have wanted to speak to you for some time."

"And coming on my wedding day to throw me off seemed like the best time?" Her tone came out harsh and cold.

Orion showed no twitch in his features that he was offended. "My presence too soon would have tempted the shadows to take command and create chaos. I also chose your wedding because I wanted to present you with a gift specific for this occasion."

"Another gift?" She held up her prosthetic hand. "Does your generosity come at a cost?"

"My debt to you is unending," he said, surprising her. "Will you do us both a favor and practice your gift on me? Sense my emotions."

She stared into Orion's pale blue eyes that were so like Sam's. "I can't always control it."

"May I walk you through some simple steps to better your gift?" At her silence, he said, "Close your eyes and picture the person before you until you sense a tether. It will feel like a phantom cord connecting you to another."

She gritted her teeth but did as she was told. She envisioned Orion sitting before her.

A feather like touch pressed against her forehead. She opened her eyes to see if his hand was there, but he still sat in the kitchen chair.

"Try again," he told her.

This time when she gripped the tether, she imagined pulling it inside of her. A warm stirring flooded her senses. Her skin tingled until it felt like she was being electrocuted. She wanted to claw at her waist as Orion's feelings roared within her. Emotion after emotion tangled her up. She couldn't name them all but the ones she recognized surprised her.

Orion appeared relaxed and yet a tornado of stress, pain, and hope twisted inside of him. When she opened her eyes, she sensed his love for her—his pride in who she had become. Sorrow bled in the whirlwind for everything that had happened and was to occur. Adia dropped the tether, her hands clammy and her breath shallow.

"Why did you want me to feel your emotions?" Her knees weakening, she sat down. "If it was to get me to trust you, it didn't work. Knowing you are as lost and as frightened as we all are makes me question why you were given so much power."

Orion smiled and Adia's frustration grew. To know that nothing she could say would surprise him was unsettling. He was too polite to interrupt her even though he was sure as to what she would say.

"The ones who hunger for power rarely execute it innocently," he said, the picture of calm regardless of what she had sensed earlier. "They become bullies, liars, cheats, thieves. I never cared for power—for the responsibility of others' fates. I was chosen because I value humility over strength. Honesty over winning. Love over vanity. In the beginning, I made wrong choices, thought too much with my heart and not logically. The payment of those actions is beyond devastating. The price had to be paid by my wife, my children, and by you.

"Helena was more than I could ever deserve. I knew she would be murdered before I met her. Could feel the ticking time bomb of our love before it even began. I wonder if I had sacrificed more worlds in exchange for time with her at home —with our children, if she would have chosen to be Reborn." Orion's eyes bore into Adia's as he said, "My next death will be my last. My reign will end, and Austin's will begin."

Heat sprang from Adia's toes to her face. She misunderstood, surely, she misunderstood.

"Austin's destiny is to take my seat as Master," he said.

Adia's torrent of thoughts cascaded until she remembered

the shadows attached to her soul. If they knew about Austin…

Orion gestured to the black box between them. "This device is called a pillar. It protects our conversation. When I turn it off, you will be unable to discuss what I am telling you. Nothing the shadows can do will ever force you to speak what you now know. Even your thoughts will be protected."

"Austin is going to be the next Master of the Universe."

"His destiny could change. I told you about my wife—showed you my emotions because my gift to you is a Union. If I were to marry you and Austin, then your souls would be connected. No separation would diminish your bond."

The part of Adia's soul that frequently broke when she was separated from Austin mended itself with hope. There would be no final goodbye. No eternity in darkness. There would be an end in sight—a paradise on the horizon with Austin waiting for her.

"It will not always be an easy marriage—nor would you be guaranteed each other's company," he continued, "but the Fates will work to bring you back together. As long as you remain worthy of each other's love. I only ask for one thing in return: Befriend Reya."

"What?"

"Your challenge is in trusting people. When you do let someone in, you give them your absolute loyalty. You give them not only your friendship but your protection, your sacrifice."

"You want me to give that all to Reya?" Adia spoke the words slowly, trying to mull over how befriending Reya could ever be wise. "To the woman who abducted me? Who hates me?"

"The Universe depends on it."

# CHAPTER TWENTY-TWO

*Till Forever Falls Apart*

**Reya**
**Mount Hood, OR**
**289 Days Left**

"What's your favorite color?" Jax asked Austin.

"Blue," Austin said distantly.

Jax typed into his wrist device and then stared at Austin with an expectant smile.

"What?"

"This is when you ask me for my favorite color. It's grey. Most people think I'll say gold but that would be so vain."

Reya resisted laughing.

"What's your favorite childhood memory?" Jax asked Austin.

"Why are you asking?"

"He's trying to prepare a best man's speech," Reya spoke, rolling her eyes. "He's forcing you to be his friend."

"I'm not forcing," Jax said. "It's premonition."

"What?" Austin and Reya said together.

"It was one of the many things Orion told me." Jax placed a finger against his lips and Reya looked away. "Although there was one possibility we turned into nemeses. Something to do with killing Adia."

The kitchen door to the living room swung open. Reya's back stiffened, and she moved to stand, but Jax caught her by the wrist. She had run to the ship when Orion first arrived. Jax and Lou had convinced her to come back inside. Nerves heated her stomach as she held her breath. Maybe if she passed out, she could evade speaking to Orion. She sucked in a shaky breath. Jax still held her wrist, so she yanked it away.

"Reya," Orion said, and a chill ran down her back. Her tongue swelled in her mouth as he took her hand. She wanted to pull away as she had done with Jax. She wanted to hit Orion, to reach for her dagger, and make him bleed. "You walk on a thin line bordering who you once were and who Shemu turned you into."

She spun from Orion's grip, her blade to his throat faster than Jax could intervene, though she still felt his sword against the side of her neck.

"Deep breaths." Jax's arm snaked around her waist.

Jax didn't understand. Nobody could. She was at the bottom of the ocean, and the surface was miles away. She needed to shed blood—to give into chaos as much as a desert-man needed water. Shemu placed Orion at the center of her evil. Orion was enemy number one, and the monster needed to feast from his dying heart.

"Reya," Adia called to her. "This is what Sam wants. You are his legacy, and nothing would piss him off more than seeing his work fail. Seeing you become an ally and not the enemy to Orion. And if you don't have enough fight in you, let us be your anchor." The darkness retreated from Reya's vision. Adia stood before her. "You're part of this team. Dark soul and all."

The blade fell from Reya's hand, and her shoulders slumped. Tears flooded her eyes as she gawked at Adia who had every reason to hate her. Jax lowered his sword from Reya's neck, and she fell against him, no longer having any strength left to stand. He whispered in her ear as his hold on her tightened, but her mind was too busy to catch his words. Jax lifted Reya up, and she didn't protest as he carried her outside. The wind bit against her wet cheeks. Gold barked in the distance, but she kept her eyes shut. Jax lay her down on the bed in the ship, brushing away the wet hair her tears had soaked. She peeked up at him, surprised to see tenderness in his golden eyes.

"Orion told you something about me," she whispered. "Like what he said about Austin becoming your friend someday."

"Austin *is* my friend."

"That's why you keep looking at me like that."

"Like what?"

*Like I'm not a monster.*

*Like you see me.*

*And you like what you see.*

Reya turned away, not wanting to see Jax's expression as she said, "Gold is my favorite color."

* * *

## Adia
## Mount Hood, OR
## 289 Days Left

Adia's shoes glistened from the setting sun that peeked over the trees. She focused on that shine until the music started. Her hold on Dallas' arm tightened as she stepped under the flowery arch. All eyes turned on her. There were many she didn't recognize but the only ones that mattered were Austin's. Air flew from her lungs as his smile melted her nerves. His emotions radiated, making her miss a step, but Dallas made sure she didn't fall.

Dallas kissed her cheek and placed her hand into Austin's.

Memories of their life together blinked in her mind as Orion read from an ancient Carinthian book. She smiled until she registered Austin's shift in emotions. His eyes were wide, and his jaw unhinged as he stumbled back.

Adia moved to him, grabbing hold of his wrist. "What's wrong?"

Orion continued reading. The memories still blinked through Adia's mind, even though all her attention was on

Austin. Her eyes darted to Orion and then back to Austin, who now had a hand over his mouth and tears in his eyes. Adia shook her head, not understanding what was happening. He was feeling too many things for her to decipher.

Adia looked to Cora who nodded, assuring Adia everything was okay.

Austin's hand shook as he gestured to Dallas to hand him the ring box. He lifted the lid and studied the ring.

"I looked at a dozen rings before I found the right one," he said, his voice thick with emotion. "I thought I would be sick by the time we made it to the ice-skating rink. I went to get our shoes and checked on the ring, almost changing my mind to buy a different one. To propose another time. A little girl saw me and squealed. I was worried you had heard her. I asked if this ring was worthy of a queen. She told me it was. Seeing the look on your face when I knelt on the ice is my favorite memory."

Their breaths were quick, the air clouding between them as they stared at each other.

"I remember," he whispered, his voice catching. "I remember everything, Adia."

Her head spun, and Austin had to catch her as she swayed.

"How?" Her voice was barely audible, but Orion answered,

"His memories were a part of him; I only unlocked the door they were trapped behind."

"He remembers the Shadow World?"

"Yes," Orion said. "His near-death experience mended the two pieces of his soul."

*Near-death.*

Adia's watering eyes returned to Austin's as she remembered the day when Sam strangled him.

*He had died.*

She also recalled how he had been the only one to ever survive a smoke creature possession.

*Unless he didn't survive.*

Austin's vows changed to him listing off other memories

of them. He spoke about how he believed their souls would reunite, that love like theirs couldn't have the ending it was being dealt. Adia desperately wanted to tell him how their souls were bonded now—how he didn't have to fear losing her forever, that they would have eternity together someday, but she couldn't.

The words died in her throat because of the pillar. Austin was destined to take Orion's place, but there were too many variables that could change his fate.

"I never wanted love." Adia cleared her throat before continuing, "Love was a weapon Sam could use against me and he did. He used and used and used. But we can use it as a weapon too." She knew the shadows were listening. "They can rip my soul apart, but I will always find my love for you. No matter how hard they bury it, drown it, smother it—I will *always* love you. I promise to never stop fighting to find it."

Orion reached for Adia and Austin's hands. He spoke in Carinthian and then translated it into English:

"May your love be like the brightest star in the darkest sky —lighting the path for which you seek. From this day forward, your marriage is a Union of Souls. No outside force except your own choice," Orion turned to Austin, "can break it. Not even time."

Understanding grew on Austin's face. "Thank you."

Orion smiled. "Kiss your wife."

Austin pulled Adia to him, and their lips met as the small gathering witnessing their Union broke into applause. Jax's voice was heard above all as he hollered to the sky that was now dropping snow. Adia laughed against Austin's lips. He rested his forehead against hers.

"Now I have memories to share with you," he said, referring to his time in the Shadow World with the other Adia. She wondered if that lost piece of her soul reconnected with hers like Austin's had. Or if Adia's body had to die instead of only a piece of her soul. Her mind buzzed with questions and Orion held the answers. She doubted she would ever get another secret conversation with him. Even if she did, not being able to share his knowledge with Austin felt damning.

Jax collided with Austin, breaking Adia's hold on him. "You did it!" Jax shook Austin by his shoulders. "A soulmate ceremony! Forever!" Jax wiped at his brow, one arm firmly around Austin's shoulders. "How scary is that?"

"Not scary at all." Austin gave Jax a polite smile and stepped out of his hold.

Her mother was the first Adia hugged.

"I love you, Mom."

Her mother's arms tightened. "I love you." She let go of Adia to hug Austin.

Dallas pulled Adia into a bear hug, lifting her off her feet.

Cora grabbed Adia's hands. She cleared her throat and said, "A Union is not given lightly nor to every couple. Hold onto it when you are in your darkest moments."

Adia wanted to ask if Cora and Dallas had received a Union, but she feared the question would only trigger an uncomfortable moment. When Cora stepped aside so Austin and Adia could continue down the aisle that was now layered with snow, she saw Reya standing with her arms folded. Adia pulled on the tether of Reya's emotions. Sadness gripped Reya but there was also joy.

Reya was happy for Adia. There were dark emotions creeping along the edge, but Adia could feel Reya's fear of them.

Adia paused and Reya's brow quirked, but her posture remained guarded.

The idea of becoming Reya's friend seemed odder than Jax becoming Austin's, but Adia would make the effort. "I'm glad you're here." Adia sensed Reya's surprise before dropping the tether. She wished she could speak to Lamarse about when to sense someone's emotions, or when it was considered an invasion of privacy.

The snowy night sent everyone inside to eat refreshments. Austin and Adia smashing cake in each other's face triggered

Jax to start a food fight, misunderstanding the custom. What surprised Adia the most was watching her mother sneak behind Jax and dump a pitcher of iced tea over him. Adia's wedding dress was stained with all types of food and drink by the time the party settled.

Austin squeezed Adia's hand as they opened the door, a whip of icy air shocking them before running to the ship Orion gifted them. They kissed as the autopilot took them to the sky, flying to a private island where their honeymoon would begin.

\* \* \*

## Jax
## Mount Hood, OR
## 288 Days Left

Music thumped off the wooden walls of the cabin as Jax threw back his head, swinging his arms to the beat. He loved this song. He wanted to marry this song.

"What's this song called?" he shouted to Reya who shrugged. Her cheeks were gloriously flushed as she took another swig of her champagne. She was coated in frosting and punch from the food fight earlier. She twirled to the song and stumbled.

Jax tried to catch her, but his mind was foggy and instead fell with her. They laughed, their faces only inches apart, lying on their sides. She plucked a noodle from his hair.

*Kiss her.*

*Kiss her.*

*Kiss her.*

*Kiss her.*

He had to squeeze his eyes shut to stop himself from foolishly acting upon his thoughts.

"What?" she asked him.

Jax rolled to his back. "This is my spot for the evening. All must dance around."

"Everyone else went to bed. It's dawn."

Jax peeked through a slitted eye, too tired to open both. A blurry Reya stood over him, smiling.

"You're nicer when you're drunk," he said.

"You're less annoying when I'm drunk." She laughed, her voice swimming in his mind like a melody he wanted to dance to; only his arms were too heavy to lift. He smiled lazily at her before giving into exhaustion.

He awoke starving. It took a lot of energy to heal the alcohol from his blood.

"Was that your stomach?" a voice grumbled.

He glanced down at Reya, her brown hair a tangled mess on his chest. She winced as she rose, slowly turning to him with a murderous stare. She was paying a different price for their alcohol consumption.

"If you need to stab me, please wait until I have eaten at least a dozen eggs," Jax mumbled. "And brushed my teeth."

She choked on a gag before rushing to the corner of the living room where she vomited into a potted plant's soil.

"I really must learn to decipher your expressions, *Reya*." Jax stood, his vision blurring as he swayed. "I thought you were going to kill me."

"I may still." She slumped against the wall, wiping her mouth with the sleeve of her crimson dress. It was a flattering dress. Jax had spent most of the wedding coming up with compliments to tell Reya, only to end up not saying any of them.

"That dress looks," he paused as his stomach growled again, "like blood."

She narrowed her eyes that were outlined in smudged makeup. "You're weird."

"And you're beautiful." His smile dropped as her lip curled. Her hands fisted before punching a hole in the wall. She ran out the door, into the snowy forest. He heard Gold bark in the distance and knew the dog had followed her. Jax cursed, his head bouncing on the stained rug as he fell back.

"It's not her you complimented," Lou said, sipping from a mug as she stood in the doorway between the kitchen and living room. "She's in another woman's body."

"It was against her will," he argued.

"The shadows still murdered an innocent woman for Reya to possess."

He groaned.

"There're muffins in the kitchen and you can cook the rest of the eggs." Lou took another sip from her mug before sitting down on the sofa. "When you're fed, I expect you to fix the damages your dancing caused. And the vomit in my favorite plant."

Jax resisted the urge to run after Reya and headed to the kitchen where he ate two muffins while he scrambled the rest of the eggs.

"How's Reya?" Cora asked, taking a seat across from Jax at the kitchen table.

He shrugged and shoveled eggs into his mouth. He was no longer dizzy, and his energy was rising, yet he still felt deflated from Reya taking off. "I told Reya she was beautiful."

"I know." Cora was giving him her pity eyes.

His irritation sizzled. "When do we leave?"

"I will send the ship to pick you two up later tonight."

"Pick us up?"

"There's a matter Dallas and I must attend to with the hunters."

"A monster matter? But I love killing dark souls."

"You're staying to clean Lou's cabin." Now Cora was giving him her stern eyes that reminded him of Helena, which reminded him of her murder, and his time in Abyss.

"I could really kill something right now." Jax tried to say it in his usual light, amused tone, but the words came out bitter. He retrieved his sword he had dropped behind the couch, a reckless move if it weren't for Orion being at the party last night. Wherever Orion showed, it meant no danger would come, or the danger was controlled at least. So Jax let his guard down and partied with Reya, a piece of his broken soul clicking back into place as she laughed and danced.

She *was* beautiful. Not because of her body, although it was an attractive one. Her dark, reckless, broken soul that was so like his was what he found breathtaking.

Jax ran through the snowy forest, Gold's barks leading him to where Reya kneeled. She jolted at his arrival, her knives at the ready.

"Leave," she said through her teeth. "I don't want your pity or—"

Jax's sword clanged against her daggers, stunning her before she spun on her knees and attacked. He blocked one of her blades, but the other sliced his chest. Blood stained the snow as they danced a much different dance than they had last night.

Even with her hangover, he couldn't get her to spill blood. She was a Lehranian warrior who was Shemu's spy. The anger fizzling inside of Jax was replaced by sorrow for all Reya had gone through. His movements slowed, but she still fought as though Jax was the enemy. Black spread over her eyes like ink as she drove her dagger through his heart.

He gurgled, his body reacting for a terrifying minute like he was dying. He wondered, as he usually did, if this would be the end. Reya breathed heavily next to him and through blurry eyes, he saw her emotions alter on her face from blinded anger to regret and then distress. Her jaw quivered as she pressed against the bleeding hole in his chest.

Jax used the little strength he had to link their hands over his wound. Golden light spiraled out around their hands, healing him.

"I need food," he said, grunting as he sat up.

"Why did you fight me?"

"I have demons too." He stared at her flushed face. "When I said you were beautiful, I meant your soul. Every dark and light piece of it."

She stared, unblinking, her tears having stopped. He cleared his throat, coming to his knees before using his sword to weakly stand. She unfroze from her dazed reaction to hold him steady.

"I already ate all the eggs. What am I supposed to eat now?"

"Gold has plenty of food."

"Was that supposed to be a joke? Because it's tempting."

Gold growled before coming to Reya's side.

"Some protector you are," he said. "Didn't even try to stop me."

Reya scratched between Gold's ears. "He knows I can take care of myself."

Jax leaned against Reya as they trudged through the snow back to the cabin.

"Cora says we have to clean while they go have fun."

"We? I'm taking a nap after a shower."

"Another joke!"

She stepped aside and Jax fell. She ran to the ship, shooting him a devilish smile over her shoulder. He stared after her in awe.

# CHAPTER TWENTY-THREE

*Work Song*

**Lou**
**Earth Guardianship**
**9 Years Before Adia's First Deal**

Lou adjusted her night goggles as she scoped the arena that had been transitioned to a war room. A buzzer sounded late into the night. Lou had been ready, unlike the other trainees, who had snuck away to go drinking on their day off. There were no free days in training. She had declined Alex's offer to roam the city the Earth Guardianship was nearest—Las Vegas, Nevada. Their location changed often and swiftly. Each Earth was different from the last. Some seemed futuristic, while others felt like traveling decades or centuries in the past. Leaving the ship to explore was a risk. There had been numerous trainees cut from the program. They never returned, not even to gather their items.

Lou wondered if she would ever see Alex again.

In the year they had been in training, their friendship grew. He trained with her every day without fail as their ranks rose. Hers was near the top, while he fluctuated in the middle.

Lou's finger curled around the trigger, shooting a group of three passing trainees—they had seemingly formed an alliance. Each shot brought a flash of nightmarish memories of her Kill Orders. Therapy helped her not to let those images control her. Her jaw ticked at the revolting images before she buried them deep and searched for more trainees to eliminate —*kill*. This was only a test, but her mindset needed it to be real to ensure she would not hesitate during battle. When her first mission came, she feared her past trauma would make pulling the trigger impossible. Her kills haunted her. She feared adding more victims to the list.

Someone snuck behind her, but she didn't take her eyes off another trainee—*foe*—crouching behind a fake tree fifteen feet away. She shot the enemy down, spinning at the last possible second to shoot the one approaching. She rolled before using her elbows to crawl to the nearest cover—a broken stone wall. The room was unusually hot, and her skin stuck to the mat, making enough noise to reveal her location.

Three foes moved in on her. She dodged their shots, gunning them down as she dove behind a fake boulder. She shot the one already hiding there and allowed herself a few deep breaths. There couldn't be many left to shoot. She anticipated showering before lying in her air-conditioned room. Where she would not let herself think of Alex.

Lou carefully shot the foes moving around the room, catching them in the split second they were visible. She pulled off her shirt, leaving her in a tank top and shorts, and threw it in the open. As shots fired at her shirt, she eliminated all but one.

"Got you," someone whispered, electrifying her nerves.

She swung and shot.

The lights switched on, making her disoriented. She yanked off her goggles and stared at a smiling Alex. His eyes lowered to her tank top before snapping back to her face. He followed as she swiped her shirt off the floor and used it to mop the sweat dripping into her eyes, ignoring the sound of him clearing his throat.

"Did they have to make the room so hot?" she asked, keeping her eyes away from his shirtless chest.

"There are places hotter than this where we will have to go." He paused before adding, "I suspect."

"You had the shot." She glared. "Take it next time."

"Lou—"

"Don't ever let me win again."

"My gun jammed."

"Alex."

"Second place helps me plenty."

Cal called for their attention before going over tactics he had seen used. They dissected the test until Lou's brain felt fuzzy. Her sweat had dried, now leaving white salty lines on her black tank top. Once excused, Alex and Lou grabbed toiletries from their rooms and headed to the shower line.

Lou let out an uneven breath. Alex was in the middle of telling her how he cornered another trainee but stopped when she turned to him. She blinked and an errant tear slipped down her face.

"I thought you left the ship last night," she said.

"I didn't want to go without you," his words came softly. He stared down at her mouth before clearing his throat and moving forward in line.

Before Lou could change her mind, she pulled his face to hers. She tasted salt on his lips as someone whistled. Everyone felt far away as they kissed. They were nudged to move forward in line. Breaking apart, they took a few steps forward. A smile danced on Alex's face, fighting between a look of uncertainty and utter happiness. She wasn't sure what her frozen expression conveyed, but she finally thawed when he gently stroked her jaw and leaned in to kiss her again.

A throat cleared behind them, signaling it was time to move up in line again. Alex dropped his hands from her face.

Silence.

There was so much silence between them and now he looked scared. Her tongue swelled in her mouth, but she found the courage to place her hand in his. His sigh was visible as his shoulders relaxed.

Lou spent her shower thinking about what to say to Alex to ease the awkwardness. She rehearsed confessing her feelings to him while she dressed and combed her hair. When she stepped out of the woman's restroom, he stopped pacing in the hall.

"Hi," she said to him, forgetting everything she had planned to say.

Alex's chest rose and fell as they stared at each other. He moved to her, his hands tangling in her damp hair. Then they were kissing again.

* * *

**Lamarse**
**Earth Guardianship**
**9 Years Before Adia's First Deal**

It had been two months since Lou and Lamarse's first kiss. Although their morning and afternoon routines were devoted to training, their evenings had transformed into the best hours of his life. There wasn't anything he wouldn't do to keep her. If they were placed on separate teams, he would quit and follow her the best he could. Waiting for her to come back from life-threatening situations would be excruciating, which is why he swallowed his pride and called his father a week ago.

He never heard back.

Lamarse's lips still tingled from kissing Lou goodnight as he lay in bed, staring at the dark ceiling of his small room. Their recent kisses were lasting longer and longer each night, neither of them wanting to part.

Anxiety tightened Lamarse's jaw as he thought about how to tell her about his identity. He desired to keep the past separate from his new life. It was like he hadn't started existing until he met Lou. Telling her who he had been felt wrong, because he wasn't that person anymore nor did he want to be. She knew some things, but his stories were always filtered, leaving out his heritage. As their relationship shifted into more, he sometimes caught her watching him like she wanted to know all his secrets. Talking about his past meant she would feel obligated to share hers, which is why he assumed she never asked.

Lamarse closed his eyes, willing himself to fall asleep. The night was nearly over by the time he did.

\* \* \*

"You didn't sleep."

Lamarse loved the sound of Lou's voice. She didn't use it as often as others, so there was a gravelly tone to it. She spoke only loud enough for him to hear. Some of the other trainees had still never heard her speak.

"I slept." *Three hours.*

They were eating breakfast and his leg was bouncing with too much energy. They would be finishing their run by this time, but the training room was closed. Earth Guardianship was in flight, taking them to wherever their mission was located.

Lou's hand closed over his. "Are you okay?" She spoke in Mata when she wanted to make their conversation more private.

He ran his thumb over hers. "I want to tell you more about my past."

She blinked. Once. Twice. "You're not breaking up with me?"

He released a surprised laugh. "No. Never."

She fought a smile, but then looked guarded again. "Your past. On Matadon?"

The alarms blared, signaling everyone to return to their rooms at once. The floor shook as the room tilted. Lamarse grabbed Lou's hand as they fought the crowd to reach their secured rooms. Each room was equipped with a pod to escape from the ship. Someone pushed past Lamarse, and he lost Lou in the wave of people flooding the halls.

"Lou!" He shouted several times.

He shouldered and pushed until he reached her room.

She wasn't there.

He searched the now emptying halls for any sign of her as the alarms blared. He retraced his steps before going down a hall that he hadn't before. A Mortal Guard scolded him to get to his pod, being cut off by a loud explosion. The whole ship shook as Lamarse and the Mortal Guard fell to the floor.

"LOU!" Her name ripped from his throat like a roar.

"Alex!"

He clung to the wall as he made his way toward her voice. Around the corner, he saw her hunched over someone who was bleeding from their head—Hannah.

"She can't walk," Lou said, her eyes large. "Help me."

He couldn't recall a single time when Lou asked for his help. They each took Hannah's side and lifted her.

"Where's your room?" Lamarse asked Hannah.

Hannah only moaned.

"There's extra ones in Sector 2," the Mortal Guard who had followed Lamarse said. He called someone and two other Mortal Guards appeared within a minute. "Go to your rooms. Now!"

Another explosion. Lou was thrown further than Lamarse. He hurried to her, crawling most of the way until he was able to stand. They walked, stumbling as the ship tilted and shook.

"Code 24, Code 24." The overhead speakers sparked and went out; so did the lights.

Code 24—abandon ship.

"Come on," Lamarse said through gritted teeth.

Lou had a red spot on her forehead and a cut along her cheek. She was bleeding but not deeply.

They froze. There were stars where Lou's room had been. The opening glowed orange before flickering. The shield wouldn't last long.

"This way." Lamarse held her hand as they hurried to where he had found Hannah.

The way to Sector 2 was blocked by rubble. They ran down

the only other path they could and reached his room. Together they pried the door open.

Another explosion rocked the ship.

"I don't think this is another test." Lou's eyes were large and beautiful.

He kissed her, his hands tangling in her hair as hers went to his jaw. When they parted, she looked dazed. He moved to the operation panel and prepared the pod. He settled Lou into the seat, fastening her belts. Her eyes sharpened, noticing there was only one seat.

"I love you."

"Get in the pod, Alex." She struggled to unclasp her belt.

He knew she would fight him to make sure he was the one to survive.

He moved quickly to the panel and sealed her in. He wished he had time to tell her everything. She had been his purpose—his destiny. He felt it stronger than anything in his life. He had little faith he would be Reborn.

He pressed eject.

# CHAPTER TWENTY-FOUR

*Lost and Found*

**Lou**
**Earth 145**
**9 Years Before Adia's First Deal**

After Lou's pod ejected into space, she saw ships surrounding Earth Guardianship. She thrashed against her seatbelt before trying to reach the control panel to change the course of her pod back to the ship —back to Alex. She witnessed the final bomb hitting Earth Guardianship before she was thrust into hyper speed, unable to see anything but streaking stars.

The pods had taken everyone to Earth 145. They hadn't received any news other than they were waiting for another ship to come get them once it was safe; once whoever attacked them had been *dealt with.*

Days later, Lou had tried running the few miles to the city. Her limbs were heavy with fatigue even as she walked. The smell of food from a burger shop made her stop to eat. She sat on a bench, watching couples and groups of friends dressed for a night out as she ate.

It all fascinated Lou, but it also broke her heart. Alex had wanted to spend a night in Las Vegas with her. She mourned for memories they could have made if she hadn't been so focused on becoming a Mortal Guard.

"I'm sorry about Alex," Hannah said, approaching slowly—

cautiously.

Lou spotted the Mortal Guard—who had taken Hannah to Sector 2—in the driver's seat of a parked car.

*If we had followed them*, Lou couldn't help from thinking, *Alex would still be alive.*

"I know you guys were..." Hannah cleared her throat, looking pained. "I came to tell you a ship is coming. Do you want a ride back to base?"

Lou entered the car wordlessly. The sun was setting but the air was still thick and hot, so she rolled down the window. Hannah kept conversing, directing her words to the Mortal Guard when Lou didn't speak. It hurt to swallow, and Lou feared she was getting sick. She rested her head against the open window, relishing the wind.

Hannah nudged her awake. It was dark now. Although it had been a short drive, Hannah and the Mortal Guard had left her in the car to sleep. There was a soft buzzing, and the car vibrated, but it wasn't on. It took Lou a disoriented moment to understand a ship had arrived. It was time to return and become a Mortal Guard—without Alex.

* * *

**Lou**
**Carinthia**
**9 Years Before Adia's First Deal**

The ship touched down on lush grass, greener than Lou had ever seen. It was a long line to exit, so she stayed staring out the window. This would be their home until another Earth Guardianship was built. This was where Orion resided, although she heard he was rarely home.

An hour had passed before Lou stepped out of the ship, impressed how many tents were already set up. She lined up to be assigned a sleeping quarter, her mind trying to focus on how wonderful Carinthia smelled and not on what Alex's reaction would have been if he was standing next to her. He was always fascinated by new places.

After her tent was settled, she decided to explore. She found a creek and dipped her hands in the chilled water before finding a tree to sit against. In her isolation, she wept. Once her sobs had subsided, she rinsed her face in the creek and returned to base. She took her container of noodles, vegetables, and bread to her tent. After a few bites, she set her food aside and slept.

She awoke dehydrated. She chugged her water and finished her cold meal. She heard people whispering outside of her tent. Peeking out, it was a group of trainees preparing to run. She needed to make up for not fulfilling a proper workout in days. She went as far as putting on her shoes before the idea of running reminded her too much of Alex.

She stepped out into the chilly morning, blinking the sleep from her eyes. She strolled along the road until she reached a town as the sun rose. She glanced in the windows of several shops not yet open. Everything was labeled in Carinthian, so she used the translator application on her wrist device. She smiled when a painting of a dog and a boy playing fetch was labeled, "Earth Canine Eats Earth Boy's Toy".

She circled the shops until they opened. She used her translator to order a tea and purchase a book. Even with the translator, the story was difficult to follow, but it kept her mind occupied. She sat at a table outside, wishing she had a warmer jacket. The book told a tale of two brothers fighting over a kingdom. The bookseller had promised it was worth reading after all the world building.

When her stomach rumbled, Lou ordered cheesy bread. It was the most delicious meal she had ever eaten so she ordered two more. She returned to base by late afternoon. The rest of the trainees were in the middle of a weapons course. She expected Cal to make a comment, but he only nodded, and she slipped into her tent. Receiving pity from someone she was trying to impress created a knot in her throat. She cried into her pillow, hoping no one could hear her.

Tomorrow, she would return to her routine.

When morning came, she panicked thinking about running without Alex. Everything she did to become a Mortal Guard involved him, and the idea of continuing made it difficult to breathe. Her chest ached as she grabbed the book she had purchased the day before. She read until her tent became stuffy. She ate lunch at the outdoor tables, avoiding Hannah's stare.

She walked back into town, purchasing another book since she was almost done with the first. She entered the art gallery after smiling again at the painting of the dog and human boy.

She was surrounded by paintings of all types from worlds she had never heard of before. She was flipping through an art collection when she stopped at a painting of Orion's three children. They had no faces. She found it odd and held her translator over the text, but it wouldn't translate.

"Lou."

The book fell. A hand held her steady as the room spun. Slowly, she met his eyes.

"Breathe," he told her.

She sucked in a stuttering breath. "Alex?"

There was an intensity in Alex's eyes. He wasn't wearing his glasses. He opened his mouth, but someone approached him with a broad smile, speaking in Carinthian. Lou blinked when Alex responded with rapid words she didn't understand. She straightened when the shop's owner saw the book she had dropped and its crumpled pages. She expected him to be scolding, but his voice was tender as he spoke to her in Carinthian.

Alex replied and the owner left.

"He is going to get you some calming tea," Alex told her in English.

"How...?" There was not a visible scratch on him. She focused on his wrist, where he had been injured during a test.

The scar was missing.

"You're not Alex." Her heart cracked because she wanted to cling to the fantastical idea that maybe it could still be him.

The owner came with her tea. Her hands shook as she held the cup. The owner bowed to Alex, pounding a fist to his chest. He spoke a word she had read a hundred times in the Carinthian novel—Prince.

When the owner left, Alex spoke with a slight waver in his voice, "My name is Lamarse Alexon, son of Orion." He picked up the book, flipping to the painting of Orion's children.

Now one of them had a face—Alex's face.

"Orion's children are blessed with anonymity." He showed her his wrist that had been bare a moment ago. A tattoo of the Carinthian crest was now visible.

"You're an Eternal Guardian," she spoke slowly. "You're Lamarse. Not Alex."

"Walk with me and I will tell you everything." His words were hushed and desperate as though he expected her to decline his company.

They had reached a bridge by the time he finished telling her about his history, filling in the parts about Reya he had left out before. About the Shadow World. About how many times he had died trying to find Reya and losing his gifts. It was painful to hear. No matter how much time had passed, their love had been real and tragic. He carried the guilt of losing her like Lou carried every one of her kills. The memory of seeing him in Matadon flashed in her mind and now she understood the shell of a man he had been.

He told her about his conversation with Orion, and how he let go of Reya the best he could. He talked about becoming Alex, and how he was drawn to Lou like their souls were magnetized. How he didn't believe he would come back from dying on the ship because he had found his purpose in her and didn't believe his destiny could be any greater than that. Then he told her that when he came back, his gifts had been returned.

"You can read minds?"

He chuckled and kissed her palm. "No need to worry. If I abused my powers by violating your privacy, I would lose them again. Or not be Reborn." He kissed up her arm. "Until your last breath, I will choose to be Reborn."

Her shoulders lowered as he kissed her collarbone. "Shall I call you Lamarse, then?" She expected him to laugh again, but he said,

"I prefer you call me Alex." He kissed along her neck and her breath hitched.

When his lips met hers, a pleasant shock electrified her nerves.

"We better head back," she said. "It's nearing curfew."

"I need to tell you…" He took a breath. "My father is granting me Earth Guardianship."

"Granting you as in…?"

"I will be leading it."

"Which team?"

"All."

She mulled over his words and what that meant for him, for her, for their relationship. How often would they be able to see each other if he was commanding wars and the Mortal Guards fighting them. Would he indirectly place her out of harm's way? Her mind and heart battled for her next words but what she said was, "Oh."

"Oh?" His smile was shy.

"I love—"

"I love you too," he was quick to say.

"I love *Alex*. And Alex loves me."

"I *am* Alex."

"I don't think you'll be able to be. Not with your status and —" She shut her eyes, flashes of the past reminding her of the trauma she never discussed with him.

"I will give it up then." He closed the distance she had placed between them. He brought her hands to his chest. His heart was beating fast.

"You don't even know everything about me. The son

of Orion cannot be with someone as..." *Broken, violent, murderous.* So many words she could have finished with and yet she couldn't say any of them. She wouldn't be able to bear how Alex would look at her if she told him detailed accounts of the victims she was brainwashed to kill.

"You were a prisoner."

"I was an assassin," she whispered.

"You were a prisoner," he repeated. "None of their blood is on your hands."

"I doubt your father will see it as that. My capability to kill got me into Earth Guardianship training, but do you really believe anyone would approve of our relationship?"

"My father sent me to Earth Guardianship to become the best version of myself. I asked to go home to better prepare, but he wouldn't let me. He sent me to meet *you*. Someday, if you ever become ready, you can tell me about your past, and I will help shoulder the burden of it." He brushed through her hair, and she shivered. "Nothing you can say will stop me from wanting to marry you."

"You want to marry me?"

"Since the day you beat me in combat." He moved closer.

"It's getting late."

"You can stay at Alexon Manor with me."

She was lightheaded and part of her was tempted to give into desire and wash away her duties and all that she had worked for. "I should go back. I have a long run in the morning."

"We could run together."

"They will question how you're alive."

"Yes and no," he said. "The blessing makes it so they will not recognize me as Alex but see someone new."

"But I recognized you as Alex."

"The blessing grants exceptions. I needed you to recognize me, so you did."

"Today was... I need..."

"Oh." It was his turn to say the simple word. "You need time to process."

"I haven't been…" Her jaw trembled. "When you died it was like I died. I've fallen behind on my training. My focus."

"I will walk you back then."

# CHAPTER TWENTY-FIVE

*Spirits*

**Cora**
**Phoenix, AZ**
**100 Days Left**

Blood splattered Cora's face and she fought the urge to spit. Jax smiled sheepishly at her.

"Was that necessary?" Cora had been readying her gun to shoot the possessed man charging at her when Jax jumped in, impressively swinging his sword.

"Maybe not." Jax looked to Reya, who was digging her dagger into a dark soul.

Cora bit any remark she wanted to say.

A shotgun fired. Adia stood before a dead dark soul. Half of his head was missing. Cora's eyes swept the area in time to see Dallas fight off a female dark soul and Austin shooting her in the back.

"That's it? Good," Jax wiped his sword on the shirt of a dead dark soul. "Let's eat."

"We need to burn the bodies," Cora said.

Jax threw his head back and groaned. "Can't we make the newer guys do that?"

"Lazy baby," Reya muttered as she passed him.

Jax joined her side, saying something quietly to her. Reya's lips tightened in amusement before she shoved Jax's shoulder. In the months since Adia and Austin's wedding, Reya still struggled fighting the darkness Shemu had merged her soul with; but she could smile again.

Dallas and Austin were already piling bodies in the field. Cora meant to direct them when her mind slipped into a waking dream.

*White eyes burned her soul as a hand gripped her wrist. Dallas screamed but she had no control over her neck to see if he was okay.*

*She fell through blackness, her stomach lurching from the incontrollable flight of her soul, moving between worlds. She stood still, looking up at five crowned demons—Lamarse stood on her other side—wrists and ankles bound by glowing chains.*

*Doors opened behind and footsteps echoed behind her. Cora wanted to drop to her knees as her father stepped between her and Lamarse, escorted by Ebony. One of the Seven stood, her lips twisting into an unnatural smile as she stood before her father. She had red hair and golden skin. Her glowing green eyes bore into Cora's and then Lamarse's. She held her knife to Ebony, who bowed to the demon before driving the blade into their father's chest.*

*A laugh echoed behind her, blending in with Cora's screams. Adia stepped forward, crown on her head. Her laughter subsided as she stroked Lamarse's face before stabbing him. She now stood before Cora, her blue eyes void of any recognition. Adia drew back her knife before swinging it forward.*

Cora gasped, her hand flying to her chest where Adia had stabbed her. Her head was lying on Dallas' lap while hunters surrounded them.

"Are you okay?" Dallas asked.

"What did you see?" was Jax's question.

Cora struggled to grip reality as what she had experienced in the vision swirled in her mind. She licked her dry lips and slowly sat up. The ghost of pain was still present in her chest. This had been her first vision since the wedding. Her eyes found Adia's before quickly moving away. Cora stood with Dallas' help. She dried her shaking hands on her pants and cleared her throat. "The bodies need to be burned."

"Cora—"

"We have work to do," she said, cutting Dallas off. "And Jax will lose his temper if he does not eat."

"What did you see?" Jax asked again.

Cora's eyes pricked. She gripped Dallas' hand and pointed at the pile of bodies on the field. "We can't burn them there. We need to move them to the street."

Nobody argued, even though it meant carrying fifty bodies half a mile. Cora straightened her posture, her vision spotting as the sound of Lamarse being stabbed by Adia echoed in her thoughts.

\* \* \*

"Tell me."

Dallas stroked Cora's face in the privacy of their room. She had always told him about her visions. He was her confidant. He helped carry the burden of knowing too much and the helplessness of changing what had to be done. A tear slipped down her face and Dallas was quick to swipe it with his thumb.

"The Seven needs me to get to my father."

"I thought they only needed Adia and the knowledge of who her father is."

"My father put extra measures on our family to ensure Carinthia is protected. He told me that I would have to make a choice to ensure the Guardianship is not compromised. Ebony is adopted, so her blood means nothing to them. Most of her knowledge of our family was protected. All she could do was point them in Adia's direction without explaining why."

Dallas held her, stroking her back in soothing patterns. "What can be done?"

Cora held her knees, tears falling freely now. "I am not sure," she lied.

\* \* \*

## Adia
## Seattle, WA
## 90 Days Left

Reya's blade flashed toward Adia, who dodged and then swung back. They stared at each other, sweat burning Adia's eyes as their swords pushed against each other. Adia's feet moved quickly, but Reya was faster. The sharp edge of her blade touched Adia's throat.

"Again," Adia said, breathless.

"That's enough for today."

"One more—"

"We have been practicing for hours. You are getting better, but I'm teaching you skills that took me decades to master in the Shadow World." She sighed, her eyes fixating on something behind Adia. "Please rescue your husband from Jax."

Adia stared over at Jax and Austin in time to see Jax laugh as he feigned slicing through Austin's waist and then his neck. Jax gripped Austin's shoulder and Austin nodded to whatever he instructed.

"I'm going for a run," Reya announced.

Adia positioned herself against the wall to observe Austin's training.

They had spent a month away on their honeymoon. With the ship Cora had lent them, they traveled to several destinations. They went snorkeling, rafting, and stargazed in the Atacama Desert. They ate every type of food and relaxed on a beach in Fiji. They were crossing items off a list Adia hadn't known she had. It was tempting to forget their duties and live the rest of Adia's time traveling on Earth.

A sweaty Austin collapsed by Adia. She stroked his damp hair while he sucked in deep breaths. "He's trying to kill me."

"Adia?" Jax wore a serious expression, his forehead pinched.

"I realized…"

"What?"

"Dallas is your uncle." Jax barked a laugh.

Adia patted Austin's back. "Want to run?"

"No," he moaned.

"I'll see you at dinner."

Austin gently caught her by the wrist. "I'll run with you." He got to his feet and Jax moved to join them. "But not *you*."

Jax feigned hurt.

They ran around the old hospital. Cora and Dallas were training recruits in the California facility. While they were away, Adia, Austin, and Lou oversaw the hunters' training in the Seattle location. Cora made a point that Jax and Reya were not allowed to interfere.

Austin remained quiet as they ran, and Adia was too tired to speak as well. Still, she enjoyed quiet moments as these. When they had run five miles, they showered, got dressed, and headed for dinner. This was Adia's favorite time in the day. Her training tasks were over, and they could do as they wish.

"Everyone should share their favorite kills," Jax said with a mouthful of mashed potatoes.

"No," Reya was quick to say.

"I'll go first." Jax shoveled another bite into his mouth, and Adia no longer wanted more food. "Agori." He raised his eyebrows but only Austin looked mildly impressed.

"Big troll-like creature with vanishing capabilities," Austin explained to Adia.

"Don't forget their fascination with turning weapons into dust. I had to fight him with nothing but these hands!" He held up his palms, his eyes wide to emphasize how enthralled they should be. He briefly looked at Reya, who made no change in her blank expression. "What's your most impressive kill, Lou?"

"King Tyron."

Adia hadn't meant to, but she reached for her mother's tether and sensed unnerving guilt.

"That was *you*?" Jax stared in awe. "I hope you made it

a painful death. His specialty was abducting children and training them to kill for him. He fed them these supplements to make them stronger and harder to defeat." He smirked. "But not impossible to kill."

Her mother stood and Adia released the tether on her storming emotions. She squeezed Adia's shoulder in assurance before leaving.

Reya shot Jax a reproachful look.

"What?"

"She was clearly one of those children he took," Reya said to him.

"Louise Miller Dawson? A Tyron Assassin?" Jax looked impressed.

Adia refrained from smacking him. Reya, however, shoved his head into his plate of food. She folded her arms, scowling until she caught Adia's appreciative nod. She nodded back.

* * *

**Reya**
**Seattle, WA**
**90 Days Left**

"I have potatoes up my nose."

Reya was meditating, something Lou taught her to help with intrusive thoughts. Her concentration was broken, but she chose to ignore Jax as he sat next to her.

"I came to meditate as well," he said. "*Oof.* It's hot in here."

She willed him to go away.

"Reya?"

She gripped her knees, her back stiffening.

"I can't help but feel you might be angry with me."

Through her teeth, she said, "I am trying to meditate."

"So am I. Although, I don't know how."

"Silence."

"Silence?"

"Inside and out."

"Inside?" He sounded appalled.

"No thinking. Just follow your breaths."

"Oh. Okay." The mat squeaked as he wiggled into a position. "Reya?"

Her face tightened. "What?"

"I don't know how to shut off my thoughts."

"Focus on your breathing."

"I keep thinking about the word *breathe* and that made me wonder if thinking about the word counts as meditating. And then I started thinking about Lou and maybe how I upset her and you. I also thought about how hot it is in this room."

"You didn't upset me."

"You pushed my face into perfectly good dinner. I didn't know you cared so deeply for Lou."

"You were upsetting Adia."

He raised his brows at her. "And you care about her now?"

"She would have broken your face with her prosthetic hand if I hadn't interfered."

"You care about *me* then?" A bead of sweat rolled down his face.

"When you are hurt, you eat like a wolf. I was concerned over the hunters who would have to work overtime to feed you."

Jax's response was interrupted by an alarm. They swiftly rose, running out of the room as the lights went out. Quietly, they crept along the wall of the gym, ducking when a figure opened one of the doors.

"Jax! Reya!" Austin called. "You're on our team!"

Reya and Jax exchanged a confused look before rising. Austin's light flashed over them as he jogged over.

"What's going on?" Reya asked, staring at the strange gun in Austin's hand. It was black with a green stripe that glowed.

"Cora and Dallas brought the California hunters." He held his gun for her to take. "It's loaded with paintballs. California vs Washington."

Reya studied the gun the best she could in the dim lighting. She aimed at the wall and shot a paint pellet. "A game?"

"Paint on you means you're eliminated," Austin explained. "Whichever team has the last person wins."

"Where's my gun?" Jax asked eagerly.

"Cafeteria. It's a safe space to load and find weapons, but you only have sixty seconds there before you're eliminated."

"What about—"

Jax grabbed Reya's hand and started sprinting toward the cafeteria. She had been about to ask if the bathroom was also considered a safe space.

"How are we supposed to know who is on what team?" Reya asked as they ran.

"We know not to shoot Austin, Lou, Adia, and..." He hummed. "I don't remember anyone else's names."

They were turning the corner when they almost crashed into an unfamiliar face. They held a black gun but instead of a glowing green stripe, theirs was blue. Reya pulled Jax down, helping him dodge a paint pellet. She shot the hunter in their shoulder. The opposing hunter cursed and walked off.

"California has blue guns," she whispered to Jax in case more hunters lurked around the corner.

"How were we supposed to know that?"

"Maybe if you allowed Austin to finish explaining the rules of the game..."

He huffed a laugh. "I'm sorry. This is just so exciting."

They edged down the hall only running into two others, who happened to be green. They looked in the cafeteria windows, spotting the hunters who were armed along the walls. There to shoot anyone who lingered too long. She observed the bathroom across the hall, witnessing someone coming out before getting shot by one of the assigned hunters. Reya ignored her full bladder and sprinted for the weapon's tables with Jax following.

They grabbed what they could, pocketing extra pellets before sprinting away. They ran down the hall where blue-gunned hunters were waiting for them. Jax expertly eliminated them as he slid, and Reya reached the door leading to the indoor track.

"We should head back to the gym," Jax said.

"I doubt Austin will still be there."

"He could."

"I say we take this outside."

"It's raining."

"Exactly." Reya didn't wait for him to deny her suggestion and ran quietly to the nearest exit.

"There won't be many people outside," he whispered.

"The object of the game isn't to eliminate the most people but be the last standing."

"Oh." Jax's face fell. "But shooting people is so fun."

"Fine. Stay." She used her shoulder to push open the door. The summer rain had slowed to a mist. She breathed in the refreshing air and jogged to the tree line that bordered what used to be a parking lot but was now full of different weapon stations. She snagged night goggles from one of the booths, handing a pair to Jax. She ducked behind an archery station, having heard something.

Jax's hand rested on the small of her back.

"I hate that our guns glow," he whispered near her ear.

A pleasant shiver ran through her as his hand slid to her hip. He was already looking at her when she faced him. He was so close, and she didn't move away. His eyes ticked across her face, pausing on her lips.

A bark startled them apart.

"Gold, my friend, you're on our team!" Jax whispered as the wet dog licked the face she almost kissed.

"I'll be back," Reya whispered.

Jax's eyes were intense when he looked at her. "Will you?"

"I have to pee. Keep a lookout."

On her way back, she paused at the sound of shooting. She used her goggles, spotting the group of blue hunters firing toward Jax. A whimper sounded from Gold. Her eyes locked on the hunter who shot her dog, blackness edging her vision. She worked to separate her emotions from the ones that wanted to slice the hunter's throat. When the blackness in her vision cleared, she aimed her gun and shot the hunter in the forehead. She took out the others before running to where Jax hid. She slid on the cement, burning her knees as she examined Gold.

"You okay?"

"I'm fine. My gun jammed."

"I was talking to Gold." She inspected the blue paint on Gold's neck.

"Gold, looks like you're eliminated. Cafeteria is a safe space."

"He doesn't know what you're saying," she told him.

"Sure he does." Gold trotted away. "He'll be fine."

"This way." Reya led him to the tree she picked to climb.

Jax arched his neck, making a face.

"What?"

"The limbs look weak."

"You're light enough, but I doubt it could hold your ego." She smiled.

He looked like he was about to laugh but then cursed, shaking his head.

"What?"

A tree branch snapped behind. Reya aimed her gun, but she couldn't see anyone there. She turned to climb the tree, but Jax caught her by the waist and pulled her to him.

"Your smile, that's what." He kissed her. She fisted his wet shirt as he kissed along her jaw. He hummed when their lips locked again, and she deepened the kiss.

At rapid speed, Jax broke away, shot two hunters with paint, and returned to kissing her.

* * *

**Austin**

## Seattle, WA
## 89 Days Left

Austin examined the welt on his ribs where Dallas had shot him. Adia was asleep on his lap. They were supposed to be overseeing the cafeteria, but so few hunters were left in the game.

He lowered his shirt and rested his head against the wall. He thought back to playing paintball with Adia in the City of Souls. Although she had described the day, he loved how he could now remember each detail. How he felt when she stared at him with her guard down. The sound of her laugh when she shot him in the mouth. He had felt hope that she could love him again.

Since gaining his memories back, the idea of losing Adia cut deeper.

The sound of the door opening startled Adia awake. Cora, Dallas, Jax, and Reya walked in laughing.

"Who won?" Adia asked, rubbing the sleep from her eyes as she sat up.

"We did," Cora said. "They were too busy kissing to hear us coming."

Austin raised his brows, taking in Jax's grin and Reya's annoyed expression.

"About time," Adia said, standing. "Jax's heart eyes were getting pathetic."

"How did you even find us?" Jax asked Cora. "Did you cheat with your second eye?"

"No, Gold led us to you."

Jax twisted to the dog wagging his tail by the door. "Traitor!" The dog yawned in reply.

"It will be nice to have a day to rest tomorrow," Jax said.

"Training starts in two hours."

"I've always loved your humor, Cora." Jax dropped in one of the chairs at the circular tables. "When's breakfast?"

"I'll see what I can find," Reya said, still seemingly annoyed.

"Is training really starting in two hours?" Dallas quietly asked Cora.

Cora laughed and shook her head. "Free day."

"Oh good." Dallas headed toward the kitchen.

"You hungry?" Austin asked Adia.

"I'm exhausted."

"How about we eat then sleep until it's night again."

"It's a plan," she said while yawning.

Reya, Dallas, and Austin brought out spaghetti, chips, mashed potatoes, chicken, and rolls. Pretty much whatever was left over from the last several meals. They ate as they exchanged stories. Adia's head found his shoulder, and she fell asleep during one of Jax's exaggerated tales. Knowing he was a god and had lived many mortal lifetimes, Austin was curious if maybe he didn't exaggerate by much.

"Time to crash," Cora said.

Austin moved to collect the dishes.

"I got them," Dallas said. "Get her to bed."

Austin gave him an appreciative smile. Adia barely stirred as Jax helped hold her up while Austin stood. He gathered her into his arms.

"I can carry you to bed too, if you'd like," Jax said to Reya while Austin walked to their assigned room.

Austin heard a thud. He glanced back to see that Reya had shoved Jax's face in his food again.

# CHAPTER TWENTY-SIX

*Just Say Yes*

**Lou**
**Earth 819**
**8 Years Before Adia's First Deal**

Covered in mud and blood, Lou filed behind other Mortal Guards to board the ship. They were leaving an Earth that had been dominated by witches who worshipped the demon lord Ruin. The invasion had occurred years before, but Earth Guardianship interfered only recently. A team infiltrated the coven while Lou fought bewitched humans on the muddy plain.

A local crowd cheered behind a barrier boarding their ship. Lou watched them, too exhausted to feel pride for saving their planet. She had a gash in her arm, but the mud made it difficult to see how deep it was. She could no longer move that arm, having still used it to fight long after it was injured. Pain made her dizzy, but she kept a stoic face until she caught the eyes of a little girl.

Lou straightened, adjusted her gun, and smiled as pain zapped through her. She saluted the girl, who beamed, looking up at the woman whose hand she was holding in amazement.

There weren't showers or rooms on the aircraft taking them back to Earth Guardianship. Lou stood, shoulder to shoulder with her fellow Mortal Guards and prayed the flight wouldn't be long. She thought about the girl and the woman, who she assumed was her mother. Lou had been nine years old when she tested into a gifted school. The night before her first class, Tyron's assassins broke into her home and killed her parents. She had hidden under her bed, hearing their faint screams, staring at the outfit she had laid out for the morning.

The room filled with smoke.

She awoke in the pit.

The drugs they had experimented on with her fellow captives had changed her. Although she wasn't as strong as she had once been, the formula altered the chemistry in her brain. She could run longer, knock out others with a single punch. She had a higher tolerance for pain.

But the cut in her arm became too much.

Her vision pulsed with the pain. She stood in a puddle of blood. In her dazed mind, she couldn't comprehend that it was her own. She said to the Mortal Guard next to her, "You're losing too much mud."

Lou's head slumped forward, falling unconscious.

* * *

**Lamarse**
**Earth Guardianship**
**8 Years Before Adia's First Deal**

Lamarse swiped through the mission commands he needed to approve. He hadn't slept since Lou went to Earth 819. The Mortal Guards standing at attention in his office were annoying him. He wished he could command them to leave, but Earth Guardianship had too many enemies and they were in flight. The Mortal Guards would need to act fast if the ship was attacked.

Lamarse's fingers tingled as he debated checking on Earth 819's status again. His relationship with Lou had been kept secret. He tried to keep his tactics unbiased, but Lou called him out when her first few missions weren't in the heart of the battle. He tapped his anxious fingers along his desk before entering the code for Earth 819's chronicle. It was projected into the air, so the Mortal Guards could see as well.

"819's team is in transit," one of the Mortal Guards said.

Lamarse's swiping halted. The mission was accomplished. He didn't have an unbiased reason to see the dead and injured list. He gritted his teeth, closing the chronicle. He returned to the mission commands.

Hours later, when 819's team boarded Earth Guardianship, he sent Lou a message. His anxiety spiked when she didn't respond. Scenarios of her mutilated body on the battlefield fed his fears.

When it was time for dinner, Lamarse walked through the medic wing. The Mortal Guards trailing behind him didn't speak a word. Staff pounded their chests in respect to Lamarse's status as he passed. They were aware he was the son of Orion, but the blessing on his identity made it so they couldn't share his description, location, or name. If they recalled his image, it would be faceless like they dreamed their interaction.

It was strange seeing people he knew as Alex stiffen at his approach. The nurse who had worked tirelessly on him after being injured during a test, having teased him during his stay, now bowed. She wasn't capable of recognizing him as Alex unless he told her.

Lamarse scanned for Lou but couldn't find her. His shoulders tensed; his heart raced. If she wasn't responding, and she wasn't in the medic room...

"Sir."

Lamarse's eyes followed where the Mortal Guard had gestured. Two medics were rolling Lou's unconscious body into the room. Lamarse held his breath.

"What is her condition like?" he asked the nearest medic.

The medic hesitated. "Abrasion in her arm from a cursed sword. She's losing a lot of blood."

Lamarse noticed the blood bags. "Is she unable to wake?"

"The cut is highly painful, even with medication. We could wake her if you had questions. There are thirty-three others with the same injury. Is there something we should know?" The medic looked concerned. When Lamarse got involved, it usually meant a priority issue.

"No, I..." He cleared his throat. "I am going to stay with her. Keep me updated."

The medic's eyes went from Lou to Lamarse. She gave him a curt nod and left. Even with their advanced medicine, Lou's cut was barely a scratch deep, but there was a suction along the wound, catching the blood she was losing. There were hives along her arm, and her fingers were blue.

Someone brought Lamarse his meal. He pushed the meetings he could to the next day, only taking the one from his father, which he did by Lou's side.

"I cannot talk," he told his father. "If this is urgent—"

"I will make this fast," his father said. "I have arranged a dinner for you and Lou to attend here at the manor. I have marked your calendar. Give Lou my best wishes while she recovers."

His father ended the call before Lamarse could say another word. He unlocked his calendar on his wrist device. The dinner was scheduled in two weeks. Hope warmed him as he held Lou's cold hand. She would be well enough to attend a dinner by then.

* * *

**Lou**
**Carinthia**
**8 Years Before Adia's First Deal**

Lou's arm burned as she fought through the fire, carrying an unconscious Alex on her back. A chilling laugh echoed around them. She moved her legs faster, nearly tripping on the last step. She could see the door, but the distance elongated as she ran to reach it.

She threw the door open and froze. Chills ran through her at the sight of King Tyron. He grew bigger, towering over her. The walls became mirrors and she saw herself as a child. Two girls she knew from the pit pulled Alex off her. He screamed as they threw him into the fire.

King Tyron grabbed Lou's chin. She stared into his purple eyes as he smiled. "I'll keep you as my own."

He yanked on her burning arm, dragging her out of the house.

She screamed for Alex, but when she twisted to face the burning house, she saw Alex at a tavern table, drinking whisky. His drooping eyes connected with hers. He lifted his glass before downing the contents as King Tyron took her away.

"Lou, Lou, Lou!"

Gentle fingers stroked her face as the nightmare faded. Her arm still burned but when she glanced sleepily down at her wound, there were no blisters but a thin scratch. Her head was too heavy to lift. Sleep was calling to her, but the lingering emotions from her nightmare forced her to blink the fog away.

Alex sat on her other side.

"Hi." Her voice was weak. She recalled the battle and losing blood on the ship. "How bad was it?"

Alex leaned back, emotions shadowing his features. "You were cut with a cursed blade. It was like you were poisoned."

"How long have I been asleep?"

"A few days. The bleeding finally stopped. Special antibiotics will help with the rest."

Lou managed to sit up. Her eyes took in the others in the medic room, most watching them. Heat burned her cheeks as she pulled her hand from Alex's.

"I can make them forget, if you would like." He looked exhausted. His voice sounded hoarse.

"How?"

"I can reach into their minds and alter their thought process as to why I have been by your bedside the past few days. Or the identity blessing can stretch to yours if you say yes. No one would remember you as a Mortal Guard unless you wish them to."

"Alex," she whispered.

"I know." His tone told her he was giving up hope they would ever marry. That their relationship would always be him running Earth Guardianship while she battled missions. Until he would inevitably lose her. "I will monitor your health. Feel free to message me if you need anything. Oh." He spoke the rest in her mind. *"My father requested our presence in Carinthia. Not work related. You can say no, but if you would like to meet him, I will share the details later."*

His fingers grazed her knuckles before he left. She wanted to call him back but didn't. Alex paused at the door, his back to her. The muttering in the room halted as he touched their minds.

* * *

**Lamarse**
**Carinthia**
**8 Years Before Adia's First Deal**

Lamarse breathed in the familiar scent of his home. Lou walked beside him and like many times before, he wished to know what she was thinking. He had never invaded her thoughts. She asked that he only speak to her telepathically when necessary.

She didn't trust him inside her mind.

They still hadn't spoken about her past. He feared while he was waiting for her to say yes to marrying him, she was gaining the courage to end their relationship.

"It's so beautiful," she said.

He squeezed her hand as they crossed the bridge to Alexon Manor. He had shown her his favorite spots on Carinthia back when they were reunited, but never took her home. She said she needed time before meeting his family.

They circled the grounds and he shared stories from his youth. Lou's smile melted his heart, but he feared this would be their last moments together. Meeting his family was sure to scare her away.

"And who is this?" Lou asked as Chancel trotted to them.

"Chancel. He was my mother's Familiar."

"Familiar? Like for witches?"

"My mother was one, although she gave up her craft to be with my father. Chancel stayed with her, losing his shapeshifting gift, but keeping his immortality."

Chancel lay by Lou's feet. She squatted down with her hand ready to pet but hesitated. "Is it offensive to pet him?"

"He may bite you if you do not."

Lou ran her fingers through the lynx's fur before petting his arched back.

"Brother!" A blonde woman with piercing blue eyes approached. She hugged Lamarse and then turned to Lou, grabbing her hands. She spoke in Carinthian as she said, "You must be his human girlfriend! Who knew my brother would find love losing his powers. Old wounds heal after all." Her smile broadened. "I am Ebony."

Lou eyed her with raised brows, pulling back her hands.

"My apologies," Ebony said in slow English, placing a hand over her chest. "You do not speak Carinthian. I said I am—"

"Ebony. My name is Lou," she said in Carinthian. "You may continue to call me human girl as I am sure you prefer."

Ebony's smile grew. "I like her, Brother. Finally, someone who puts the effort into learning the dominant language of the Guardianship. You will make it far as a Mortal Guard. My apologies if I offended you. I did not expect you to know our language. The last one did not."

Lamarse jerked back, his face tightening as he gaped at Ebony.

"I am only teasing." Ebony nudged his arm and laughed.

"I do hope, Ebony," Lou continued in Carinthian, "you will be kinder in your teasing. Or I may believe Cora's prophecy went to the wrong sibling."

Ebony's eyes snapped to Lou's.

Lamarse reached for Lou's hand. "We will see you inside, Sister."

"She cannot speak to me like that, Brother. Knowing of things only family should know."

"You did refer to her as a human girl and not kindly," Lamarse said and smiled. "Be more mindful of your words next time you speak to us, and we will do the same."

He ushered Lou to the front doors, his smile growing. "I do not believe anyone has ever spoken to her like that."

"Should I sleep with my knife?" Lou asked, no amusement in her words.

He faced her, halting their steps. "I would never let anything happen to you here. Regardless, Ebony is self-righteous, not murderous."

"If that was Ebony, I fear meeting Cora."

"I believe you will favor Cora. You can trust her."

"Lamarse! Your father has requested a meeting," Nexa said, coming from behind them.

"I thought we were headed to dinner." Lamarse's grip on Lou's hand tightened.

Nexa gave him a scolding look for questioning his father's orders.

"Let me get Lou settled somewhere."

"I will show her around," Nexa said, smiling at Lou.

Lamarse hesitated.

"I'll be fine." Lou gave him a reassuring smile and kissed him. "Go," she urged.

\* \* \*

**Lou**
**Carinthia**

## 8 Years Before Adia's First Deal

"You made quite the impression on Ebony."

Lou tore her eyes from the painting of Lamarse as a boy. A petite woman with short brown hair leaned against one of the doors along the corridor. She searched for Nexa, but she wasn't around.

"You must be Cora."

Alex's other sister tilted her head. "What has he told you about me?"

"Only what he could."

"The identity blessing works differently for every person. We must be able to trust you if you know about my prophecy."

Lou did her best not to show how nervous Cora's stare made her feel. "My words were only meant to defend myself from Ebony. I'm sorry if I overstepped."

Cora surprised her by smiling. Not a plastic smile like Ebony's, but a genuine one. "You do not like Ebony."

"I…" Lou considered. "…don't know her."

Cora faced the painting of Alex as a child. "He never stood up for Reya."

"What do you mean?"

"Lamarse asked Ebony to mind her words around you. Nobody tells Ebony to do anything. Lamarse was the born leader, but Ebony wields power in her own way."

"What about you?"

"Hmm." Cora moved on to another painting. "Has he proposed yet?"

Lou didn't answer.

"I was only wondering when your wedding might be. My visions are like dreams. The details fade over time." Cora faced her.

"I want to marry him." Lou blushed. She had no idea why discussing her relationship triggered such a reaction.

Cora placed a gentle hand on Lou's forearm.

"I will age. Or die in battle." Lou's nose stung as her throat ached. "He looks at me like I am everything. He's told me how I resurrected his purpose. I fear what losing me will do. Whom he will become."

"If you were to lose him, and not the other way around, would you let him run away to spare your future pain?"

"We react differently to loss." Lou nearly choked on her words. She recalled the pain when she believed him to be dead. The loss of motivation. The spiraling grief. "But no. I wouldn't let him."

\* \* \*

**Lamarse**
**Carinthia**
**8 Years Before Adia's First Deal**

Lamarse had been waiting for his father for ten minutes when the door opened.

"Hello, Lamarse."

"Why did you make me wait? Nexa was insistent when she told me to meet with you."

"Cora is helping with Lou's doubts."

Lamarse's hands shook. "You..." He bit back the nasty words he wanted to say. "Meeting her was orchestrated. Why?"

"Time—"

Lamarse pounded a fist on the desk. "Do not feed me some spiel about Fate and Time. *Tell me*." The last two words he sent to his father's mind.

"Lou holds an important key in destroying the shadows. You wanted them gone. She will provide the way."

"No."

"Lamarse—"

"No! She will have nothing to do with those demons. She will not face them. Defeating them means deals—becoming a core. I will not have her soul damned by—"

"Her soul will never enter a Shadow World. Your child's

will."

* * *

## Lou
## Carinthia
## 8 Years Before Adia's First Deal

Lou broke from Cora at the sight of Alex walking on the grounds. Cora had been telling her childhood stories she shared with Alex, and Lou's heart swelled with affection for him. She had to run to catch up, for he was walking in the other direction.

"Alex!" She caught him by the elbow, her smile growing.

He turned and she saw whatever dark emotions lingered from speaking with his father. She said the words fast, in case she lost her confidence, "I will marry you!"

His chest rose and fell. She expected him to beam once her words registered. He shut his eyes, squeezing them tight and said, "No."

"Alex—"

"We cannot marry." When he opened his eyes, they were hard.

"What did your father tell you?"

"I cannot be with you."

"He told you that?"

"Quite the opposite."

"Something will happen to me then."

The composure he fought to keep broke. "Please do not convince me to marry you."

She held his tearful face. He leaned into her touch.

"Our Union will help defeat the shadows," he said at last.

Her thoughts fumbled as her heart raced. "Isn't this what you want? For them to be destroyed? To rescue Reya's soul?"

"Not this way."

Lou stepped back and faced the other way so she could

properly think. When she turned back to him, she said, "They will come after you with or without us together?"

"I…" His throat bobbed. "Yes. I was reckless while trying to find Reya. I told them my name."

"Your father sees multiple futures," she stated, trying to piece together the puzzle. "Our marriage will defeat the shadows."

"Lou—"

"So, we get married."

"It is not *us* who will be defeating the shadows." He looked pained.

Her knees weakened as the realization hit.

Hours later, they sat in the grass in silence. It was well past dinner time, but no one came to order them inside.

"We could be careful," Alex said. "Take precautions to ensure we are childless."

"What about the other children?"

"Other children?"

"The children the shadows take every second of every day." She searched his face in the dark. "They need to be stopped. It's our child's destiny to stop them."

"I will not put any child in that position, let alone ours."

"You would sacrifice your soul to defeat them?"

"Yes."

"Our child will be as strong and as willful as you. They won't be a child when the time comes, right?"

"I still cannot bring a child in this world, knowing their soul will be damned."

"We marry but never try for a child."

"If Fate wishes us—"

"Alex. Marry me. Please?"

He loosened a breath. "Yes."

"Okay." Her mouth found his.

"Okay," he echoed, kissing her back softly and then fiercely.

# CHAPTER TWENTY-SEVEN

*Adia*

**Lou**
**Matadon**
**6 Years Before Adia's First Deal**

Lou pressed her back against the stone wall. Shutting her eyes, she counted the footsteps drawing nearer. She allowed herself to dwell on memories she kept hidden deep within her.

Men invading her home.

Her mother's screams.

Her father's gurgles as he choked on his blood.

Her innocence being stolen.

Blood seeping over her hand after plunging the blade into her first victim.

His laugh.

Tonight would be the end of her nightmares.

She would never allow herself to dwell on the past again.

Opening her eyes, she swung her sword into the chest of Tyron's guard. She kicked him, removing her blade only to stab another. She moved swiftly, keeping her breaths even so not to lose momentum. She barreled through his guards, killing them before they could make out who was attacking. Her special suit from Orion shielded her from her first blow. She slid in blood, nearly falling but managing to recover. She withdrew her gun and rounded the corner, shooting while running to get to Tyron's Throne Room.

An energy blasted from her suit, striking the closest guards. She continued down the corridor.

Bullets struck through windows, assassinating his guards.

Alarms blared.

Lou kicked the door open, aimed her gun, and shot Tyron in the head. He collapsed by the hidden entrance. His guards reacted quickly, bullets flying off her suit that sent another energy shock throughout the room.

She shot at the closest window before jumping through it. Her suit slowed her fall, but the impact was still jarring. She sprinted through the desert surrounding Tyron's castle as bullets hit her suit.

It wasn't until the ship's door was closing and her team of six were seated safely next to her when Lou allowed herself to relish in what she had accomplished.

She assassinated King Tyron.

\* \* \*

**Lou**
**Bend, OR (Earth 323)**
**6 Years Before Adia's First Deal**

The ship touched down near Todd Lake. Lou turned to her team and nodded her appreciation. She doubted she would ever see them again.

"Take it easy, Lou," one of the assassins named Sal said.

She stepped out into the wintry night. A car was waiting for her to drive the hour to her house. She took her time brushing the snow from the windows as the engine warmed. She thawed her hands on the heater vents and fiddled with the radio.

The drive was longer than usual due to a few skidding moments, but she managed to reach her neighborhood before midnight. She sat in her car, staring at the light through the living room window. She checked her reflection, fixed her ponytail, and counted her breaths.

She opened the car door. The push of wintry air was shocking. She pulled up her hood and stopped at the front door. Her hand shook as she twisted the knob.

Alex stood in the glow of the hallway. He stepped aside to let her in. She kicked off the snow from her boots and hung her jacket on the coatrack. Then she warmed her hands by the fireplace.

Alex watched her every move in silence.

She feared he could hear her heart race from where he stood. More so, she feared him reading her thoughts. He said he never would, but promises can be broken. Like the one she broke.

"There's soup in the fridge," he said quietly. "When you are ready for bed, I will sleep on the couch."

"Alex."

"I left the heating instructions on the counter."

"Alex."

"You may also want to shower. You have blood on your neck still."

"I had to do it."

Alex's face crumpled as he fell against the wall. He covered his face, taking stuttering breaths.

Lou's jaw trembled as she neared him. He shook off the hand she placed on his arm.

"I will not... We cannot..." He lifted his head and she wondered how many times he had cried since she was gone. He shook his head, unable to speak.

"It's too late," she replied.

"How could you do this?"

Tears slid down her cheeks. "Orion can be convincing."

"No. Do not put this on *him*. You—" He looked as though he was going to be sick. "When?"

"Early last month. After decorating the tree. I stopped taking my..." Lou choked on her words at the intensity in Alex's eyes. "S-she will have a life. A purpose."

Alex slid down the wall. "My father promised you Tyron to bring an innocent girl into this world to be damned?"

"She will be a hero. She—"

"He sees many futures, Louise! He is desperate to make the one she will succeed come true. But what about the ones she will fail? She will suffer as Reya is suffering now. Forever."

Lou struggled to speak. "I-I needed him dead by my hands."

"I know." Alex's tone softened. "I would have helped you."

"But we wouldn't have had Orion's resources. His plan. His…"

"I hope you made Tyron suffer at least."

"It had to be fast to be successful," she muttered.

Alex rubbed his eyes. His tears had stopped, and he looked exhausted. "How far along are you?"

"She will be born on August 25$^{th}$."

"Are you feeling sick? Tired?"

"I'm okay," she whispered. She felt like she had been hit by a bus.

He straightened. "Go ahead and eat. Shower. Rest. I will sleep on the couch."

"Is that necessary?"

"I need to be alone to think. To figure out a plan to ensure it is my soul they shall take and not hers."

\* \* \*

## Lamarse
## Bend, OR
## 5 Years Before Adia's First Deal

"Where are the bags, dear?"

"On the bed," Lou answered from the kitchen.

Lamarse rushed to the bedroom, placing his toothbrush in the side pocket. He stared with a hand in his long hair, trying to remember what else they needed. "Blanket!" He rushed to the closet in the hallway.

"They will have blankets there." Lou leaned against the door to the kitchen, taking a bite from her bagel. Crumbs dropped on her pregnant stomach. "We have time. Relax."

"Relax?" He ran back to the bedroom. He stuffed the blanket in a third bag before changing his mind. He grabbed Lou's favorite pillow and wrapped the blanket around it. "Where is that stuffed lion?"

"Adia will be too small to care about toys."

He poked his head down the hall, catching Lou rolling her eyes with a smile. "I won that stuffed lion for her. He needs to be there for her first day of life."

Lou took another bite of her bagel.

"Any contractions?"

"Nope."

"Water breaking?"

"I think you would notice."

"Nausea? Dizziness?"

"I'm fine, Alex."

"Are you sure he said August 25$^{th}$?"

"Yes, but it's the 24$^{th}$."

"Labor takes hours. Sometimes a day."

"Can we please get ready for bed?"

"Yes! You sleep. Get rest. I will clean the house."

"You cleaned this morning."

He ushered her into the room.

"Why is my pillow covered by a blanket?" she asked.

"The hospital has thin pillows and blankets. Here." He untangled the pillow and placed it behind her back as she sat on the bed. "I can always quickly wrap it when it is time."

She finished eating her bagel and made a face.

"What? Are you okay? Is it a contraction?"

"Just heartburn. I miss salsa."

"What if you cannot feel the contractions because of your high tolerance to pain?"

"It's not that high. Otherwise, my back wouldn't be aching like this."

"Your back?" His eyes widened. "Lou! What if you are in labor?"

"It's fine." She patted his hand. "I'll let you know when it's go-time."

\* \* \*

**Lou**
**Bend, OR**
**5 Years Before Adia's First Deal**

Lou awoke to a pop sensation then she was peeing. *No.* Her water had broken. She sat up to find Alex's side of the bed empty.

"Alex!"

He pushed their door open, gloves on his hands from cleaning.

"Go-time?"

"Go-time." She winced as her back cramped.

He guided her to her feet and noticed her pajamas were soaked. He helped her dress into clean sweats.

"What about the bags?" she asked as her back cramped again.

"Already in the trunk." After helping her to the car, he sprinted inside and came back with her pillow, blanket, and a bottle full of ice.

He was breathing heavily as he started the engine. Lou placed a hand on his forearm, willing him to look at her. When he did, she kissed him. "You're going to be a great dad."

It was night when Lou held Adia for the first time. Alex's arm was wrapped around her sweaty shoulders as they beheld their daughter. Adia's unfocused eyes moved across their faces.

"Well," Alex said, his voice catching. "She is beautiful."

# CHAPTER TWENTY-EIGHT

### *Smile*

**Adia**
**Mount Hood, OR**
**65 Days Left**

"Happy birthday, Adia!" her mother sang as Adia stepped into the kitchen. "Oh wait!" Her mother pulled out a cake from the fridge. "Austin, could you hit the lights? I know it won't make a difference for you."

Austin chuckled as he let go of Adia's hand to flip the light switch. Her mother lit the thirty-three candles on the chocolate cake. Then they sang her *Happy Birthday*.

"Are we eating cake for breakfast?" Adia asked as her mother handed her a plate.

"Of course! It's tradition."

Adia didn't want to say how she couldn't remember her birthdays before the Shadow World.

"I'm thinking I'll mow the lawn this morning," Austin said as they ate cake. "Then I'll head to the market to get supplies."

"Supplies?" Adia narrowed her eyes. "There's salmon in the fridge for dinner."

"We're expecting some guests," her mother said. "Cora and Dallas will be here tonight. They're bringing Reya and Jax. And some other hunters. There are dark souls in Portland they plan to take care of tomorrow morning."

"We can handle it," Adia said. "They don't need to come."

"That's what I told her," her mother said, "but I think they also want to see you."

Adia took the last bite of her cake and carried her plate to the sink. Austin snagged the dish from her hands.

"I can wash my own dish."

"Not on your birthday," he said and then kissed her. "Are you sure you want salmon for dinner? We're supposed to eat your favorite meal, not mine. I can pick up the stuff to make lasagna."

"Salmon," she confirmed.

He dried his hands on the kitchen towel. "Go watch TV. Or read. Or do whatever you want while we get things ready."

"I'm going for a run."

After changing, Adia stretched by the ship. Her mother came out dressed to run as well. "Mind if I join you?"

The summer heat burned the morning dew as they ran along the familiar trail. Adia memorized everything: The smell, the sound, the sight. It was all so beautiful. She wanted to hold onto this forest forever.

A few miles in, her mother slowed to a stop.

"What's wrong?" Adia asked. "Are you hurt?"

"I need to tell you something that will make you hate me."

Adia placed her hands on her hips. "What is it?"

"I told you about your dad. How we met. How we eloped and moved to Bend while he ran Earth Guardianship from home. I had done missions time to time for Orion, but he stopped assigning me them once I was pregnant with you.

"He had told us before we married the shadows would come for our family. That our child was destined to destroy them."

Something touched Adia's mind, like a fingernail scraping along her skull.

"We decided we would not bring a child into this world with a destiny such as yours. Orion sees many futures, and the odds of you succeeding were slim. We knew what it meant for your soul if you failed.

"I wish I could tell you it took a lot of convincing, but I struck a deal with Orion in a single conversation. He arranged for me to kill King Tyron in exchange for bringing you into this world. It took your dad weeks to speak to me again. Even when he promised I was forgiven, I knew he resented me for taking away his choice in the matter. His feelings got worse when we had you. He wanted to protect you from everything. Your dad never trusted anyone we passed on the street. Not even the preschool you were attending. We bought this cabin to help ease his worries. The shadow found you anyways.

"We had moved to the Earth I was from—the Earth that would be targeted if I, or my child, would be taken as a core. At first it was for sentimental reasons. I stayed as punishment for making the deal to kill King Tyron. My punishment for failing you.

"When you awoke, I genuinely believed it was over. I didn't know you were a core. All I knew was your dad was still in the Shadow World, fighting them from within like he promised he would do. His plan was always to make sure it was him over you. We hadn't anticipated they would make you a core so young.

"I am sorry, Adia. If you never wish to speak to me again, I will understand. It is why I took so long in confiding this to you."

"King Tyron kidnapped you when you were a child?" Adia asked.

She nodded.

"I'm glad you were the one to kill him. We all have made foolish deals, but I don't hate you for bringing me into this world. You never forced my choices."

*Her blood on your hands.*

Adia shut out the small voice. The shadows were desperate for control. "Can I ask you something?"

Her mother's throat bobbed as she nodded again.

"Tell me about the day I was born."

Her mother laughed, swiping at a tear on her cheek. They continued running as she told Adia about her birthday and many other memories. Adia learned how stressed her father had been, trying to keep their location a secret from the shadows. They were walking back to the house when Adia started sharing things about her life in the Shadow World. Things she regretted. Memories she was desperate to keep.

"If it had been me," Adia said as the cabin came into view, "I doubt I would have made a different choice. If offered to kill Sam..."

"You would have," her mother said. "You have too much of your dad in you to be as foolish as me."

"Did the nightmares stop after you killed King Tyron?"

"No."

"I thought I would have better dreams once Sam was gone," Adia said after a sigh. "I sometimes dream that I am back in that alternate reality where he makes me love him. He manipulates me into killing the people I love."

"Do you talk to Austin about your nightmares?"

"Not always."

"You should."

Adia's chest swelled with emotion. "Will you check on him when I'm gone?"

"Of course."

Adia's shoulders relaxed. She felt exhausted from their conversation and run. "You can shower first. I'll sweep the front porch."

"It's your birthday."

"And I was supposed to sweep yesterday."

Her mother laughed. "True."

* * *

**Austin**
**Mount Hood, OR**

## 65 Days Left

Music blasted as Austin and Adia shared a log in front of the bonfire. Reya and Jax were jumping around, singing along to a song. Dallas laughed at something Cora had said, sitting directly across from them. Adia's head rested on his shoulder as she stared up at the stars. Sounds from other hunters partying were heard in the distance. Lou had gone to bed not long after presents.

"Happy birthday," Austin whispered.

She smiled up at him. "It was a good one. Thank you."

"Come dance, guys! Dance!" Jax hollered to them even though he was a short distance away. His drink sloshed into the fire, causing it to blaze angrily.

Reya pulled him back to the grass, laughing when he stumbled. She shrieked as he chased her. Austin changed the song from his phone to one with a slower melody.

"Dance with me," he said into Adia's ear.

"One dance." She grabbed his hand as they stood. "Then I'm going to bed. Birthdays are exhausting."

They swayed under the stars as Austin quietly sang to her. When he took his eyes off hers, he saw that Cora and Dallas were slow dancing as well. Reya and Jax were more kissing than dancing.

The song ended, transitioning to a more upbeat one. Adia looked near asleep when he pulled from her. He tucked her hair behind her ears and kissed her. "Time for sleep."

"Party pooper," Dallas said to Adia as Austin walked her back to the cabin.

"Good luck handling those two," Adia said over her shoulder.

Austin looked toward Jax and Reya who were now lying in the grass, kissing.

Dallas dropped his head on Cora's shoulder in defeat and Austin laughed. Adia leaned against him as they walked through the dark living room. She didn't bother changing out of her jeans as she collapsed on their bed. He tucked her in.

"I love you," she muttered, her eyes already shut.

"I love you too." He kissed her forehead.

Austin left for the bathroom to shower and brush his teeth. When he returned, Adia was fast asleep.

\* \* \*

## Lou
## Mount Hood, OR
## 64 Days Left

Lou awoke parched. She blindly went to her door, flipping on the hallway light. She squinted until her eyes adjusted. She used the restroom first and then headed to the kitchen. She smiled at the Carinthian painting of a dog and human boy playing fetch that was hung in the hallway. Her fingers brushed the dust from the frame. She would make time to clean it properly tomorrow.

She passed Reya and Jax who were asleep on the living room floor. She tried not to fixate on their spilled drinks as she entered the kitchen. She opened the fridge door, lighting the dark room to reveal Adia sitting at the table, stirring a cup of tea.

"Can't sleep, honey?"

Adia's shoulders were slumped. "I'm having the strangest dream."

"Adia?" Lou flipped on the kitchen light. Adia didn't react to the brightness, only continued to stare into her cup, stirring it with a knife.

"You birthed her to kill us." There was an echo to her voice. She blinked and her eyes glowed white.

"You're breaking the deal." Lou grabbed hold of her daughter's shoulders. "You can't possess her. Bring her back!"

Adia angled her head. "Gullible humans."

\* \* \*

## Adia
## Mount Hood, OR
## 64 Days Left

"No, no, no, no, no, no, no, no…" Adia pressed her hands against her ears.

Sam yanked her mother's hair, his blade drawing blood from her throat.

"Stop! Stop!"

"Don't you understand?" Sam asked. "She knew you would be damned. She knew you would fall victim to us. She threw you into your pathetic world with a slim chance you could defeat us." He removed the knife from her mother's throat, twirled it in his hand, and offered Adia the handle side. "You should be the one to kill her."

"This isn't real," she said slowly. "This is a dream. I'm dreaming."

"Adia," her mother said. "Adia, wake up. Wake up!"

Darkness was closing in on Adia. The walls moved with it, and soon she would be crushed.

Sam stood at the center of the room, still holding out the knife. She grabbed it, staring at it as her surroundings flickered between dream and reality. She saw her mother standing with fear, blood sliding down her neck from Sam's cut. Then her mother was in their kitchen, her eyes fierce as she gripped Adia by the shoulders.

"She doesn't love you," Sam said. "She would sell you to kill Tyron again. Become powerful. Unstoppable."

"You're strong, Adia," her mother said. "You are so strong!"

The dream faded as Adia gained control of her body. Her mother held her shoulders, smiling when she saw that Adia had returned.

"I don't understand." Adia looked around the kitchen, seeing that dawn was breaking through the window. "Was I sleepwalking?"

"You fight them with all you have," her mother said. "They will try to turn you into one of them. That is not you. Whatever they make you d-do…that is not *you*."

"Mom?" Adia's eyes dropped to the blood on her fisted hand and then to her mother's bleeding stomach. Adia dropped the knife in time to catch her mother. Adia's knees buckled, dropping them to the floor.

Blood smeared across Adia's cheek as her mother cupped her face. "This is not your fault."

"Mom?"

Her mother struggled to speak.

Her breaths rasped.

The light in her eyes went out.

"Wake up." Adia shook her mother, still in her arms. "Please wake up. This can't be real. Wake up!"

**It is real.**

# CHAPTER TWENTY-NINE

*Safe & Sound*

**Lou**
**Mount Hood, OR**
**1 Year Before Adia's First Deal**

"Earth 819 is gone?"

Alex nodded solemnly. "They are searching for us. Or sending me a message."

"But I was the one who fought to protect that planet. Not you."

"I oversaw the decisions for that battle. Or maybe it is a threat to you." He stood from the couch and moved to the fireplace. I asked my father if he would give Cora Earth Guardianship."

"What about Ebony?"

"I saw something in her mind last time I spoke to her."

Lou shifted in her seat. It was unlike Alex to reach inside anyone's mind unless they were his enemy.

"What did you see?"

"My mother being murdered."

"What about Jax?"

"I have been thinking over the past a lot lately, and my father's reactions to certain events. Cora's prophecy. Why Ebony asked to work on Earth Guardianship when she has always found your kind to be far beneath her liking. I fear it all has to do with the shadows."

"Ebony doesn't know where we are. Does she?"

"My father has promised to not disclose our location. Then again, you were on a mission with others to kill Tyron. They were present on the ship with you when it touched down on this planet."

"They were Orion's people. I'm sure he trusts them."

Alex ran a hand over his mouth. "He also anticipated my mother's murder. Whatever Ebony's next betrayal will be, he has seen it. Expects it. Wishes it."

"We are not safe here."

"Nowhere will be safe."

"What can we do to protect Adia? Tell me you have a plan."

"The last time I turned against my father, I lost all my gifts. We will have to be careful to ensure the shadows will not target Adia. I will also need to train her to fight."

"She's four."

"I started training as soon as I could walk. But it is not only fighting I will need to teach her. I will have to strengthen her mind, but you are right—she is too young."

"How much time do you expect we have before they come for us?"

"If Adia is to be the core, I suspect whenever her emotions are desperate enough to sell her soul. We will also need to assume they will offer one of us the deal."

A chill ran through Lou. "Meaning the shadows will take Adia. Since we will both be desperate enough to save her."

"If I am taken as a core, then Carinthia will fall to the shadows. Adia is my blood, so she will be taken as well. I may not be an ally to her in the Shadow World."

"What if—"

Alex held up a hand. "Adia, it is well past your bedtime!"

Adia stepped into the living room from the dark hallway.

"Oh honey, let's get you back to bed." Lou stood from the couch, shooting Alex a look for his abrasive tone.

"I'm sorry, Adia," Alex said from behind them as they walked up the stairs to her bedroom.

"I need a drink," Adia said, getting back into bed.

"Oh, you mean like this one?" Lou handed her the cup that had been on her nightstand.

Adia giggled but then her eyes grew wide.

"What is it?"

"I'm scared of shadows."

Lou's breath hitched. "What?"

"You told Dad the shadows were going to take me."

"Oh honey! We were just talking about a bad dream your dad had."

"Bad dream?"

"Yeah, grown-ups have bad dreams too."

"Did you sing to him?"

"I did. Now take ten sips so you won't wake up thirsty again."

Adia counted after each sip, grinning.

"You are to go to bed…" Lou pointed at her daughter, making an exaggerated angry face. "No leaving your room until the sun wakes."

Adia laughed.

"I mean it!" Lou tickled Adia's sides.

"Stop it!" she squealed.

Lou kissed Adia's forehead. "Okay, Princess Adia."

"Queen Adia," she corrected.

"My apologies, Queen Adia. It's time to be asleep."

"Sing to me." Adia reached for her stuffed lion and hugged it tightly.

Lou brushed her fingers in her daughter's dark hair. "I sang ten songs two hours ago!"

"Please!"

Lou dramatically rolled her eyes. She continued brushing her daughter's hair as she sang, *"Rest your head, go to sleep. The stars will watch over you. Have no fear, the light is near. I'll see you in the morning."*

"Again!"

Lou shook her head.

"The shadows will take me unless you sing."

"Sweetie," Lou struggled to keep the emotion from her voice, "there are no shadows here."

"Are you okay, Mommy?"

"I'm okay. Why?"

"You felt sad."

"Strange, because I am *so* happy."

"I'm still scared."

"Now, now, Adia. You have nothing to fear. Besides, you have your lion to protect you from bad dreams."

"I only fear what I can't see," Adia said.

Lou was overcome with love and fear for her smart little girl.

"Please sing again?"

"I'll sing two more songs."

"Five!" Her eyes lit up and she giggled.

After singing, Lou stepped out of Adia's room. Alex stood in the hall, looking exhausted.

"She heard—"

Lou placed a finger to her lips and nodded to their bedroom. Once they were inside, he whispered,

"She heard us talking about the shadows?"

"Yes. She's a great listener, unfortunately."

"Not when I talk to her," Alex said. "She does not want me even tucking her in bed. I used to be her favorite."

"You've been stressed lately, and she can sense it. We should talk to Orion about what gifts she may have."

"You think she is an empath?"

"She sensed I was sad just now. Sometimes she'll come to me when I'm feeling overwhelmed. I wonder if it was our emotions that woke her up."

"I do not have experience with empaths, nor do I know how that gift could fight against the shadows. I doubt my father will give much insight, but I will ask."

\* \* \*

## Lou
## Portland, OR
## Day of Adia's First Deal

"Adia. Come along," Lou said as they tried to cross the street.

When their daughter still stared up at the sky, Alex yelled her name, startling her to attention.

"She never listens," he muttered to her.

"She's a child."

"She's vulnerable."

Lou was exhausted by the time Alex had found a suit for a meeting he had arranged with Cora and Ebony on Earth Guardianship. He had been on edge the entire day, dreading the conversation he would need to have with Ebony regarding her status. His plans were to demote her, against his father's wishes.

They decided to make a day out of visiting Portland. They had gone to a museum and had exchanged some Christmas gifts. She was eager to get home.

It was snowing by the time they reached their car. Lou helped Adia into the backseat, picking up her stuffed lion from the floor.

"It's a bit of a drive home. If you sleep, we'll be home before you know it."

She handed Adia the lion and then rounded the car to her seat. Alex was tight with stress as he drove.

"We could stop at a hotel," she suggested.

"We will be fine."

"Alex. What's wrong?"

"I have this feeling. Like déjà vu." He looked over at her, his throat bobbing.

She placed her hand on his arm and squeezed. "We'll take it as it comes."

"She is so innocent." Alex's tears sparkled in the darkness. "I feel powerless to help."

"We don't know when the shadows will come. We can't ruin our little time with her by worrying we will lose her. Worrying about what will come."

"She hates me."

"She doesn't understand. She senses your negative emotions and thinks you're feeling them for her, not about her. Be in the moment with her. Show your love a different way—one she will understand."

He nodded. It was a while before they spoke again. A song played on the radio.

"I didn't know Frank Sinatra covered this Ink Spots' song," Lou stated. "Remember how it played at Hannah's wedding?"

"Which wedding?" Alex's face broke into a smile and Lou laughed with him.

"The one on Earth 49," Lou said, resting her head on the back of her seat, watching him. "We only went to two of her weddings."

"She invited us a third and fourth time," he joked, "because of your generosity in presents."

"Remember how she drunkenly mentioned my past love, Alex, to you? How your death affected me so much, and she was glad I moved on with someone more *important*."

"Remind me why we attended her second wedding?"

"I have no idea." He stared over at her and they laughed. It was so beautiful to see Alex smile again.

Lou twisted her head at the sound of Adia's seat unbuckling. "Adia! Get back in your seatbelt!" The car skidded and when she faced forward, bright lights of an oncoming truck blinded her.

\* \* \*

**Lou**
**Carinthia**
**Two Weeks After Adia's First Deal**

Lou watched Alex's coffin lower into the ground. Unlike

Adia, his body and soul's connection were severed. She had no idea whether his soul had passed or was trapped in the Shadow World like Adia's. Adia was being looked after by Cora on the ship. Alex never wanted anyone outside of them, Orion, and Cora to know of her existence.

Eyes were on Lou as the service concluded, but the person she stared at was Ebony. Lou tried to see any sign of guilt as Ebony dabbed at her crocodile tears.

"I do not understand how he has not been Reborn!" Ebony's voice shook. "I just—"

"Excuse me." Lou ignored Ebony's gasp and walked to Orion. Mortal Guards stopped her before getting too close. "I need to speak to you. Please."

Orion held out his hand to Lou and the Mortal Guards parted. She declined his offer to guide her into the castle and walked ahead. Once they were alone in his office, Orion having excused his Mortal Guards, she began pacing.

"It was too soon. She is only a child!"

Orion's pale blue eyes held hers.

"What can you tell me?" she asked, begged.

"Your part in this is to care for Adia's body."

"She will return?"

Silence.

"Just tell me what's going to happen. Tell me I will see them again. Tell me I won't. Just tell me!"

"I cannot."

Her jaw shook. "I can't do this. I can't go back to my planet and watch it be destroyed. I am not strong enough for this. You —" She bit her words that were being fueled by anger. "I will fail her!"

"Take a seat," he asked her kindly.

Lou's fingers trembled as she sat.

"I will tell this and this alone," he said, pouring an amber liquid into a glass. He slid it over for her to drink. "In all the futures I have seen, you never fail as her mother."

# CHAPTER THIRTY

*Gallows*

**Jax**
**Mount Hood, OR**
~~**64 Days Left**~~
**Day of the Broken Deal**

J ax coughed himself awake. He could barely see Reya
sleeping next to him, her hand on his naked chest. He
blinked, but his vision wouldn't clear. He coughed again
then jolted at the taste of smoke.

Reya's hand dropped from his chest, remaining asleep as he
rose.

He staggered to a stand. Healing from alcohol consumption
never made him this dazed. He fanned the smoke, trying to
find its source. He caught sight of flames near the stove. And
Lou lying on the floor.

He called for Reya, but no sound came out. He held the
kitchen table, waiting for the dizziness to pass, and wondered
if this was a lucid dream. A vague memory of another time he
awoke feeling similarly floated around his mind. He had been
poisoned then.

Adia stepped into the kitchen as he registered the puddle of
blood Lou was lying in. He reached for his sword, but it wasn't
attached to his bare back.

He tried to voice a warning to Adia as she came close.

Her knife stabbed through his chest. He saw double as he

failed to catch her wrists. She slashed his throat, her eyes glowing white in the rising smoke.

\* \* \*

## Cora
## Mount Hood, OR
## Day of the Broken Deal

"Wake up!"

Dallas wouldn't stir, no matter how roughly Cora shook him. They were on the ship. She had been about to go to sleep when a message from her father told her to remain awake. Believing he would call soon, she moved to the other part of the ship, so not to disturb her husband. When no call came, she returned to bed, tripping over Dallas' shoes. She caught herself on the glass medicine cabinet, but the commotion knocked over vials of sleeping draughts. She had been surprised Dallas remained asleep until realizing the vials were empty.

The sleeping draughts didn't cause drowsiness, but once the dosed person fell asleep, they were comatose.

"Dallas!" She smacked him, breathing heavily through her nose. When he still would not awake, she searched for the counteractive to the sleeping draught. They rarely used the sleeping draught, but it came in handy when transferring an enemy or operating on someone injured.

Cora found the antidote but had no idea how much Dallas had been drugged.

A memory of Adia bringing out drinks surfaced. Cora shut her eyes, recalling how many drinks Dallas had. Maybe two? She placed a few drops of the counteractive on his tongue then prayed that wasn't too much. She armed herself with guns and stepped off the ship. She ran toward the burning cabin.

She found Reya first, lifting her the best she could while keeping her gun at the ready. Reya's legs had been burned, but she remained asleep. She was returning to the ship when

Dallas stepped out, looking dazed and then shocked to see fire.

"She needs help." Cora had kept her voice quiet but couldn't fight the coughing fit. Her eyes burned trying to resist.

Dallas grabbed Reya from her.

"There is a vial next to the bed with a green label," she managed to say before coughing. "Give her five drops on her tongue. If she still doesn't wake, give her two more. Take care of her burn so she can fight. Find the other hunters in their tents and give them three drops until it works. Keep them away from the cabin."

"Fight whom?" His eyes told her he feared the answer.

She kissed him, making him nearly drop Reya. "They broke the deal," she whispered before running back to the cabin.

She discovered Jax crawling toward Adia and Austin's room. She knelt near him, seeing all the wounds glowing on him.

He mouthed Reya's name.

"*Ship,*" Cora mouthed back. "*Go!*"

He shook his head, but she glared back at him, forcing him to listen.

"*Lou,*" he mouthed before shaking his head with a grim look.

Cora's chin wobbled as grief gripped her. She nodded for him to go back to the ship. He gritted his teeth and crawled toward the door.

Cora shut her eyes, trying to Vision Walk. She could not. She set the weapon for activation and typed out a message to Dallas but didn't send it. The door was already opened a crack, so she pushed it using her gun. Adia sat on her bed, covered in blood, holding Austin's hand.

"It's okay," Adia said. "We're okay."

Cora wouldn't allow her eyes to linger on Austin's slit throat. She shot Adia multiple times in the chest and head. Adia slumped against the headboard, blood seeping through her clothes.

Cora sent the message to Dallas.

Adia's white eyes popped open.

Cora triggered the weapon using her wrist device.

Adia charged for Cora.

The cabin exploded.

\* \* \*

### Reya
### Mount Hood, OR
### Day of the Broken Deal

Someone was touching Reya's face, speaking to her, but the sound was muffled. Jax's face was distorted. She moaned at the pain radiating from her legs. Another figure moved and there was a small pinch in her shoulder. The pain faded as her vision cleared.

"Time to fight," Dallas said, handing her a gun.

"Dark souls?" she mumbled, still fighting the grog of sleep. "They sure picked an exceptional time when everyone was hungover."

Jax cocked his gun, which she found unusual since he preferred swords. "We were drugged." His usually golden eyes were a dark amber. "The shadows killed Lou."

Dallas' phone beeped. After reading the message, he sprinted for the ship's door. "Inside! Inside!"

A line of hunters shuffled in, Dallas roaring at them to move faster. Reya and Jax exchanged a puzzled look.

"Everyone, get down!" Dallas stared at the door, contemplating, and then moved to exit.

Jax jumped for him, holding Dallas down as the door shut. Reya's foggy mind was fighting to catch up.

The ship rocked violently.

Reya hit her head on the medicine cabinet. She scrambled finding a gun and when she looked up, Dallas was kneeling by the now opened door. Smoke and ash billowed in making everyone cough. Dallas remained kneeling, his shoulders hunched.

Jax stepped behind him, his face mirroring Dallas' shocked

horror once some of the smoke cleared.

The cabin was gone, as well as the trees surrounding them. If they hadn't been in the ship, they would be dead.

Dead like Lou.

Dead like Austin.

Dead like Cora.

Jax came to Reya's side. His eyes had darkened to brown. He dabbed at the blood from her forehead with a cloth before bandaging it. "I need food," he said weakly.

"Our friends are dead and you're thinking about food?"

"If you want me to fight for our side, I need to eat. Even Gold's food would suffice." There was no humor in his tone.

Jax held his stomach, falling against the wall of the ship. "Any food. Please, Reya." His eyes were onyx now. "Eating helps me… The shock is triggering…" He cursed. "Gold and his food are in California. Is there seriously *NOTHING* to eat on this ship?"

Dallas sprung to his feet, but not in reaction to Jax now breaking things. Reya moved behind Dallas to see Adia standing where the cabin had once been, eyes glowing white in the smoke.

"I thought she made a deal," Reya said through her teeth.

"Shadows make and break their own rules."

"Jax needs food. If we want him to be strong to fight," she added.

A crash sounded behind them.

Dallas rounded his shoulders. "If Jax comes for you, run."

"What's happening to him?"

"His immortality came with a price."

Figures emerged in the distance. "Dark souls."

"Are you prepared?" Dallas asked her.

"To die? Sure. Whatever Hell has in store for me, it must be better than the Shadow Core."

"Cora wanted to tell you, but Orion told us we couldn't," Dallas said. "The Shadow Core is the only place dark souls go when their body dies."

Reya swayed. "No," she said faintly. "I am not ready. But it's not like I ever have a choice." She stared at Adia's glowing white eyes, and they glowered at each other. Reya stepped forward but something blurred past her.

Jax ran at incredible speed toward Adia. She caught his fist, but he punched her in the gut with the other, and she flew into the woods. He chased after her, a monstrous roar ripping from him until he was out of Reya's sight.

"Hunters!" Dallas called, pointing at the dark souls drawing nearer. "Fight!"

* * *

**Jax**
**Los Angeles, CA**
**5 Days Before the Broken Deal**

"You have that look in your eye again."

He and Reya were lying on a blanket in the park as Gold chased birds.

"What look?"

She moved to him, her lips only an inch from his. "Like you're already missing me even though I'm right here."

He chuckled but didn't feel amused. "I was only thinking..."

"About?"

"Coming with you."

"With me where?"

"Wherever you go."

Due to Orion's pillar, he was unable to share everything with her. Like how her soul was bound to go to the Shadow Core once her body died.

Jax originally agreed it was best Reya wasn't aware of her fate. They needed her mind healed to be well enough to fight against the shadows as opposed to joining them. Now Jax pleaded with Orion daily to tell her.

"I'm not going anywhere," Reya said, giving him a quick

kiss. Then, because their conversation was bordering around feelings they held for the other, she stood and chased after Gold.

* * *

**Jax**
**Mount Hood, OR**
**Day of the Broken Deal**

Reya's scream put the monster controlling Jax to sleep. Adia's throat was in his hands. Her laugh echoed as though there was a chorus of demons inside of her. Jax panted as he searched around for Reya. Then he was flying through trees and the monster awoke.

"Jax! Jax!"

Reya's voice brought him back again. He stared at her, dazed as sounds of battle surrounded them.

He had his foot on Adia's throat as he held an unconscious Dallas by the shirt. He dropped him and staggered, catching himself on a tree. Adia's broken body remained limp as he tried to catch his breath. His burning eyes met Reya's, who stared back in shock. She had a bleeding cut running along her cheek. Her bandage had fallen off.

"Are you okay?" he asked her.

"You're you again." She ran and hugged him.

He dropped to his knees, pressing his cheek against Reya's stomach as they held each other. His lungs pinched with every breath. He scanned the field, seeing countless bodies and other hunters fighting the remaining dark souls. He tried to stand but was drained. He could be able to fight if he gave into the voice whispering to take over again. The monster didn't have allies or enemies—only a thirst to destroy. If he closed his eyes, he doubted he could remain conscious.

Adia rose, her bones mending back into place. Jax tried to push Reya behind him, but it was a futile attempt.

Adia grabbed Reya.

"Stop," Jax croaked.

Reya swung her dagger, cutting through Adia's human hand. Jax managed to rise. The monster within him roared to return. Someone grabbed his arm, and he yanked it away, growling.

"Jax." Reya reached for his hand and placed it over her thumping heart.

The monster retreated as he timed his breaths with hers.

"You knew I would return to the Shadow Core," she said, her eyes intense on his once he calmed.

"Orion made it so I couldn't tell you," he said weakly.

"Why?"

Jax's eyes moved to Adia whose hand had healed and was moving toward them. He pushed Reya away. "I want to make a —"

Reya's dagger pressed into his throat. Her eyes darkened as she narrowed them. "I'm ready to return."

"And I will—"

She cut off Jax's words by pushing him down, kneeling on his throat. He needed to make a deal with the shadows. Needed to come with Reya. Otherwise, he would never see her again.

"I will willingly return and serve you," Reya said to Adia—to the shadows. "Only if you leave Earth and fulfill your promise. I have grown tired of these playthings. Although some of them were pleasurable."

Adia smirked as she said, "Lou and Austin are dead. Our second agenda was to make a deal with Cora, but she chose to blow up instead. Everything else *is* rather dull."

Dallas stirred on the ground behind Jax as though mention of his wife's demise shook through his consciousness. Dallas lifted his head only to drop it back down, unable to fully awake. Jax had little energy to mourn Cora, but something had broken within him, and he was sure the pain would wreck him once the storm settled.

The shadows gestured to Jax. "What was it you wanted to

say, Son of Aurum?"

Reya's black eyes held Jax's. There was a hint of desperation in them before she masked her true feelings.

Reya pressed her knee harder on his throat. "Don't take his deal. He only wishes to fulfill a mission from Orion, which he has kept secret from everyone else. As his lover, he foolishly told me of their plans. He is to help Adia defeat you. His curse will make him unstoppable in our world."

"I see," the shadows said. "That would be clever. Though I doubt any creature could overpower us. We will consider."

Adia's body collapsed as the shadows conferred in their world.

"What are you doing?" Jax rasped once she released him.

Her eyes returned to brown as she stared at him, shaking with anger. "You told me days ago that you would follow me wherever I went. You meant the Shadow Core. Did Orion tell you to follow me?"

"No, but—"

"Then don't be a fool, Jax!"

"Reya, I—"

"I will hate you if you make that deal!" Her dagger moved to his throat, making her words seem more like a threat than what they really were.

"As opposed to what?"

Her beautiful eyes watered.

"I love you too." Pain was clear in Jax's voice. "Orion warned me I couldn't keep you."

Reya kissed him fiercely. Moments of their time together blinked in his mind. When she pulled away, her eyes were black again.

"I love you," she said before sliding her dagger across his throat.

* * *

**Reya**
**Mount Hood, OR**
**Day of the Broken Deal**

Jax bled out in Reya's quaking arms. She dropped him before facing a rising Adia, whose complexion darkened at the sight of Jax.

"He attacked," Reya lied.

"We decided against taking him anyways."

A growl vibrated in Jax's chest. As Reya had expected, he would attack. He stood, turning his onyx eyes on hers. She kept her darkness present as she drew out her daggers. Jax moved for her. Reya spun, gaining momentum. Her blade hit nothing. Her surroundings had changed so abruptly, Reya dropped onto her knees.

Hours ago, she was dancing with Jax.

Now she stood at the heart of the Shadow Core.

# CHAPTER THIRTY-ONE

*Where the Shadow Ends*

**Austin**
**Mount Hood, OR**
**Day of the Broken Deal**

Austin rolled to his side, blindly reaching for Adia but felt grass instead. He bolted up. He was on the field's edge with no memory of how he got there. Smoke wafted in the air, making him squint.

The cabin was gone.

The forest was on fire.

Austin ran, but as he ran, his surroundings blurred. He skidded to a stop, his feet burrowing in the dirt and ash. A ship flew overhead, pouring water over fire, but Austin's eyes stilled on the pile of dead bodies.

Dallas stood before them.

"Dallas!" Austin shouted.

Dallas' reaction was slow as he turned to Austin. His eyes were bloodshot and his face bruised. His clothes were torn and bloodied at the waist.

"What happened?" Austin asked.

Dallas looked drunk as he stared back at Austin.

"You…" Something sparked in Dallas. He gripped Austin by his shirt. "She's coming back. She's coming back."

"What happened?" Austin asked again as Dallas repeated the phrase.

"The shadows broke their deal," Jax spoke from behind. He took a large bite of an apple. His pants were also torn and bloodied. "Welcome back. Though I bet you wished you had remained dead."

Austin stared at his feet, covered in the dirt he had sprinted too fast in. His eyes were large as he took in Dallas' crazed expression and Jax's look of defeat. "Where's Adia?"

"In the Shadow Core," Jax answered. "Reya got them to leave, making them believe they had her loyalty."

The world pulsed around Austin as he lost control of his breathing. "We had 64 more days," he said and then yelled the words.

"Yeah..." Jax stabbed his sword into the ashy dirt. "Might as well feed you the rest of the bad news. Cora's dead—"

"She's coming back," Dallas said.

"Sure, yeah." Jax nodded in assurance.

"She had this vision..." Dallas looked in the distance as though he would see Cora soon. "If the shadows had taken her soul, then they would have gotten to Orion. She blew up the cabin before they could manipulate her into a deal."

"Where's Lou?" Austin asked.

There were hunters wandering the fields, searching through the dead bodies of dark souls. He looked up at the ship dropping water and wondered if Lou was up there.

"She's gone," Jax answered. "The shadows possessed Adia and..." He cleared his throat. "They also made Adia drug our drinks last night so we would sleep through the fire. My body healed it out of my system. I woke to find Adia...in the kitchen. I was trying to get to you, but Cora stopped me and told me to go to the ship. I know now it's because she had plans to blow up the cabin."

"How am I...?" It was all too much for Austin to process. He was struggling to breathe again. "Why me?"

"Third time's the charm." Jax winced at whatever emotion Austin conveyed on his face.

Adia was in the Shadow Core being tormented by her

mother's death and most likely his own.

He had been Reborn.

Austin pounded the dirt and screamed his voice raw.

\* \* \*

**Cora**
**The Passage**
**Time Unknown**

Cora fell into her mother's arms.

"You have been so brave." Her mother's soothing voice echoed in the vast, white room.

Cora was flooded with things to say but her words were pushed down as she sobbed.

"It is over, my strong girl," her mother said.

"The shadows… They broke the deal!"

"I know."

"I had to set off the bomb."

"That was very smart of you, and why you were gifted with that vision."

Cora pulled away and her mother wiped away Cora's tears.

"What of Earth 323?"

"Earth 323 is safe. Adia and Reya are in the Shadow Core. There is still much to do."

"I know I will not remember any of this," Cora said. "Like I did not remember the last time we met." The memory of seeing her mother after being killed by Ebony was now apparent in her mind. "I still have so many questions."

"We have time."

"Is Dallas okay?"

"He will heal of his injuries. Austin has already returned with a more durable body."

"Will I know what our next objective is? While we wait for Adia to defeat the shadows?"

"The dark souls have returned to the Shadow Core. Earth

Guardianship will recruit the hunters, those that are willing."

Cora stepped back, noticing the sadness in her mother's eyes. "I am not returning."

"Your work will continue when you Pass On."

"He thinks I will come back," Cora said. "He thinks—I cannot do this to him!"

"Dallas is a great man," her mother said. "Grieving you will be his greatest trial."

"I wish to go back. I—" Cora's knees buckled. "I failed! I failed! If I did something differently...I would be worthy to return!"

Her mother held her tightly. "You are worthy, only your work is now for the Beyond."

"I cannot leave Dallas without explaining..."

"Your father still believes I chose not to come back. I will see him again and be able to explain. As you will see Dallas again."

"But time can be cruel to lovers," Cora said. "He could move on."

Her mother continued brushing through her hair as Cora wept. Peace touched her heart, and the pain diminished enough for Cora to stand. She held her mother's hand as they walked. The white room grew brighter as Cora passed through.

* * *

**Adia**
**Shadow Core**
**1 Day After the Broken Deal (ABD)**

Adia sat on the floor of her room, banging the back of her head against the wall as hard as she could, trying to wake up. Glimpses of Austin and her mother's dead bodies burned in her mind.

*It wasn't real.*

The door opened and Adia stood, holding onto the wall, wishing she could move through it.

"Hello, Adia," Talena, one of the Seven said. "We must make

you presentable for your crowning."

It clicked then as though her mind cleared of fog. They broke their deal. They killed her mother. They killed Austin.

Adia became feral, running for Talena and pulling at her hair, throwing fists, and kicking. A force pushed her back as someone entered the room, laughing.

"Happy birthday!" Ebony crooned, using her telekinesis to hold Adia into place.

Adia focused on Talena's red marks that were already healing from her attack.

\* \* \*

**Austin**
**Los Angeles, CA**
**1 Day ABD**

Dallas, Jax, and Austin sat at one of the tables in the food court of the LA Market the night after the broken deal. It had been some time since any of them had spoken. People passing by gave them concerned looks. They had cleaned up the best they could after dropping off the hunters who had survived, but it was their haggard faces and slumped postures that drew attention.

The hunters had returned to either the Seattle location or Los Angeles. Many were waiting for instructions that neither Dallas nor Austin were capable of providing.

Austin still hadn't wrapped his mind around how he had come back from the dead until a single thought floated in his mind. "I won't age."

Dallas seemed to not have heard him, too caught up in his own thoughts.

Jax, who was petting Gold's fur while staring off, looked at Austin.

"I won't age," Austin said again. "I…"

"It's one thing waiting for your mortal life to end," Jax

began, his eyes large as though he was still in shock from all that had happened, "knowing the rest of your waiting for Adia will be in Heaven. Entirely different when you know you are stuck...*here*...in this universe of trials and death and suffering."

"Why me?" Austin asked.

"Couldn't tell you." Jax tapped his fingers on top of Gold's head, who moved away in annoyance.

"Jax." Austin pinned him with a tired look. "You know something."

"I *can't* tell you. When Orion lets you in on secrets, he has a way of making it so you can't talk. Anything I spew out, it's because he allowed me to. As a way of—"

"Manipulating us," Dallas said, his expression growing angry. "She would be back by now. Her purpose is over. We have no assignment regarding the shadows. Our job is done. Just left to pick up the broken pieces Orion is too mighty to fix." Dallas stood. "Send the hunters wherever they want to go. I quit."

"Dallas." Austin swallowed.

"At least you knew you would lose Adia. You were able to cherish your moments knowing the end was coming. We did not. Jax was supposed to follow Reya. Cora was supposed to be Reborn. You're the only one with a Union on your relationship. No matter what, your souls are bound to reunite."

"I need a drink," Jax said, and Gold barked. "There's this great tavern on Plea. It's only 100 ports away. We could be back in a month. I say we go for it."

Austin could still see the anger rolling through Dallas. "It hasn't been long," Austin said. "She could still come back."

"She had a vision," Dallas said through his teeth. "If her soul was taken then they could have power over Orion. She's not coming back. Not while the shadows are still alive."

# CHAPTER THIRTY-TWO

*Seven Devils*

**Reya**
**Shadow Core**
**1 Day ABD**

Reya counted her breaths, willing her heart to slow its beating. She placed a hand on her chest, remembering she no longer had a body. Her skin was pale again, and her hair white. She mourned for the body she had on Earth that had no evidence of her Lehranian heritage. No resemblance to the cruel parents she hated.

By the time Reya reached the Throne Room, she stopped trembling and schooled her features to appear cold and fierce. How she often appeared when she was by Shemu's side. Her heels clicked along the stone floor until she reached the velvet carpet leading to the seven thrones under the canopy. She had been to the Shadow Core enough times that she managed to walk without seeming intimidated or awed by the Seven staring back at her. She recognized four of the Shadow Cores she was now bowing to. The Seven cycled through cores. A detail she had been working to tell Adia, but her nerves always bested her.

Adia was dressed in a black dress, her shoulder-length hair twisted in an elaborate braid. Her makeup, which Reya had rarely seen Adia wear, was done so severely she was almost unrecognizable.

Although Reya had meant to seem indifferent, her throat bobbed at the sight of Adia staring back as though she had been betrayed. As though Reya could have something to do with their time ending so abruptly on Earth. Reya yearned to have Lamarse's telepathic gift to convey the little she knew to Adia.

Reya smirked, hiding her unease. The other Shadow Cores needed to believe her smile was of pride.

At Ebony's high-pitched hum, Reya's jaw ticked as she turned to Lamarse's sister.

Talena raised her hand to silence Ebony. Reya stepped to the left where the other Core Guards stood at attention. Her stomach clenched at the sight of her brother Coye, who refused to meet her eyes; not that she stared at him for long.

Talena smiled as the last of the Core Guards bowed to the Seven before taking their stand on the right or left side of the Throne Room.

Then shadows flew in, filling every available space. Some transitioned to various people or creatures, many remained in their shadowy form.

Talena called for order even though everyone had already been standing in silent observation of one another.

"As tradition, we will start with the Crowning of the Queen. Adia. Rise."

* * *

**Adia**
**Shadow Core**
**1 Day ABD**

An invisible force lifted Adia from her throne. All evil eyes were on her as she was made to walk to the center throne —where she had been branded with the Allegiance Bond. Her soul's heart pounded, and she feared every devil could hear it. She was still reeling from seeing Reya bow her loyalty to the Shadow Core. Orion had promised Reya would help take them down. This couldn't be the future Orion had worked to come true. Otherwise, he would have warned her about the two months stolen from her time on Earth. Would have warned her about her mother dying by her own hands.

Adia had little hope Austin had been Reborn. Nothing Orion said comforted her anymore. Not when she was sitting before monsters and demons, being crowned to be one of them. The throne buzzed beneath her. Her Allegiance tattoo warmed until it burned. Adia made no expression of pain.

Ebony approached, grinning. She raised her hands, and a silver crown that was on a pillow near Talena flew into Ebony's hands.

Talena's eyes darkened, shooting the back of Ebony's head an annoyed glance before smiling.

Talena also rose her arms, but instead of a crown, she conjured dark clouds as she chanted unfamiliar words that sent chills through Adia. Her tattoo burned hotter causing Adia to hiss, arching her back.

Ebony's maniacal smile grew as she placed the crown on Adia's head. The silver melted onto Adia's skull, searing her skin as it glided down her face. Adia could no longer stop from screaming out in pain. Through her tears, she caught Reya's eyes and saw not joy but distress. Reya schooled her features, but Adia was no longer fooled.

The burning stopped, so Adia reached for her forehead and discovered the crown was intact. It didn't move with her touch, so she pressed harder then tried to take it off. It was sealed to her like her Allegiance tattoo.

"Queen Adia," Talena announced.

An invisible force pulled Adia to a stand again as everyone in attendance bowed.

"Camar!"

At Talena's call, one of the Seven whose face was in shadow stood. Closer examination made Adia see that the shadow wasn't from his cloak. His hands were also fading into blackness.

"We will be celebrating the Shadowing of Camar next," Talena announced.

The cloaked Seven stood too close to Adia. She wanted to step away but was forced to stand still, the memory of pain still radiating in her wrist and forehead.

Camar removed his cloak and knelt. He raised his silhouetted arms as Talena recited an incantation. The other five Shadow Cores joined in. Adia noticed Ebony struggled matching their pronunciations.

Camar became a shadow before Adia's eyes. She dared look at the other Shadow Cores and focused on the one with no face—Hesta, the shapeshifter. Since Adia last had been in the Shadow Core, the blank face had shadowed some.

Adia's breaths became shallow. If it weren't for Ebony holding her in place by her telekinesis, she would have fallen.

The Seven were not superior to shadows. They were souls collected to power the Shadow Core—until they *became* a shadow.

Adia was still processing this when a trial began. Ebony released her hold, and Adia moved mechanically to her throne. Black spots clouded her vision as a shadow approached them, transforming to a little boy. Talena and Ebony spoke over each other until Talena held up her hand and Ebony fell silent.

Adia half-listened to Talena read the shadow's crimes. Most were how many times they failed to bond to a soul. The shadow boy pleaded his case, but Talena wasn't moved. He was instructed to kneel. Terror flashed in the boy's eyes, and Adia's chest squeezed, almost forgetting he wasn't a child but a demon.

"Seren!" Talena called.

The Seven Core with claws and teeth like a feline stepped to the shadow boy. Her red eyes grew hungry. The shadow boy tried to flee, but Seren moved to him lightning fast. Her teeth sunk into his neck, and he bled dark goo that Seren drank. The boy returned to his shadow form and fought back. Seren suffered a scratch along her face before ripping the shadow apart, feasting on him. Black blood leaked from his wounds until he disappeared. Smoke lingered in the air before evaporating.

Adia blinked, staring in stunned disbelief. She fixated on two ideas:

One, that shadows could be killed in the Shadow Core.

Two, that she could die as well.

Something like hope sparked in Adia. Maybe she could take them down from within. If not, she could die and spend eternity somewhere else.

Hours of trials continued. Each of the Shadow Cores took their turn killing shadows. No one's pleads were granted.

Adia learned the other Seven's abilities.

Talena breathed fire. Adia wondered if she had been the same species as the dragon lady—a draemaki. She could also hypnotize, which was the power she used to coerce Adia into making the Allegiance Bond.

Hesta, although their soul was shadowing, could shapeshift not too unlike shadows. Only Hesta's capabilities to become beastlike far outperformed what Adia had seen most of the shadows transform into.

Eris, the purple devil, could conjure any weapon in his hands, from a dagger to a bomb. Adia had witnessed him destroy shadows using a wide range of weapons. Adia only saw him smile when he killed.

Camar could kill by waving his hand. Talena explained to Adia that he had once been a sorcerer. That the shadows took a piece of their power with them even in shadow form. Talena also mentioned how he would be replaced soon.

Ebony used telekinesis to kill her shadows. She took her time making the shadow suffer before eventually snapping their necks.

Talena always wore a bored expression when it was Ebony's turn to execute.

"Adia," Talena called, her face coming back to life as Ebony walked back to her throne. "You shall experiment with your power."

"I sense emotions," Adia said.

Talena hummed. "Have you tried...placing emotions? Like sorrow? Or *pain*?" Her sweet voice deepened on the last word.

Adia's hands shook. She had avoided looking at Reya during the trials. They locked eyes before Adia stood. The trembling shadow on trial was a young woman who reminded Adia of Crystal.

Adia gripped the tether between her and the shadow, sensing not fear but anticipation. Amusement. Adia hesitated, caught off guard, before she tried forming the idea of fear and pushed it down the tether. No change. Adia tried something smaller like worry. Still, all Adia could sense was the same excited amusement. The woman's fearful face shifted to express what Adia could sense. She smirked before standing, brushing invisible dirt from her clothes. Her laugh deepened.

Dread zapped through Adia.

The woman's features changed into Sam's.

# CHAPTER THIRTY-THREE

*Demons*

**Adia**
**Shadow Core**
**1 Day ABD**

"Hello, my dear. How I have—"

Laughter broke through Sam's words. Adia first looked to Ebony, but the laughing came from Reya. She held her stomach, head thrown back, her eyes squeezed shut. Sam joined her in laughing until Reya stopped so abruptly, Sam tilted his head in question.

"I missed you too, Reya Queen."

Reya's smile twisted, her eyes blazing as she said, "I am looking forward to tearing you apart." She sprinted—weaponless—to Sam. Adia pushed everything she felt, all her burning emotions that were spiraling like a madhouse, down the tether connecting her to Sam. He turned curious eyes on Adia as he caught Reya blindly by the throat. Reya twisted and kicked, breaking herself free. Adia jumped on his back, choking him while Reya threw rapid punches to his face. He was bleeding black before Ebony froze Adia and Reya.

"As fun as this is to witness," Talena said, "we do have a schedule to keep. Deals to make. Shemu, take your queen as part of our arrangement."

Sam spat some blood before folding his arms behind his back, shooting the Shadow Core a charming smile. "I was curious if I might not have them both?"

Talena was considering when Ebony whispered something, making them laugh.

"Reya is to join Orion's son in the cages," Talena announced. "Coye? You will join Shemu and Adia in their kingdom. And transport your disloyal sister to the dungeon." Talena's green eyes glowed as her smile stretched. To Reya, she said, "We knew you were never one of us."

"I still carry hope," Sam said.

Reya shook with rage burning in her black eyes, unable to fully break from Ebony's hold.

"If there is no one left to kill," Eris spoke in a quiet scratchy voice, "let this meeting be done."

* * *

**Adia**
**Consumption**
**1 Day ABD**

Adia pulled from Sam's grip on her waist. He had teleported them between worlds as quickly as taking a breath. Coye held Reya by her upper arm. The moment their feet touched grass, Reya yanked away and swung at her brother. Once he managed to grip her again, they vanished.

Adia breathed deeply through her nose as she searched the unfamiliar town. The sky was a grayish purple, with black cracks spread like broken glass. They stood before a gated mansion. There was a forest on one side with a street on the other.

"I know you don't remember being here, but welcome back to Consumption," Sam said and then added, "A broken version of it."

At her silence, Sam laughed and walked away. Over his shoulder, he said, "I need to visit with Reya for a bit. I'll see you in our castle later. Don't be late." He placed his hands in his pockets. So casual. So calm. Then he headed into the mansion.

Adia sprinted down the road, finding a deserted neighborhood with burnt houses. She reached a black gate that opened upon her arrival. There was only darkness beyond it. She searched around, considered her options, and then stepped into the unknown. She knew she couldn't really escape. The Edge was gone. There was nowhere she could go where Sam wouldn't find her, which was why he let her leave. She wondered what would happen to her soul if it were to die here. Any Hell away from Sam would be solace.

Yellow light broke through the darkness. Adia stepped onto grass. She was at the Park, though there were no souls roaming. Tables were toppled over, tents were torn. The pond littered with discarded clothes and lockets. Once Adia broke the Shadow World, the souls were freed but their things were left behind.

Adia walked through the trees toward Mountain Village, coming across an abandoned campsite. She halted, unbelieving, until she stepped closer to a tree. She pulled out a hatchet and examined its blade before testing its sharpness by slicing the tip of her finger.

Black blood.

Fisting her hand, Adia shook with fury. She was going to fight. Fight them until they burned in Hell. The scar on her wrist heated with pain. Dread washed through her. They could control her. She would need to be clever.

She reached the river and cleaned the black blood dripping from her finger. She eyed her surroundings finding no other soul or monster around. She reached Mountain Village and her hands tingled at the familiarity of seeing all the cabins. Her eyes lingered on Austin's name carved on a door as she passed.

She headed to Alternate Earth through the Dark Forest.

She shivered as she passed through the trees. She had been walking too long. She was surely lost.

The trees disappeared, and wind blew across her face. She stood at an intersection. Abandoned cars were everywhere;

some had crashed. The starry night was perfect above her like she was in a movie, and the sky was a greenscreen. It was a wonder she ever believed it to be real.

She crossed the street. Based on license plates, she was in Alternate-Arizona. She walked through neighborhoods and shops. Walked until dawn. She entered a random house and searched, making sure it wasn't already occupied. She took off her shoes and examined her bloodied feet. She winced placing them back on. Her hand cramped for how tightly she still held the hatchet as she sat on the couch, her eyes on the door. Her chest quaked as emotions from the day caught up to her.

She was back in the Shadow World.

With Sam.

She had killed her mother.

And Austin.

Reya was being tortured.

Adia abandoned her.

She pulled up her knees, hugging them, and cried until she felt faint and nauseated. She couldn't catch her breath. She dropped her hatchet, falling onto her hands and knees. Wave after wave of dizziness hit her.

Her eyes rolled back.

* * *

## Reya
## Consumption
## 1 Day ABD

Reya kicked at her glass cage. Coye stood on the other side, watching her silently. She cursed at him in every language she knew. He teleported away as she continued to thrash against her prison.

"Are you done?" Lamarse sat in the glass cage nearest her, looking haggard. She tried to speak to him with her thoughts, but he shook his head.

"I cannot hear your mind beyond this glass."

Footsteps echoed down the steps, and Reya's eyes ticked across every glass cage, where Lamarse's hunters were imprisoned.

Shemu approached. He smiled at her before transforming into the image she had been most familiar with. He had bright hazel eyes, long black hair, and tanned skin.

"Reya Queen," he said, shaking his head. "Why did you try and kill me? I thought we were *everything* to each other."

*You are everything to me.* She declared those words before vowing she would stay in the Shadow World to be with him. Now his crooked smile triggered Reya's darkness. She slammed her body against the glass. Exerting all her energy into breaking something that would never break.

Shemu laughed. "I guess she has moved on from me as she did you." His hazel eyes turned to Lamarse before transforming into Jax. "Now Reya Queen," his voice even sounded like Jax's, "I am going to visit you often. Since the Core will not force you to be with me, I will have to convince you. Again." He laughed at Lamarse, who watched in silence. "Not tonight. I have plans with Adia."

Lamarse stepped to the glass.

"If it's a deal you wish," Shemu said to Lamarse, "I'm afraid this new arrangement with her is *everything to me.*" He returned to smiling at Reya.

It wasn't Jax's amusing smile. His laughing rhythm was wrong too. Reya ached for Jax but was glad he wasn't here for Shemu to torture.

"Your brother will be back for you," Shemu told her.

\* \* \*

**Adia**
**City of Souls**
**2 Days ABD**

Adia hurried her steps, her heart racing. She frantically searched around until she found the trail leading up the mountain and began climbing. Her breaths were painful by the time she reached the castle grounds. She saw two White Guardians posted by the grand door and waved to them.

"Excuse me! Excuse me! Is he here? Am I late?"

The White Guardian looked stunned. "He's inside."

She shot him a look of disapproval. "Is that how I am to be addressed?"

"Your highness," he added quickly.

Adia ran inside the castle. Two females met her in the hall. "Hurry!" she called to them. "All of this is wrong! So wrong! Please help me!"

The females exchanged amused looks. "What is wrong, exactly?"

Adia threw up her hands, annoyed by their reaction. She would deal with them later. "Everything! My outfit! My hair! Fix it, now! Before he sees!"

"Of course," one of the females said.

Adia widened her eyes. "Does nobody respect royalty anymore?"

"Your highness," they said together, their lips twitching.

"Come now," one said.

"We are running low on time," said the other.

Adia was bathed in special water that healed her blistered feet. She was dressed in a silver gown that sparkled. As the ladies started twisting her hair, Adia stopped them.

"He prefers it long," she scolded.

"Of course, your highness."

Adia's dark hair grew to her waist. One of the ladies braided the top half below her crown.

Adia gasped at the jewel selection, picking a necklace and bracelets. She was ushered into the Great Room. Her braids were twisted so tightly, her head ached. Her shoes pinched her toes, but she smiled through the pain as she walked to *him*.

"My queen," Sam said, bowing.

"My king!" She curtsied. A giggle bubbled out of her as he kissed the top of her hand.

"Are you ready?" he asked.

"This is the most excited I have ever felt," Adia replied, her smile growing. "I am faint!"

"Then let us waist no more time and be married."

\* \* \*

**Adia**
**City of Souls**
**2 Days ABD**

Adia's neck pinched as she straightened. She sat on a gold throne, only it was encased with glass. Celebratory chaos was before her. People danced to music, drinking and throwing things across the room, shouting their cheers. She saw Sam at the center of a mosh pit, jumping with the crowd. Someone threw a gauntlet at Adia's throne. Energy zapped through the glass, and she gasped at the unexpected pain. Someone laughed and another gauntlet was thrown at her. She was electrocuted again.

"My queen!" Sam shouted, barely audible above the thumping music. "Welcome back to the party!"

Horrifying memories flooded Adia's mind. She recalled marrying Sam. Sharing his bed. And celebrating. It was as though she had been hypnotized, unable to control her actions. She had been transformed into exactly who Sam had always wanted her to be—a submissive queen.

Adia screamed, slamming her hands against the glass. Another energy blast electrocuted her. She stomped her feet, as if she could break through the marble floor. She thrashed and was electrocuted repeatedly, hoping one of the times her soul's heart would give out.

Sam stepped to her glass prison. "Better rest, my queen. You have much to do tomorrow. But maybe we could spend it in bed."

Adia attacked the glass where he stood.

Sam threw his head back in laughter as she was electrocuted.

"You hate me now," Sam said. "Give it a few thousand years. You won't even remember Austin's name."

Adia's vision pulsed as she became unable to take in enough breaths. She slumped on the floor, fighting to stay conscious because she knew when she awoke next, she would return to being Sam's queen. Still, she drifted off.

*"Adia."*

Adia gasped, finding herself surrounded by darkness. A slight breeze touched her face as she searched around. Her eyes fell on the Ferris wheel.

"I'm in Echo," she said to herself.

"Yes."

Her father stood as a man before her. Adia couldn't find the words as she stared at him. Reya appeared by his side, three swords in her arms. She handed Adia one of them, the other went to her father.

"You have much to learn," Reya said.

"I…" Adia got to her feet. "How am I in Echo?"

"We are sleeping in our prisons while you sleep in yours," Reya said, not answering Adia's question. "This is when we must train."

Adia's eyes welled as she continued to stare back at her father. She feared telling him what happened to her mother, but he needed to know. He raised a hand, stopping her from forming the words.

"It was not your fault," he said.

The tension broke in her throat as she sobbed. He raised his arms, and she fell into her father's embrace while Reya stood silently by. When Adia pulled away, Reya was staring past them, her eyes watering.

"You said train?" Adia asked.

"Yes." Reya cleared her throat. "You have much to learn."

"With my Allegiance Bond, they have control over me. I won't be able to help."

"We will not only train by sword," her father said, "but by mind."

"I will train you to fight," Reya said, "but Shemu will die by my sword." Reya's hardened eyes softened. "Maybe we will flip for it."

# CHAPTER THIRTY-FOUR

*Fade*

**Adia**
**City of Souls**
**30 Days ABD**

Celebrations continued with no break. Demons and monsters visited from other Shadow Worlds. Adia would cater to them as Sam's queen.

"Wait! Watch this!" Sam handed Adia a pistol. "Shoot me!"

"What, my lord?" Adia's eyes were large.

"Shoot me!"

"I could never!"

"Precisely!" His fingernails dug into her bare shoulders.

She stared at the pistol. It was heavy in her hands, which shook as she examined the unfamiliar weapon. Sam kissed her cheek before biting her shoulder, leaving a mark. Adia continued smiling. Sam jogged to the other side of the Great Room, shaking off his overcoat and rolling up his dress shirt. His tie was already hanging loosely around his neck. He stood against the wall.

"Come on, my dear! Shoot me!"

Adia's hands were now vibrating as she lifted the gun. She tried pulling the trigger, but it wouldn't budge. "I cannot!" Tears were slipping down her face, but her smile remained the same. "The trigger is locked!"

Coye stepped to Adia's side, removed the gun, and shot. A

laugh burst from Sam, seeing the bullet hole a half inch away from his head.

"She cannot harm me but also has to obey orders!" Sam continued laughing.

"Did I fail?" Adia asked Coye who stared back at her with an annoyed expression. She tried to recall what she could have done to make the White Guardian hate her.

Sam skipped to them, taking the gun from Coye. It vanished at his touch.

Adia swayed, catching herself on Coye's sleeve.

"Is it that time already?" Sam looked thrilled.

Coye removed Adia's hand from his arm and disappeared.

"Time to sleep." Sam lifted Adia into his arms and started kissing her. Her dizzy spell spiraled, making her float in and out of consciousness. Sam didn't break the kiss until they reached her gold throne.

"Tomorrow, I'll remember to time the day better," he said. "So, we can make it back to my bed."

"Hmm?" Adia sat, feeling every bruise and sore muscle, unsure how they came to be. Her head slumped before snapping back up.

"Hello, my dear," Sam said to her.

Adia kneeled on the small space of floor she had. Sam smirked, and Adia knew he was expecting her to start yelling as she had done before. Give him her meanest glare. Fight him with only words because she couldn't reach him past the glass. She curled up on the floor, and rolled to face away from Sam. If she wasn't touching the throne or the glass, she didn't get electrocuted when something was thrown.

Sam cleared his throat.

She ignored him.

He scoffed.

She shut her eyes and pictured Austin sleeping next to her. Imagined the feel of his hand resting on the curve of her waist, his breath touching the back of her neck. She had the urge to roll over, but she would see Sam not Austin. Sam, who was now singing the Frank Sinatra song that once fueled her anger as he hit her glass prison.

She practiced the breathing techniques Reya taught her to meditate. Sam's singing faded as her consciousness dropped through the floor and rose in the darkness of Echo where Reya and her father were already waiting for her.

\* \* \*

## Austin
## Los Angeles, CA
## 30 Days ABD

Every morning, while Austin's eyes were still closed, and his dreams lingered, he forgot she was gone. Then he would see that his hand was resting on a pillow he positioned to trick his subconscious into believing Adia slept next to him. This morning, he refused to open his eyes.

A knock disturbed his fantasy.

Austin had moved into Dallas and Cora's Los Angeles apartment near the Hunters' Training Facility. Dallas had traveled to San Diego to visit his father weeks ago. He stopped answering Austin's calls.

"Time to go!" Jax said, rushing into the apartment with Gold by his side. "Pack! We're leaving, friend."

Austin shut the door. "What are you talking about?"

"New orders. We are to take the hunters to train at Earth Guardianship. You will be training as well. After you graduate, Orion agreed to let you partner with me on missions." Jax paused his pacing and narrowed one eye at Austin. "You do need to practice your villain smile. If we are to fool anyone into believing I would consort with you. They would see right through our rouse with those kind eyes." Jax picked up a bag from Austin's closet and started stuffing it with an assortment of random items. "Dallas may take some convincing, but he is meant to be leader over Earth Guardianship. Orion said

Cora's death wasn't initially anticipated, but once he's finished mourning—"

"Jax. Stop." Austin walked to the kitchen and started the coffee maker. He inserted several bagels into the toaster. Austin needed Jax to be in a good mood for what he would soon say.

"Have you talked to Dallas?" Jax asked, dropping into a kitchen chair. Gold curled into a ball by his feet.

"I spoke to his dad. Dallas went to get things for dinner last week, but he didn't come back until the next morning. His dad said he had been drinking all night. Every afternoon since, Dallas leaves for a bar and doesn't come back until dawn."

"Drinking's normal considering," Jax said.

"Not for Dallas." Austin got out the cream cheese and a knife. He loaded a plate with toasted bagels and handed them over to Jax.

"We all have our ways of coping." Jax's smile was weak as he spread cream cheese all over the bread, top and bottom. His messy fingers danced on the tabletop as he took several bites. "Is it better knowing you were going to lose her?"

"Every time I've lost her," Austin said with a knot in his throat, "I knew it would happen. It still felt unexpected. Still felt like the ground broke beneath me, and I dropped into a cold, dark place."

Jax slowed his chewing, his fingers stilling. "I'd prefer the cold, dark place as long as it meant we were together." He laughed. "Reya, I mean. Although I am grateful to be with you. I think I would let the monster take me over if I lost you as well."

Austin took a scolding sip. "Are you training the hunters, then?

"Only for a little bit while you all adjust to the new setting. Orion has a mission for me soon. Some old friends I need to infiltrate. But I'll visit you during training. And Dallas too. Once you convince him to come with you."

"I can't convince him," Austin said, taking another painful

sip.

"Sure, you can. Once he understands his importance with the Guardianship—"

"I can't convince him because I don't want anything to do with Orion. Or Earth Guardianship. I'll stay here. And hopefully that choice will allow me to grow old. Maybe then I can find Adia in the afterlife."

"But your purpose—"

"I don't want to be a game piece Orion manipulates anymore."

"What will you do?"

Austin leaned down to pet Gold's head. "I have no idea. How are you holding up?"

Jax's leg started bouncing. "I'm good. I didn't know Reya that long. I'll move on." Jax gave a breathy laugh as he added, "I keep doing this weird thing where I call her. It's especially weird because calling her wasn't something I did often. But I can't stop. I don't even realize that I'm doing it until it's ringing." Jax laughed again before reaching in his pocket. "Speaking of ringing...rings."

Austin's stomach dropped at the sight of Adia's wedding ring. He reached for it, surprised how shinny it looked.

"I had it cleaned," Jax said. "It...was dirty with ash...from the explosion."

"Thank you," Austin whispered.

"Listen. You don't have to train right away. Just chill with me until you feel up to it." He paused before adding, "Please."

"I'm sorry, Jax. My fight has always been for Adia. I have no interest in continuing without her."

"Right." Jax stared at the picture of Dallas and Cora on their wedding day. He stood abruptly, startling Gold who barked as though danger was near. "I'll see you around, Austin. Best of luck."

\* \* \*

**Adia**
**Echo**
**60 Days ABD**

"I can't." Adia heaved deep breaths, hands on her knees. "It's impossible."

"Try again," her father said.

"It's pointless."

"Adia. Again."

Adia caught her breath, staring at her father with weary eyes. While her soul slept, she exerted her consciousness in Echo. Her days were strange and never easy. When she exercised in Echo, she felt sore and bruised in the City of Souls even though she didn't have a mark on her. The healing baths helped, but she couldn't always take them.

"I'm exhausted," Adia said. "Taking off this *damned* crown is impossible."

"Your soul and consciousness are only reacting how your body once did."

"It's sealed to me."

He gave her a tired look. It was strange to see her father's emotions when all she used to be able to see was his eyes in a lion's face. He stepped to her and touched the crown. It slid off easily. Adia, without meaning to, moved the crown back into place.

Reya observed from one of the Ferris wheel cars. She was to train Adia next. Physical fighting was easier to Adia than her father working on her mind or her gift.

"Removing the crown means overpowering your Allegiance Bond," her father said. "Try again."

# CHAPTER THIRTY-FIVE

## *The Monster*

**Shemu**
**City of Souls**
**5 Years ABD**

Shemu watched the celebration carry on from his throne. Adia danced with a viper in the form of a gentleman. Shemu watched and watched, until the viper took a bite from Adia's arm.

"Fight him," Shemu whispered. "Kill him."

Adia's forehead pinched as the monster continued to drink her soul's blood.

"Weak, stupid girl," Shemu snarled as Adia collapsed.

Coye wordlessly picked Adia up from the floor, looking bored as he stared back at Shemu, who waved at him to take her away. The Seven wouldn't appreciate needing to resurrect Adia.

The next day, Shemu strolled down the dungeons with Adia. She gripped his arm, frightened by all the monsters locked in glass prisons. It took restraint not to push her down the stairs. He wanted Lamarse to see her. It had been some time since their last visit.

"Hello, Father!" Shemu called once he caught sight of Lamarse's prison.

Reya stiffened at their approach, and Shemu's smile turned genuine.

"Reya." Shemu kissed Adia's hand before stepping away from her hold. He feigned concern as he said to Reya, "You look dreadful. Are they not feeding you here?"

Her white hair was a tangled mess, and her pale complexion glowed in the darkness.

"You can always join us up at the castle," Shemu continued. "Lots of food and drink there. And plenty of room in my bed. Isn't that right, Adia?" He smirked at Lamarse's darkened stare.

"Room in your bed?" Adia asked in an annoyingly sweet tone. "It is a rather large bed."

Reya trembled with beautiful rage.

"I do believe you would find it more accommodating." Adia wrung her fingers, staring around the glass cages as though one of the prisoners would break free and attack. "Can we bring them to the castle?"

Shemu slapped Adia and laughed. Lamarse disappointed him by remaining still, but Reya threw herself at the cage. Shemu hit Adia again.

"I'm sorry," Adia whispered, holding her nose. "I'm getting blood all over the floor! I'll clean it up."

Shemu kicked her in the stomach. Again, and again.

Reya shouted, "Stop!"

Shemu stepped to Reya's glass, studying her anger. "You used to love me. You were my most devoted servant." Her eyes blackened as he turned into Jax. "My bed is yours at the cost of an Allegiance Bond."

Adia moaned on the floor and Lamarse's eyes were locked on his daughter. Shemu resisted rolling his eyes at the pathetic sight.

"She's *boring* like this," Reya said.

Shemu slowly turned his head back to Reya, who was smiling.

"No fight. No anger. If I made the bond, I would be the same." Reya's smile grew. "Then you would be stuck with two *boring, boring* queens."

Shemu slammed his palm against the glass. He slowly

shook his head as he walked backwards toward the stairs, still looking like Jax, and left Adia to suffer on the floor.

* * *

**Shemu**
**Shadow Core**
**15 Years ABD**

Shemu approached the Seven, locking eyes with Adia who stared back at him as though she was no longer his queen but also not the Adia he desperately wanted back. She was under Talena's hypnosis.

"I come to amend my arrangement with Queen Adia," Shemu said, putting on his best smile. He remembered when he had been a Seven, slowly transitioning to a shadow. Remembered the power struggle and how they often made decisions based on their own interest. He turned his attention to Ebony, knowing it would anger Talena. "She is rather boring, and the celebration has run its course. I ask that we change scenery. And alter her personality. I recall a scenario when she believed to be an FBI agent."

Ebony raised a brow and smirked. "You mean the version of her who broke your Shadow World?"

"It did need to be done in order for her to become a Seven, correct?"

"It was not planned nor permitted."

Shemu bowed while smirking. "But it did work out in our favor."

"Orion has a plan to destroy us," Ebony said. "Nothing will change until he is trapped in our world."

Shemu turned to Talena. "Imagine this. She believes she returned to Earth. Believes the shadows are already destroyed. And she reunites with what's-his-name! I'll play the part, of course."

"I do enjoy your imagination, Shemu." Talena giggled. "Only

Adia is not your reward but punishment."

Shemu locked his jaw, he could feel his form shifting into a shadow as smoke billowed around him.

"During your trial it was a choice between damning you to Hell or creating one," Talena said, looking pleased. "Since she broke the world not out of her own power but due to your attachment, she is your penance. Adia?"

Adia stood, her features transitioning to the soft smile he hated. Hated so much he once tried burning it off her face.

"Yes, Queen Talena?" Adia's large eyes were doe like.

"Take Shemu back to your world. His punishment for asking such a thing will be to never leave it again."

"You cannot—" Shemu's words were cut off by Talena raising her hand.

The floor cracked beneath him. Shemu dodged the falling rubble and locked eyes with Mal, who had replaced Camar. He had also been a sorcerer.

Shemu had little time to decide whether the breaking floor was an illusion before Adia gripped his arm and transported him back to their world. He tried and tried again to return to the Shadow Core. Teleporting within his own world was also lost to him. He tore at the grass of the castle grounds.

Coye approached calmly.

"They trapped me!" He charged at Coye, gripping him by his tunic. "Take me back to the Shadow Core!"

Coye held on to Shemu's shoulder and disappeared, leaving Shemu in the City of Souls. When Coye returned, his silver eyes were a fraction larger.

"*Adia!*" Shemu spat. "You must try!"

"My lord?" Her doe eyes fluttered in confusion.

Shemu cursed, kicking at the shrubs. He grabbed Adia by her throat. "I will kill you! I will kill you and free myself from this Hell!" Her face darkened from being strangled, but she didn't struggle.

"There is the chance," Coye spoke evenly, "that if her soul were to die, this world you two created would also...*die*." Coye examined his nails before looking at Shemu. "It is only a theory. Go ahead. I've grown tired of her as well."

Shemu shut his eyes and dropped Adia to the ground. She croaked, clawing at her throat. "I'm sorry, my lord," she rasped.

Shemu stormed off to the dungeons. He needed to break bones, and Lamarse was the perfect candidate.

* * *

**Adia**
**City of Souls**
**30 Years ABD**

Adia limped to the bath. She awoke in her glass prison as she did every day feeling exhausted. She greeted the White Guardians she passed, some kissing her hand, others groping her. She laughed with them and cheerfully continued to her bath. She hoped she would see Sam today. Coye had informed her that Sam had traveled to Alternate Earth but would return soon. *Soon* became two years. He often left for lengthy periods of time, came back, and it felt like their honeymoon again.

Adia undressed and placed her hand into the already filled bath. She never knew which servant to thank for always making sure it was the perfect temperature each morning.

She sighed and smiled at the short time she would be able to relax alone. It never lasted long enough before someone pounded on the door. They weren't allowed to come in.

She folded her dress neatly and placed her jewels on top. She was about to step into the bath when she stopped. "Oh!" She removed her crown and set it down next to her jewels, so it wouldn't get wet.

# CHAPTER THIRTY-SIX

*Cosmic Love*

**Austin**
**Vancouver, WA**
**30 Years ABD**

Austin's dream was to see Adia again. And his nightmare took place ten years after he had lost her. He had awoken one morning and hadn't dreamt about her. Had moved through the day and didn't think of her. He taught his class at the University and didn't picture Adia sitting in the front row, absorbing the information he taught his students. He made it all the way through dinner, busying himself grading papers as he ate.

Someone on the news had said Adia's name, but the picture displayed was not his wife.

He stared at the television in utter disbelief. How had he gone an entire day without thinking of her? He hurried to the dresser in his bedroom and pulled out her wedding ring. He vowed it would never happen again.

And now, twenty years had passed, and he had kept his vow. Never once did a day go by without him paying some respect to their love.

Austin approached the visitor's desk, his chest tight.

"The resemblance is uncanny!" a young woman said to his left.

"Excuse me?"

"Are you Winifred's grandson?"

Austin hesitated before nodding.

"She has a picture of your dad. You look just like him. Except the beard. I just started working here a week ago. She didn't mention having a grandson." The woman's eyes lit with interest. "I can show you to Winifred if you'd like?"

Austin's smile faltered. He rubbed his forehead, drawing attention to his wedding ring. "I'm okay. Thank you."

Someone called her name from the desk and Austin hurried to the elevator, his heart racing. He hated lying. He hated looking twenty-five when he was supposed to be in his sixties. Hated when people asked about his wife after noticing his wedding ring.

When the elevator took too long, Austin used the stairs. His anxiety made him forget his strength, and he threw open the door. He winced, examined the damage, and felt grateful it was only minor cracks along the wall.

He stepped into his mother's room. "Hi, Mom."

Her mumbling stopped as well as her rocking. She sat in a cushioned chair next to a stand with three water glasses on top.

"Speaking of Austin!" She clapped her hands. "He was just telling me..." Her brows furrowed. "I can't remember. What was it you were saying?"

Austin collected the water glasses when he saw they were littered with dust. His mother's lips were cracked, her complexion grayer since his last visit.

"Guardian...something."

Austin paused and searched the room. He heard the faintest creak of the floor and a light reflected in the mirror for a split second. "Who were you talking to?" he asked his mother.

"Your dad, of course. I told you this yesterday." She continued rocking. "He forgives me for marrying Grant. That lying cheat! Marrying his mistress like some..." She squinted, losing her train of thought.

Grant had passed away ten years ago. Austin's mother

attended his funeral wearing the white dress she had worn when they eloped. She told Austin that story every night for several months when her dementia worsened.

"You saw dad?" Austin asked.

She jerked back. "Of course not. What's wrong with you?"

Austin sighed and went to the small kitchen counter to clean her dishes. He placed a clean glass of water before her and, throughout the repetitive stories she told him, reminded her to drink.

"I hope he'll have me," his mother said, staring at the picture of their family hung on the wall as she mindlessly rocked. "When I see him again. I hope he'll have me."

"I'm sure he will, Mom," Austin said softly. He held her hand as she wept.

* * *

**Austin**
**Vancouver, WA**
**30 Years ABD**

Austin sat in a cushioned chair as people socialized at his mother's wake. He played the part of her grandson, giving vague answers, and explaining how Winifred's son was too sick to travel. Nobody questioned him. Nobody knew him enough to see the lie.

"Wow."

Austin was too slow in stopping his recognition from showing.

Judy smiled knowingly and took a seat next to him. She had aged graciously. Allowing her blonde hair to gray and her wrinkles to shape her features.

"I'm sorry for your loss," she said.

"Thank you," Austin said faintly before clearing his throat.

"I brought my family. Over there."

Austin spotted an older man and a young blonde woman

standing near the table of photos. Judy's daughter looked at the picture of Austin and then over at him to compare.

"I heard you started teaching," Judy said.

"I had to quit."

"Are you going to stay in Washington?"

"I'll be leaving soon." He was still working on a plan on where he would go. The World Union had given him proper identification and would fake papers of his death for the few people who may look too closely into his past.

Judy gestured to the ring on his finger. "Will you be leaving alone?"

Austin ran his thumb over the gold band. "Yes." He could sense the questions Judy wanted to ask. She surprised him by remaining silent until Austin started asking questions about her life. He discovered she had married but divorced after her second child was born. Then she met Howie. They took their time before he convinced her to marry him. They had a daughter together.

Austin tried not to show the ache he felt in hearing about Judy's life. He pictured what his children with Adia would have looked like as young adults. What it would be like to grow old with her.

When Judy said farewell, Austin was left with exhausting emotions from the day. He drove back to his apartment in silence, rubbing anxiously at his wedding ring. He took some medicine for his headache, dressed in comfortable clothes, and climbed into bed to read. He stared at the empty side of the bed, no longer able to focus on his book.

The doorbell rang.

He ignored it.

The bell rang rapidly followed by pounding knocks.

Groaning, Austin went to answer, checking the peephole first. He threw the door open.

"Finally!" Jax said, already heading inside. "He made us wait. I told him I have a key."

"Dallas?" Austin hugged his old friend. "What are you doing

here?"

"Why is he happier to see you than me?" Jax questioned, plopping onto the couch.

"Because I saw you last week," Austin answered.

"Still." Jax threw his feet on the coffee table and turned on the television. He played with his beard he had recently grown to match Austin's.

"What's going on?"

"We came to see you," Dallas answered. "Thought maybe you could use a friend."

"And discuss—"

Dallas cut Jax off with a look.

Austin took a seat by Jax. "Discuss what?"

"Relax, my friend. We are here to help you. Your crazy mother died and—"

"Jax!"

Jax raised his hands to Dallas. "Sorry, sorry!" He returned to looking uneasily at Austin. "Orion sent us because…you are at a pivotal moment in your life."

"We can talk about this later," Dallas said calmly. "We are here for you, Austin."

Austin noticed Dallas no longer wore his wedding ring. Their last conversation was four years ago when Dallas urged Austin to move on, claiming he couldn't live mourning Adia forever. Austin had told him it wouldn't be fair to anyone he dated because his heart could never belong to them.

Dallas caught him staring. "You were right." He examined his bare hand. "It wasn't fair to Sofia. She left me about a year ago."

"I never faulted you for trying to move on," Austin said.

Dallas gave a short nod.

To Jax, Austin said, "I'll do it."

"Do what now?" Jax worked on unwrapping a candy bar he had taken from Austin's stash of food reserved for Jax's spontaneous visits.

"I'll train with Earth Guardianship," Austin said. "I've been thinking about it for a while."

"That was easy," Jax said around a mouthful of chocolate.

"Are you sure?" Dallas asked.

Austin smiled. "You can come."

"Old man like me." Dallas chuckled. "Imagine."

"They have these special suits," Jax said, pointing at Dallas. "You could if you wanted to. Orion could also get you in touch with a Timekeeper to reverse your age."

Dallas folded his arms and for a second, Austin could see the young man he once knew. Could see the hunter behind the wrinkles and sad smile. "I'm going to work on bettering myself. Pray Cora will have me in the next life."

Austin envied how close Dallas was to seeing Cora again. He looked at Jax who had stopped eating, staring at the television with unfocused eyes. He rarely talked about Reya, but Austin could see his grief in his aura. He had been prepared to follow Reya into Hell. That type of love wasn't dulled with time.

"I was planning on seeing you, actually," Austin said to Dallas. "I was still figuring out when I would leave. You're the only person left I needed to say goodbye to."

Dallas shuffled his feet. "I'm sorry I..." He cleared his throat. "I should have been around more."

"All forgiven."

# CHAPTER THIRTY-SEVEN

## *Raise Hell*

**Adia**
**City of Souls**
**80 Years ABD**

Adia smiled at Sam as they ate. She cut her steak into perfect squares and chewed elegantly. The steak tasted off, like she was eating liver instead. She fought gagging.

Sam had been away for the past ten years, in that time, Adia had become ready. She controlled the emotions of those around her whenever she slipped into her true self during the day. Last year, she even killed a White Guardian without notice. She made White Guardians feel indifferent toward her, stopping them from cornering her in dark corridors.

Even Sam had found her less appealing. His travels through Alternate Earth were longer every time he left. She would need him to stay this time. As Adia took another bite, she reached for his tether, planting desire.

"You look…" Sam dropped his fork, eyeing her. "New dress?"

"No." Adia dabbed at her face, keeping her smile in place. "Only changed the color. Red is your favorite. I wanted to please you." She fed him more desire.

Sam hummed, his eyes lingering on her neck. "Stand."

Adia obeyed. She could feel his yearning grow. It took control not to smirk as she tucked her steak knife in the pocket of her dress while she sat back down.

"I wasn't done admiring!" Sam slammed his palm, making the small table shake.

Adia obeyed again, slowly twirling.

"What was that?" Sam rose, his hands planted on the table.

"What, my lord?" She paused, trying to not appear dizzy.

"You clenched your teeth." He moved to her, his smile growing. He pinched her chin, tilting her head back and laughed as he examined her eyes.

Adia moved to stab him, knowing it would ruin the plan Reya and Lamarse had constructed.

Sam caught her wrist, cackling as he held her tightly against his chest. "There you are."

She broke from him, teleporting away.

"Coye!"

Arms snaked around her as her surroundings changed. She was in her glass prison. Coye bowed slightly and vanished. Adia rushed to the glass, but she was electrocuted. Years of planning and she had failed. All because she gritted her teeth. Coye would alert the Seven and then eighty years of training would be used against her.

* * *

Adia awoke in the Great Room, but she was no longer trapped in her glass prison.

"Good, you're awake." Reya stood from sitting in Sam's throne. She offered Adia a cloak that matched hers. It was aligned with an assortment of throwing knives.

"How are you here?" Adia whispered. A White Guardian bleeding black from his neck was struggling on one of the tables. He vanished in a puff of smoke.

"Lamarse didn't only have one plan."

Adia tore off her crown and threw it on the ground. She stomped on it, the sound echoing. "I can't fight in this gown."

Reya stepped aside, revealing the two large duffle bags. "Change and load quickly."

Adia held back a gasp when she opened the bag to reveal not only a change of clothes but guns. Her hands tingled as she met Reya's silver eyes. "We really are doing this."

"Yes."

Adia changed and strapped on her guns. "Coye left for the Seven. They will be here soon if not already. What's the plan?"

"Our plan is to kill the White Guardians and get to Shemu."

"Then what?"

"Then we will initiate the next plan."

"Which is?"

"Which will only exist if we accomplish this one."

"Are you being cryptic on purpose?"

"Yes." Reya flashed Adia a smile.

"I hate not knowing everything."

"I know. Our plans revolve around you turning against us."

Adia tried not to look offended. She finished adjusting her bullet belt. "Where is Sam?"

"Waiting for Coye's return in one of the meeting rooms."

"There's over a hundred meeting rooms."

Reya's brows twitched as she smirked. "Come on, Adia. It was never going to be easy. No matter how many years of training we had."

"You're loving this," Adia said. "We could fail."

"Not without taking him down first."

"How did you escape your prison?"

"The same way Lamarse could pull you into Echo every night."

Adia sighed, knowing she wouldn't receive a straight answer. She had been asking that question for years.

"Ready?"

Adia examined her weapons, making sure she knew where every knife and gun was placed. "Yeah."

"Good," Reya's eyes turned black, "because I don't think I can wait any longer."

Reya kicked the door open, and Adia shot at a passing White Guardian with a shotgun. His headless body smoked as it stumbled before vanishing to Hell. Reya's cloak flowed beautifully as she took out two more White Guardians with her daggers. Her fighting always looked like dancing to Adia. Even with years of training, Adia doubted she was as elegant while digging her sword into a White Guardian's throat, kicking him off the blade, and shooting another in the chest.

Adia pumped her gun and shot someone running down the hall. She was attacked from behind. Reya slid, killing Adia's attacker before disappearing around a corner. When Adia caught up to her, the hall was littered with dying demons. Adia ran through the smoke as their souls passed on to Hell.

They ran down the halls, killing servants, killing White Guardians, killing everyone who had aligned themselves with Sam.

They searched several meeting rooms to find them bare. They halted at the sight of Coye appearing down the hall, and Adia's heart hammered. It was over. The Seven were here or he was ordered to take her to them. She caught Reya's eyes momentarily before they both charged at him. He was a better fighter than Adia had anticipated. Adia remembered what Reya had told her about their childhood. About how their parents would pit them against each other in battles. Coye was older, and Reya would be abused every time she lost. Then it was Coye losing and his punishments turned him bitter.

A laugh echoed in the hall and Adia dodged Coye's hit as she saw Sam.

"Adia, no!" Reya called, still fighting her brother as Adia charged for the shadow.

Adia teleported behind Sam, but before she could stab him, he snaked his foot under hers. She fell and his hands were on her throat. White Guardians surrounded them, one locking her arms behind her back. Adia thrashed, trying to teleport, but she hadn't been able to practice the gift in Echo. She only recalled doing it occasionally as Sam's submissive queen. It took her years to slowly gain control of her actions. Even when she had, she was always being watched. She wished she had more time to practice teleporting as Sam squeezed her throat. She was too panicked to even work her gift on him.

Sam released Adia's throat after a dagger struck his back. Reya breathed heavily from down the hall, a collapsed Coye behind her.

Reya smiled.

Sam transformed into his shadow self and flew to Reya. They fought as shadow and warrior while Adia feebly caught her breath.

Adia stumbled as she ran to them, crashing against a wall. She pulled out her gun, thought better of it, and reached for her knives. Once her dizziness passed, she ran until she was jumping on Sam's back, and stabbed him. She was pulled off by a White Guardian. She fought tirelessly, exerting more energy than she had left. Adia heaved painful breaths as Reya was thrown down the hall.

Her body rolled.

Her eyes fluttered before shutting.

Sam strode to Reya and picked her up by her white hair.

She didn't struggle.

Adia's hands slipped in black blood as she crawled to them. She tried to call Sam's name, direct his attention to her, but she had no voice.

Reya's eyes snapped open, and she smirked as a sword broke through Sam's chest from behind. Reya dropped to the floor.

Adia's father strolled casually down the hall, his hands in his pockets. White Guardians charged at him before spasming. They all vanished in clouds of smoke. Her father stepped next to Coye, whose sword had penetrated Sam.

# CHAPTER THIRTY-EIGHT

## *Power Hungry Animals*

**Coye**
**Lehran**
**Age 8**

Coye's lip curled at the sound of his baby sister's crying. She was a weak, pitiful thing. Her screaming was her only strength. His parents shared his opinion. Or maybe it was their opinion to begin with. Coye struggled remembering which were his true feelings and which he had been molded to have. Either way, his parents' bedchamber was far from the baby's while Coye's was next door. He used a pillow to muffle the wails. There was a pause, and he lifted the pillow, hearing a distinctive slap.

Her crying grew louder.

Another slap.

Coye crept out of his room, armed with his favorite sword. He slowly opened the baby's room to see one of the maiden's lifting his sister from her bed as she bawled. The maiden reeled her hand back.

An anger Coye had never known fueled him. He drove his sword into the maiden. He caught his sister awkwardly with one arm, bringing her to his chest. Her breathing hitched many times as her crying subsided. He paid the dead maiden no attention as he carried Reya back to his room.

Reya was a pitiful thing, but if she died, he would be forced to become king someday.

Coye made a spot on the floor for Reya to sleep. When her crying wouldn't ease, he carried her to the kitchen to make a bottle.

"You!" Coye called to a passing maiden. "Fetch me a bottle for the princess. Now!"

"I can take the princess," the maiden said.

Coye's nostrils flared. "Bottle, *now*."

"Of course, Prince."

Coye held the bottle for Reya on his bed and watched her fall asleep. Something shifted in his chest. His scowl softened. Then he smelled poop.

"Repulsive thing!" he grumbled as he carried Reya back to her room to change her cloth diaper.

\* \* \*

## Coye
## Lehran
## Age 16

Coye spat blood.

"Weak, repulsive thing!" King Amol—his father—shouted at him. "She is a female! She is a child! And she bested you!"

Coye's hands shook as he pushed himself back to a stand. His vision tinted red as he stared back at the king, who adjusted his rings that were stained with Coye's blood.

King Amol eyed him. "You lost out of *kindness*."

Coye did his best to look repulsed by the idea. Still, he suffered a blow to the skull. Hot blood slid down his neck as his vision pulsed. Another blow, this time to his stomach. Coye spat more blood.

"She is your *weakness*! You will never be king!" He grabbed Coye by the throat. The jagged rings bit into his skin. "You won't even be a warrior prince!"

Coye was released, falling hard on the stone floor. He shut his eyes as he bled from his skull. His father left, commanding the maidens to leave him.

When Coye awoke, he was in a bath, fully clothed. The water was a mixture of red and blue. Reya poured blue powder into his bath. Her knuckles were raw from their earlier battle. Coye grabbed her wrists and forced her hands under the water. She didn't resist, only stared at him in silence with her large silver eyes. If they spoke, the maidens would hear. They would tell their parents. Coye would need another healing bath.

*"You did good,"* he mouthed.

*"You let me win,"* she mouthed back but smiled. When she retrieved her hands, they were healed.

He matched her smile. *"Never."*

\* \* \*

**Coye**
**Lehran**
**Age 28**

Coye passed Reya in the hallway of their home without meeting her eyes. He had long stopped letting her win their battles, but she had grown stronger and faster than him. Now, she would be crowned Queen of Lehran. A fate worse than death. Once he saw that Reya would be the one to inherit the kingdom, Coye replaced his kindness with cruelty. Not because he stopped loving his sister, but to ensure she would leave Lehran and strive for the future she deserved. Since King Amol had two children, one was permitted to forfeit the kingdom for the other child to inherit. If both were to leave, there would be a tournament to win the kingdom. The winner would be whoever slayed the king's children.

Coye opened the door to leave but stopped at the sight of a blond, blue-eyed man holding flowers. Reya brushed past Coye, shooting him a warning look. Their parents were away at an important meeting on Alden.

The man was there for Reya.

The flowers were for Reya.

They were a *romantic* gesture.

Coye's mind spiraled as he continued outside, resisting the urge to glance back at Reya and the man. He had walked all the way to the river when an idea struck him.

Coye watched Reya return with *her date* hours later. Coye remained hidden until Reya stepped inside.

"You wish to threaten me regarding your sister," the man spoke in perfect Lehranian.

Coye smirked. He kept his hands in his pockets and slowly approached the stranger. "I want you to marry her."

The man arched his brows.

"If she stays, she will inherit the kingdom. If you know how to speak in Lehranian, then you must know what ruling a planet like this could do to someone's soul. Convince her to marry you, leave with you, and never come back."

"You want to rule this world so much you would have your sister marry a stranger?"

Coye stepped closer. "What is your name?"

"Lamarse. Son of Orion."

Coye tilted his head. "You would give away your identity to a stranger, Son of Orion?"

"I believed you to be a threat when I first saw you, so I searched your mind."

Coye breathed through his rage until it settled into annoyance. "If you do not wish to marry her, will you offer her refuge protected by Orion?"

"She thinks you hate her," Lamarse said.

Coye looked to the starry night. "My kindness gave her scars."

"What did your cruelty give her?"

Coye refused to answer.

"She has my heart, Coye," Lamarse said. "I will marry her if she allows it. If not, I will do everything in my power to convince her to make Carinthia her home."

"Thank you, Son of Orion."

\* \* \*

**Coye**
**Lehran**
**Age 29**

Coye sprinted down the path to his father's ship. Guards were on his tail. He had been caught listening in on a meeting discussing Lehran's attack on Carinthia. They would strike during his sister's wedding to Lamarse. Reya foolishly gave away Lamarse's heritage when their father threatened to kill her fiancé. She believed her revelation would save Lamarse from their father's wrath. It only fueled it more. Their parents' plan was to attack Carinthia. The goal wasn't to win but assassinate Reya and anyone whom she favored.

"Why are you running?"

Coye slowed at the sight of a beautiful woman in the river. He ran faster, not allowing his confusion to distract him from reaching the ship to call Reya.

The woman was now before him and Coye swung his fist, but it went through her.

"That wasn't nice," she said.

Coye fell through the ghost, trying to hit her again. "What are you?"

"My name is Shemu, and I'm here to offer a deal."

\* \* \*

**Lamarse**
**Portland, OR**
**Day of Adia's First Deal**

Lamarse was a ghost standing outside of his wrecked car.

His body sat unconscious next to Lou. His father stood, holding out his hand to Adia. No, not his father. The shadow.

"ADIA, NO!" Lamarse stepped forward.

"If you join her, you will never be Reborn again." His mother stood as an angel behind him.

"I-I have to," he said. "Please, Mother. Help me save my little girl!"

"I understand."

Lamarse wanted to speak to his mother some more, wished that time would stop long enough to embrace her, but Adia was now touching the shadow's hand.

Lamarse's eyes lingered on Lou before he jumped to Adia and the shadow. When he came to, he was in the form of a lion.

\* \* \*

**Lamarse**
**Shadow World**
**Time Unknown**

There was no way of tracing time as Lamarse remained hidden with the other lions, watching from afar as his daughter befriended Shemu. He had witnessed Adia's outburst of wanting to go home and watched as Shemu chased her. Lamarse broke out in a run only for Coye to teleport before him.

Lamarse moved to attack.

"Search my mind, Lamarse. Search it!"

Lamarse tried to move around Coye, halting at the sight of Adia running through a barrier. Shemu paced before it, unable to pass.

"She will be safe in Consumption for now," Coye said from behind. "Once Shemu moves onto a new world, the souls in Consumption are freed. Since this is her world, she will be able to come back. I've seen it done before."

Lamarse turned to Coye, still in his lion form.

"Search my mind," Coye said. "*Please.* Reya needs your help. She is…" Coye's eyes blackened. "He owns her."

"*You did this,*" Lamarse spoke telepathically.

"Search. My. Mind." Coye looked to where Shemu still paced. "Before he discovers you."

So Lamarse did. He saw Coye's life sped through passing thoughts. Saw his deal with Shemu. Saw how Shemu tricked him into believing the deal would save Reya and not trap her soul. He believed his soul would be the only one taken. Believed Reya would be safely on Carinthia. When he discovered Reya was trapped in her personal hell, he fought Shemu and lost. He slowly gained back Shemu's trust, moving from world to world until he became Shemu's second-in-command, and Reya became Shemu's loyal queen.

"*Your father visited me once in my dreams,*" Coye thought. "*Told me you would arrive as a lion with blue eyes. Told me to be loyal to Shemu. To be patient. Because one day, I would kill Shemu.*"

# CHAPTER THIRTY-NINE

*Fire*

**Adia**
**City of Souls**
**80 Years After Broken Deal (ABD)**

S am's face flashed many emotions as Coye twisted his sword. Black blood poured from the shadow's mouth. He let out a gurgled laugh before vanishing.

Sam was gone.

*Dead.*

The hall was now deserted of enemies as Coye sheathed his sword. He walked to Adia and held out his hand. "We have time for you to take a healing bath," he said and there was no menace in his tone. No cruelty in his silver eyes.

She took his hand, wishing she could speak the questions spinning in her mind, but she still had no voice.

"I'll help her," Reya said, and stepped to Adia's side.

Coye moved to her father, and they gripped each other's shoulders before hugging.

"You did well, Brother," her father told Coye.

Adia stared back at her father, wondering if this was somehow a trick being played by Sam before limping with Reya to the bath chamber.

It only dawned on Adia as Reya filled the tub that the Seven hadn't been alerted by Coye, so they weren't coming. She realized other things, like how her healing baths were arranged by Coye, and he enforced privacy while she was taking them. How he had been the one to open her father's cell every night so they could train in Echo. How Reya looked rather well even though she was supposed to be getting tortured daily by Coye.

"Did you always know about your brother?" Adia asked when her throat healed enough to speak.

"No." Reya stood guard by the door, even though they were sure no other foes roamed the castle. "Not until he opened Lamarse's door the first day we were here. Before we visited you in Echo."

"Did Austin know?"

"Only Lamarse and Orion."

"What do we do now?"

"You, Lamarse, and Coye will teleport us to the Shadow Core. It will take some time, but they won't see us coming."

"Four against thousands. I don't like those odds."

"We won't be alone. Like I said, it will take some time...to transport all the monsters and hunters locked in the dungeon."

* * *

**Adia**
**Shadow Core**
**80 Years ABD**

Adia, Reya, Coye, and her father stood before the Shadow Core's castle with an army behind them. Adia's back warmed. She twisted to see the dragon lady blowing flames. The monster made no expression of apology. Adia faced forward and locked eyes with her father. He smiled back.

They marched to the castle doors. Adia aimed at the first Core Guard, but before she could shoot, the dragon lady charged past her. The sounds of the Core Guard's screams as he was eaten alerted more to come. Adia was swept into battle, unable to pay attention to anyone else's fight while she fought.

Her goal was to kill as many Core Guards as she could before Talena came out. Once she did, Adia would be hypnotized. Then her fight would be internally.

Adia cut the head off a large snake as Reya jumped over its tail to attack a lizard-looking monster. Adia was losing track of which monsters were allied to them, so she focused on the ones dressed in black with the Shadow Core crest that matched her scar.

Adia halted at the sight of Talena. Adia tried to flee but was caught by Eris. She could feel her mind altering. Feel her fear changing to hatred toward her allies. Talena's gift was not too differently from Adia's. She yanked the tether connecting her to Talena and pushed those emotions back.

Talena was too strong. While Adia may have had eighty years to practice her gifts, Talena had centuries. Adia leaned into Eris' hold that was now easing.

"Thank you," Adia said to him.

She placed a shaking hand on his chest as she turned to face him. He sneered in revulsion. Then jolted as her dagger dug into his stomach. She stole the hatchet he had conjured, but before she could aim it for his head, Talena's powers burned through her. Talena screamed for Adia to obey her. Adia gritted her teeth, fighting for her will to remain strong.

A massive lion jumped over Adia, his claws digging into Talena's chest.

Talena screamed as Adia's father broke through her mind. He roared in her face.

Adia sprinted for them and stabbed through Talena's skull with the hatchet. She laughed in victory, her watering eyes meeting her father's as he transformed back into a man. His smile dropped as he turned, but it was too late. He was pinned by a sword to the ground. Ebony stood feet away, wearing a devilish smile. Her father took one stuttering breath. A bright light exploded from his wound.

Her father disappeared.

Adia threw the hatchet, but Ebony dodged. Adia chased

after her, yanking on Ebony's tether, but the only emotion Adia could recall was rage. She sent it to Ebony, who twisted, snarling. Adia ducked, evading the dagger Ebony used telekinesis to throw.

Ebony continued down the hall of the castle. She was almost to the Throne Room when arms snaked around Adia, teleporting her away. She twisted out of Coye's grasp.

"What are you doing?" she yelled at him. He had taken them to a dark room.

"Fulfilling Lamarse's plan," Coye whispered.

Someone stepped from the dark. It was Adia. Or someone pretending to be.

"Go," Coye told Adia's doppelganger, who sprinted away.

"I don't understand," Adia said.

"She is the piece of your soul who was trapped in Consumption," Coye explained.

"But she died."

"She hid. Lamarse needed two of you. He made everyone believe she had died. Made sure Austin would believe it. That he would make the Shadow Core believe it as well."

"Why?"

"Time will tell." Coye gently guided her to a tunnel hidden behind a painting. He stopped abruptly, turning to her. He handed her something small. "Make sure all are there. Before Talena is resurrected from Hell. When the time comes, aim for yourself."

Coye disappeared before she could ask him to elaborate his confusing command. She listened for voices and heard the new Seven, Mal, chant. The tunnel glowed and Adia's stomach plummeted as she feared she would be discovered. She couldn't see what was happening inside the Throne Room but heard Eris walk in. There was a pounding. A scream. Adia hurried back to the tunnel's entrance, but she couldn't pass. Whatever Mal chanted trapped her within the tunnel.

Coye popped into view. "Please go back, Adia."

"I heard Reya get hurt. What's going on?"

His eyes sharpened, but before he could answer, a beast jumped on him. The monster's teeth bit into Coye's shoulder, dragging him away. Adia pounded on the enchanted barrier.

"Go!" Coye yelled, and then his voice was silenced.

Adia trembled as she headed back through the tunnel, stopping at the door that would lead her into the Throne Room.

"What is this?" she heard Ebony ask. "Mal? What have you done?"

"They are trying to destroy us," Mal replied. "No one can enter. No one can leave while we resurrect Talena."

"What of her?" Eris drawled.

"Reya will be Talena's meal when she resurrects," Ebony answered cheerfully.

"I meant *her*."

"There will be nothing human about Adia when we are done," Ebony replied. "Maybe Talena will share Reya with her. Adia?" A beat of silence. "Where is your tattoo?"

Adia stared down at the small object Coye had given her. She took a deep breath through her nose and stepped into the Throne Room. She saw her other self was stripped of clothes and weapons. Her skin shined with oil. Adia met Reya's knowing eyes and then Ebony's shocked ones. Adia lit the lighter Coye had handed her and threw it at her other self, who lit up in flames.

"Mal! Release us!" Ebony yelled, climbing onto her throne as the fire spread.

Mal was kneeling, his arms raised as he chanted. Flames moved as though they were alive and hunting. Eris conjured a shield, but the fire twisted, burning his hands. He tried shaking the flames off, yelling.

Hesta burned too quickly for Adia to see.

Seren moved as a blur throughout the room. She wouldn't be able to outrun the flames forever.

Adia held Reya as they watched the others burn. Ebony sprinted around the room, screaming as the fiery waves chased her.

Mal's chanting slowed as he stood. He locked eyes with Adia and bowed. Adia wasn't the only Shadow Core to overpower their Allegiance Bond. She wanted to know the sorcerer's story. Wanted to know if Orion was behind him selling his soul or if Mal had been tricked like Adia. She watched him die, praying for his soul and Reya's. And then her own.

# CHAPTER FORTY

## *Never Let Me Go*

**Adia**
**Passage**
**Time Unknown**

Adia continued hugging Reya, her eyes shut tight, teeth clenched as though the flames were still burning them.

"Adia?" Reya moved away.

They stared at each other, wide-eyed in an unfamiliar white room. They laughed, unable to stop. Adia lay on her back, wiping her tears of joy away.

Reya examined her cloak and gasped. "Where are my daggers?"

Their laughing stopped for a beat before bursting from them in unison.

"Did you see Ebony's face?" Adia asked, taking calming breaths, her smile still large.

"Ebony's? What about Shemu's? I'll be living in that blissful moment forever. If this really is..." Reya searched the white room, doubt growing on her face. Reya never believed that even if they did defeat the Shadow Core, she would reach Heaven.

Heels clicked against the white floor. Adia and Reya sat up, composing themselves. Reya's hands were clenched, her guard up.

A female stopped before them. Her smile was radiant as she said, "They are waiting for you." She continued walking and the white wall became two grand doors as it opened.

Reya and Adia exchanged the same startled look. Music sounded in the distance. Birds were singing. Sunlight filtered into the room.

Reya stood and reached down a hand for Adia to take. "Come on."

Adia hesitated. She survived on nothing but a sliver of hope that all her training and torture for the past eighty years would lead to this moment—paradise. She would break if she stepped out and saw the Seven laughing because they had gripped her mind and made her hallucinate defeating them.

"We've been through much worse than walking through a heavenly door," Reya told her.

Adia's smile didn't last long. They approached the grand door and stepped through it, smelling fresh air. The sun was blinding, but when her eyes adjusted, Adia flinched. She stood on a large platform overlooking a sea of people. Birds small and large soared in the sky. The music was drowned out by the multitude's applause.

The unfamiliar woman stepped to the microphone. "The Shadow Core has been destroyed! You are free!" The cheering became an eruption of sound.

"All of them were trapped in Shadow Worlds?" Adia asked.

"Most, yes," the woman answered.

"I know you." Reya's voice was quiet, looking at the woman in awe.

"I am Helena." Her eyes locked with Adia's. "Your grandmother."

Adia stared in a daze as Helena turned back to face the crowd.

Helena lifted Adia's hand to the heavenly sky. "Adia will hereby be known as Queen of Shadows!"

The crowd parted at the center as they cheered.

Adia turned to Reya, who had stepped back. Adia reached

out her hand, but Reya shook her head. Mal and Coye also stood on the platform. Reya walked to her brother, and he pulled her into a strong hug. Adia and Coye's eyes met, and he nodded in greeting.

"Go on," Helena said to Adia, gesturing to the path.

Adia walked down the path as people offered their gratitude. They touched her cloak, kissed her hand. They became a blur of tears and joy as she tried to greet them all. She wished Reya was by her side, but as she turned back to the stage, she saw a crowd had formed there, praising Mal, Coye, and Reya for their heroic acts.

Adia never exhausted as she continued to meet the saved souls. She was sure hours or maybe days had passed. Time moved differently after spending so much of it in Hell. Her former self would have hated being surrounded by this many people, but she rejoiced in their love and grace.

She reached another parting in the crowd, stilling when she recognized Crystal. She was older than she had been in the City of Souls. Crystal assured Adia she had lived a long life, but her soul appeared twenty-five after passing on Earth. Brianne stood by her, offering Adia a tentative hug.

James Reddick greeted her next, having not seen him since she escaped the Shadow World. Elizabeth and Garrett stood next in the line.

Adia remembered her time in Consumption. Remembered everything with clarity and peace.

Countless souls she had only known on Alternate-Earth were assembled. She shook the hands of hunters she fought with on Earth and in the Shadow World. She held back tears as she received each of their thanks.

Peter Starling beamed at Adia, and she saw Austin in his smile. Adia wanted to say so many things to her father in-law, but what came out was, "I really enjoyed reading your book."

Peter laughed, tears overlapping his hazel eyes. He told her how lucky his son was to have found her. Adia assured him she was the lucky one.

Adia's emotion broke seeing Dallas and Cora holding hands. She ran into Dallas' arms, and he gave her a bear hug. Cora told her how proud she was as they embraced. And how sorry. Dallas caught Adia up on the little he knew of Austin. How Dallas reunited with Cora in Heaven and were given a Union ceremony by Helena. They walked Adia through the crowd as she greeted more souls. She stopped at the sight of her parents.

Her father dropped the arm around her mother's waist and ran to Adia. He picked her up and swung her around, making her feel like a child. Adia held on tightly, breathing in his familiar scent. Memories of her childhood sparked to life. She remembered him teaching her how to read. Remembered him smiling at her as she helped him make pancakes. Recalled dancing with him in their living room while her mother laughed from the sofa before joining them. She remembered eating cake for breakfast on her birthdays. She grasped even her memories as a baby. Him holding her for the first time, the pure love in his eyes as he beheld his daughter. Him waking up at all hours of the night to make sure she was safely in her crib. Him whispering how much he loved her while rocking her to sleep, vowing to always protect her.

"I am so proud of you," he said, pulling from their hug. Tears streamed down his face. "You were incredibly brave."

Adia sobbed as she fell into her mother's arms. "I'm sorry!"

"Hey!" Her mother held Adia's face. "*You* have nothing to be sorry for. You..." Her eyes brimmed with tears. "You are amazing. Look around, Adia. You did this. You freed them."

Adia searched for Reya, even though she was out of sight. "I didn't do it alone."

\* \* \*

**Jax**
**Alden**
**80 Years ABD**

"You brought the bars, right?" Jax asked Austin as they stared down the tunnel.

"You mean the protein bars you told me ten times to pack? Yeah. Next to my gun."

"Good. Because I am definitely getting stabbed."

"Come on."

"Woah." Jax gripped Austin's arm. "We can't go in blindly."

"Is this about your fear of caves?"

"I don't fear anything. I'm immortal."

"You hate caves."

"They're cold, dark, and often slimy." And they reminded him of Abyss.

"We won't be going in blindly. I can see the curve of the tunnel already." Austin held up his palm and a small orb glowed in his palm. "For you, friend."

Jax blew out a breath, shaking the nerves from his hand. "I have this feeling. Like maybe…we didn't think this through."

"This is *your* plan!"

"Exactly! Aldens are crazy!"

"You said children are in there." Austin didn't wait for Jax to be convinced; he entered the tunnel cave.

Jax cursed, pulling at his hair, before following Austin.

They walked for an hour before reaching the opening of the cave where cloaked men chanted as they circled terrified men, women, and children. Torches of blue fire were lit at every curve of the cave.

Austin made to move, but Jax stopped him. "We have to think this through," he whispered.

Austin's eyes were intense. "Backup?"

"Maybe."

Austin looked incredulous. "It's too late. I told you we needed more people." He jabbed Jax in the chest. "You said we could handle it."

"We can," Jax whispered. "I just really don't want to be turned into a goat. You know?"

Austin ran a hand over his face. "Is that a possibility?"

"They are sorcerers."

"What?" Austin's eyes were large. "Jax!"

"Okay, okay! Let me think."

The cave wall shook. A gust of wind pushed them out of the tunnel to the circle of Aldens. Gunshots fired, and Jax jumped into action, joining Austin's side as they fought. Invisible hands gripped Jax, throwing him across the cave into blue fire. He rolled, hissing as the burns healed. The blue fire chased him.

"This one won't die," one of the sorcerers spoke as Jax panted.

Austin was using his light to fight, but it was weakening. He hadn't practiced it as well as his other gifts.

"Put them with the others," a deep voice said.

Jax and Austin were bound by invisible ropes.

"Hey," Jax whispered to him. "I need those bars."

Austin shot him a look. "Sure. Let me just reach into my jacket and get them for you."

"Thanks, friend."

Austin nodded to the blue fire where his jacket was being burned.

"I won't die," Jax said, looking at the innocent people they were amongst. "I will kill everyone here!"

"I. *Know.*" Austin tugged at his invisible restraints.

Jax noticed their wrists were bare. Somehow, the sorcerers had removed their weapons and devices. "Some rescue team we are," Jax said. "Next time, you plan the mission."

"You said that before."

"And you keep giving me control."

"You're the god!"

"You're the future—" Jax's words were ripped from him.

"Future what?" Austin pinned him with an exasperated look.

"Can't tell you." Jax was starting to shake, the monster eager to take control. "I hope you're Reborn with a more useful gift than an *orb*."

One of the sorcerers approached Jax. Holding a sword made of blue fire against his neck. Jax clenched his teeth through the pain.

"Amazing," the sorcerer spoke, burning Jax again. "What would happen if I were to cut your entire head off?"

Jax shut his eyes, waiting for the inevitable.

A gunshot sounded and when Jax opened his eyes, half of the sorcerer's head was missing. The cave darkened as each of the blue flames went out. Jax caught sight of a cloaked figure running along the walls before darkness fell on them. He heard grunts and the sound of a blade cutting through flesh.

Austin's orb partially lit the cave, and Jax realized his hands and feet were free as he came to stand. He caught sight of the cloaked figure moving through the sorcerers as someone shot at them from the shadows. He wondered why the sorcerers weren't using their magic to defend before theorizing the blue fire had been their power source.

"I really should have let you do the research first," Jax said to Austin, who stared at the darkest corner of the cave, where the shooter killed the last sorcerer. His orb grew brighter.

The cloaked figure approached Jax. She removed her hood and threw something at his chest. He stared down at the roll that had dropped to his feet. Slowly, his eyes moved to meet Reya's.

* * *

**Austin**
**Alden**
**80 Years ABD**

Noise faded as Austin's world stopped. He stared at the shooter, who stood in darkness even though Austin's gift made it so he was supposed to see through it. His orb shook in his hand as he stepped closer. His light broke through her darkness until he saw her face. She lowered her gun and straightened. He focused on her aura: on the star surrounded by shadows. Only this time, the shadows weren't closing in on her light, controlling her actions. They were hers to wield.

His chest rose and fell as she moved to him. She caught him by his forearms, and he stared down at her bare wrist, unable to believe she was real.

"It's over?" he whispered.

Adia nodded.

"You were Reborn?"

She nodded again and held his face. He let out a stuttering breath. Then she was kissing him.

\* \* \*

Austin couldn't stop looking over at Adia as they guided the people out through the tunnel. Couldn't take his eyes from her as they organized the route to fly everyone home. Memorized every detail of her face as they sat around a table at Earth Guardianship a day later, and she told the story of defeating the Seven Core. Stared at her in awe as she showed them how her shadows worked, explained how she used them to put out the blue fire in the cave and controlled their emotions to not fight back.

Jax said to Reya, "What gift did you get?"

Reya rolled her eyes, but her smile was bright. She looked as she did on Earth, even though that hadn't been her natural form. She let go of Jax's hand, and a dagger appeared from nothing at the tips of her fingers.

Jax gawked at her. "Do it again, please."

She did, creating a longer blade this time.

Jax kissed her. She hesitated at first, but then her hands went to his messy curls as their kissing became more passionate.

Austin was back to staring at Adia. He looked for signs of the hell he knew she went through. Her eyes shined as she observed Jax and Reya. She met Austin's stare and her smile faltered. "We have a lot to tell each other."

"We do," he agreed, his voice sounding hoarse.

"You won't like hearing most of it."

His throat tightened. No, but he still needed to hear it. Needed to understand the source of her fear when she woke up screaming in the middle of the night. Or why he needed to assure her that no one was controlling her—that her thoughts were her own.

Austin reached inside his pocket, remembering what he had grabbed that morning—the first morning in eighty years that he didn't need to imagine waking up next to Adia.

"A story for a story?" she asked him, a tear rolling down her cheek. "It may take a while."

He grabbed her hand and kissed her knuckles. Then he gently placed her wedding ring back where it belonged. "We have time."

# EPILOGUE

## *I Bet My Life*

**Adia**
**Carinthia**
**100 Years ABD**

The wind swept through Adia's short hair. She smiled at the scenery flying by them, sitting in the backseat of a car they borrowed from Alexon Manor. The sun warmed her face, and she remembered how for eighty years, she lived without sunlight. Austin held Adia's hand in the backseat. His gasp matching hers as the ocean came into view.

Reya's arms were resting outside the window, her gold wedding ring sparkling as Jax drove down the winding road. He had been Reya's husband for eleven years. Orion performed their Union.

They found a secluded part of the beach and set camp. Jax's innocence had been declared by Orion earlier that day, and they were celebrating. Orion invited them to dine at Alexon Manor, but Reya mentioned a beach perfect for stargazing.

The sun was setting, but the air was still warm. Adia and Austin set their tent and changed into their swimsuits. Jax chased Reya. She spun around and shoved him into the water.

Adia laughed and then she was being lifted by Austin. He carried her over his shoulder as he ran for the water. "No!" Adia screamed as a wave crashed over them. There was a dizzying moment under the warm water before she found the surface.

Adia coughed and saw Austin's sheepish smile.

She gave him a challenging smile before conjuring her shadows beneath the water. They snaked around Austin's ankles, pulling him to her.

"I'm sorry, I'm sorry, I'm sorry!" he said quickly, kissing her all over her face.

Another wave crashed over them. Austin lit his orb underwater, and Adia found the surface quicker this time. They swam to the shallow edge, where the waves were kinder. Adia threw back her head, her hair tickling her shoulders as she slightly sunk into the soft sand. The moving water was like a warm bath. Austin's kisses along her neck felt divine.

Jax built a fire at nightfall. They exchanged stories, eating a noodle dish Reya had cooked. Jax embellished as he always did while Reya corrected the exaggerated parts, looking both amused and annoyed by her husband.

Adia stared up at the stars, feeling peace like when she was in Passage. Reya didn't remember their time between worlds. Nor did Austin whenever he was Reborn. Adia did, though. She remembered every face she had passed in the crowd. Recalled seeing her friends and parents. She pictured Dallas and Cora in Heaven. Pictured the life they continued together and knew, without a doubt, they were happy. Still, she yearned to see them again.

"Lamarse," Austin said, using Adia's arm to point up at the night sky that was so different than the one on Earth 323. He moved her hand, tracing the stars until she noticed the lion. Austin directed her to another constellation in the shape of an eye. "Cora." He then traced a sun out of stars. "Adia. That one is my favorite."

"I wonder what constellation name we'll soon choose."

Austin slowly lowered their hands. "What?"

"We will have to carry on the tradition." She smiled, keeping her eyes on the night sky until she slowly met his.

"Really?" The hope he radiated made her heart burst.

"Really," she confirmed.

"I am so sorry for throwing you in the water."

Adia laughed as her throat stung with emotion. "It was warm at least."

"How far?"

"Not far. I found out this morning."

"You told him?" Reya's smile was bright. She moved away from Jax who continued kissing her neck. She pushed him away.

"What's going on?" He sounded dazed.

"Adia's pregnant," Reya answered.

"She knew before me?" Austin asked.

"She was there when I found out," Adia said.

"This calls for a celebration!" Jax turned up the music that had been quietly playing in the car. He grabbed Reya by her hips, and they danced around the fire.

Austin's hands were shaking as he reached for Adia's. "We wanted this for so long. How are you feeling?" He walked backwards on the sand, gently pulling her along. They started swaying to the music, their bodies pressed so closely, she could feel his heart beating against hers.

"I feel as you do," she answered.

"Excited but also terrified?"

Adia sighed. "Exactly."

"Hey." He lifted her chin, staring deep into her eyes. Moments from their past blinked in her mind. Good and bad. Terrifying and peaceful. They survived a lot. Except this was new. This was their child being born into a universe of monsters. A universe Austin will become Master of someday. "We got this," he said.

"We got this," she agreed.

### The End

## TO MY BOOKTOK FRIENDS,

You revived the spark in me that lit my motivation to finish this trilogy. My first attempt at publishing Souls was a disaster. My second, I rewrote and released without much thought. I only wanted something tangible for me to read because I love this world and the characters so much and I owed it to them to try. Then I found readers on booktok, read the reviews, applied criticism to my future editions, hired an editor (Sharina Wunderink), and now we're here. At the end of the third book. I'm so glad we made it. Thank you for coming along this journey with me.

Happy reading,

*Megan Wolters*

# SNEAK PEEK

## Blood and Fire
*Coming Soon*

### *Arsonist's Lullaby*

E ldrin searched the dimly lit tavern, pausing on a hooded figure staring back. He ground his teeth, fighting the paranoia sweeping over him. He had seen the hooded man spying on him before.

Eldrin chewed his food mechanically as another threat entered his peripheral.

"Caro!"

Eldrin cursed under his breath as a nasty looking group stalked toward him. They all varied in skin color. Green, silver, and blue. Three men from three different worlds. Worlds that the Caro Empire invaded.

The silver man—a Gyan—spat on Eldrin's plate. "You will pay for my people!"

Eldrin pushed his half-finished meal away, feigning causality. "Wasn't me."

"You Caro warriors are all the same!" the blue man—a Percian

—said. He withdrew his sword.

Eldrin noted the blue tint of poison on the Percian's sword and considered his options.

*Run.*

*Fight.*

*Die.*

"I am not a warrior of Caro," Eldrin spoke, his tone calm.

"Your brand says differently." The green man—a Velchi—nodded to Eldrin's scar.

"A long, unbelievable story I'm afraid." Eldrin studied the design that had been magically burned into his skin over a century ago. Three rings intertwined around his wrist like snake tails. At the center was the head of Caro. Only the most loyal of Caro warriors were branded with an Allegiance Bond.

One of the men growled in response.

*Maybe today wouldn't be a bad day to die,* Eldrin thought. *I was given more years than most mortals were granted. More years than Calla was given.*

At the thought of Calla, Eldrin decided today he would die.

"Shall we go outside?" Eldrin suggested. "Easier to clean up my blood and vomit out there."

The men eyed each other before shoving Eldrin to the sticky floor. They yanked him to his feet and dragged him out the door, into the snowy night. They threw him on the road.

Eldrin welcomed the rocky snow against his face; the beautiful contrast of fire and ice it created. He closed his eyes and waited for the blade to strike him. They would be too dumb to keep his body, although selling his remains would make them beyond rich.

"Eldrin?" a female voice spoke from a distance. "Eldrin!"

"Another Caro?" one of the men asked.

"Don't..." Eldrin could only manage the one word, meeting the eyes of a Caro lady. She had been as foolish as him for not hiding her Allegiance scar.

Undiluted anger glinted in the men's eyes.

The heat started in Eldrin's back. He didn't think over his

options or the consequences. There was only one choice he would make. Only one option he would always choose over running, dying, or fighting for his life.

*Protect.*

Fire spewed from his body. It was a release Eldrin craved but rarely gave into. Fiery wings sprung from his back, burning his clothes to ash. His brown skin became impenetrable scales.

He was a man but also a dragon.

The silver man swung his poisonous blade.

Eldrin sucked in the icy air and exhaled. One breath was all it took. The men became ash.

Eldrin looked at the lady—a woman he had only met once before. He was supposed to kill her back on Caro but helped her escape.

His wife, Calla, paid the price.

The lady looked well enough, if not cold and hungry. She stared at Eldrin before understanding flashed in her large eyes.

Eldrin was never a Caro.

He was a Fire Lord.

A draemaki.

One of the last.

The woman stepped forward, ignoring the people shouting at Eldrin's monstrous appearance. The pain of loss stabbed at Eldrin, electrifying his senses. His wings flapped once, and he shot into the air.

* * *

Eldrin landed in a small forest where his scales softened into smooth skin. The Caro brand on his wrist never went away no matter which form he took. He nakedly trekked until he reached a hostel near a river where he stole some clothes before checking in. He was exhausted, not from the power he had released or the miles he had traveled, but from the emotions that spiraled inside of him.

Tonight, he would sleep.

Tomorrow, he didn't know.

His throat burned as he collapsed onto the thin mattress tucked in the corner of the room. He stared up at the cracked ceiling and let his tears fall. Another release he rarely allowed.

He awoke hours later no longer alone.

Eldrin beheld the cloaked stranger from the tavern. He stood against the door, his legs crossed, and his arms folded. Eldrin searched the man's face, but it was in shadow.

"I require your help," the man said, "but first, I must tell you a story."

At Eldrin's silence, the cloaked man continued.

"There was a god, Aurum. He ruled over Gradia."

At this, Eldrin broke his silence. "Gradia no longer exists."

"It does in reincarnation form."

Eldrin's fingers twitched, but he let the stranger continue.

"Gradian blood is cursed. Those who drink it, enhance their life—their power. Drink a Gradian god's blood, and you will conquer worlds.

"Aurum wished to retire into the heavens, not realizing his blood was cursed."

"His mistress cursed it," Eldrin said. "She was a Ruin witch."

"You know some of the story."

"I know the witch's son, Jax."

"The curse worked differently for each family member. Aurum was cursed to spend eternity in purgatory. Jax is cursed with immortality tainted by monstrous triggers."

"And Annora was cursed to be reincarnated, living out the same tragic ending. Jax speaks a lot about her."

"None of my Mortal Guards could ever stop Annora from being murdered. Stop her lover, Ignis from conquering. Stop the planet from being destroyed. Ten worlds I have failed. Now, the curse has reached an eleventh." The man lowered his hood and Eldrin gaped at the famous face.

"Orion," Eldrin spoke, standing to respectfully bow.

"I ask for your help, Eldrin, Lord of Fire. To infiltrate, spy, and protect. To break this curse before more planets are lost."

Orion held out a metal box—a chronicle of the mission he was anointing Eldrin.

"I'm not a Mortal Guard anymore," Eldrin said, sorrow tightening his chest. "I will fail as I have failed before."

"I see many futures," Orion said. "This *curse* has me in the dark. I prayed for a solution. A month ago, I dreamt of you. I know you are no longer one of my Mortal Guards, but I beg you for your help anyways."

Eldrin stared into Orion's pale blue eyes and shivered at the desperation in them.

"Aurum and Jax are my friends," Orion said. "Breaking this curse is important to me." The Master of the Universe's throat bobbed. "I will ensure your debt with Caro is paid."

Eldrin stared at his Allegiance Bond branded on his wrist before holding out his hand.

Orion placed the chronicle into his palm.

"What planet have the Gradian people been reincarnated on?" Eldrin opened the chronicle. An image of a beautiful young lady projected above the metal box.

"Earth 118," Orion answered. "The Gradians have been there for fifty years. The curse resets differently every time."

"I'll be working with Earth Guardianship, then?" Eldrin asked. "Starling's team?"

"You will be solo. Your mission is to spy as an Ignite—a Gradian with fire magic. And break the curse."

Eldrin studied the projection of the female. She had a delicate beauty that reminded him of Calla.

"Norah Parks," Orion spoke. "This is the reincarnation of Annora. It will be your job to protect her at all costs. Ignis is not her only threat."

"She's so young," Eldrin noted. "I thought you said they have been on this Earth for fifty years. Do they age slowly as I do?"

"The goddess has only been on Earth for eighteen years."

"What will be my role to her?" Eldrin asked.

"A classmate," Orion stated.

"I age slowly, but I cannot pass as a youngling."

"I have a Timekeeper who can reverse physical age."

Eldrin returned to staring at Norah Parks with a heavy heart. "I won't fail her."

# ABOUT THE AUTHOR

## Megan Wolters

I grew up in Washington State but now reside in Utah with my husband and two daughters, Penelope and Eleanor. I have been creating stories since I was a child and wrote my first book at age 12. I was first published in 2012 at the age of 21. It was a psychological thriller titled, Scarlet River. In 2017, Souls was published. When the publisher went under, I decided it was time to publish independently. I received the rights back for Souls and published the second edition in 2020 and the third in 2021.

www.meganwoltersbooks.com